JESSICA PRATHER
THE TRAITOR'S CRUX

OFTOMES PUBLISHING
UNITED KINGDOM

Copyright © JESSICA PRATHER 2017

This edition published in 2017 by
OF TOMES PUBLISHING
UNITED KINGDOM

The right of JESSICA PRATHER to be identified as the author of this work has been asserted by her in accordance with the Copyright, Designs and Patents Act 1988.

All rights reserved. No part of this publication may be reproduced, transmitted, or stored in a retrieval system, in any form or by any means, without permission in writing from the publisher, nor be otherwise circulated in any form of binding or cover other than that in which it is published and without a similar condition being imposed on the subsequent purchaser.

All characters in this publication are fictitious and any resemblance to real people, alive or dead, is purely coincidental.

Cover art by Tara Spruit
Cover & Interior design by Eight Little Pages

FOR MY FAMILY - FOR EVERYTHING

PROLOGUE

WHEN THEY CAME, IT WAS in the black of the night as the world around us slept.

I was about to scream when I heard the shouts, but my father thought differently. He clasped his large, calloused hands across my mouth as he swept me into his arms, a shelter in the raging storm about to set.

There was always a spot I hid when Eli and I played hide and seek. Our father built a food storage into our tiny home, preparing us for long winter months without food. It was deep and dark, nestled behind a picture on the wall.

That's where he hid me that night. I remember crying for him, clutching his flannel shirt firmly with my knobby child fingers as he frantically set me on my feet.

"Be back soon, *Mija*," he whispered in his sweet, Spanish cadence. His eyes said differently. They were wild with fear, and that's what frightened me the most. The pitch-black room swallowed me as he shut me in; the painting of two children, hand in hand in a meadow, was the only thing hiding my presence in our home.

The sounds were the worst of it. I identified the soldiers by their angry tones, vicious, like a dog with rabies, mad, ready to kill. Then my father's voice, usually so calm, so confident, now pleading.

The thunder of bullets echoing through our home.

My mother's scream.

I couldn't help it. I was curious, afraid. I burst from my hiding spot, shoving the back of the frame until it fell, shattering to the ground.

My world became a funnel; everything blurred around the edges. Hazy, like I was in a dream.

My father was face down in a pool of blood, riddled with bullets. I didn't hear the scream that came from me, only felt the crippling weight of grief.

Snickers from the soldiers, arrogant, cruel. Vile men, vile acts.

My mother's cries. She was still pleading.

I was so lost in the moment that I hadn't noticed the real reason for their raid. Handcuffed, limp in their hands, was Eli.

My only brother, his head bashed, dripping with blood. His long arms cuffed behind him as he slumped over, his head drooping as they dragged him.

I tried to fight for them. I tried to kick and scream, throw the biggest fit I could muster. They couldn't take him from me. They would have to take me too.

I leapt forward like a venomous snake, striking, trying to find weakness. I wasn't going to let them take him. I couldn't. Immediately, my forehead was met with the butt of a gun smacking down on me with brutal force.

My world crumbled around me. The last thing I saw was my father's lifeless body and a pool of blood.

I think they left right after that. I'm not sure of anything anymore.

1

I REMEMBER A TIME WHEN life was actually worth something. Or at least I thought so. Now, as I stand with Joshua Rivers' corpse at my feet, I realize just how naïve I really was.

I've known the Rivers family ever since I was a little girl. Eli and I would play for hours with Joshua, weaving in and out of the trees, lost in the throes of some whimsical game. After Eli was taken, I sought refuge with Joshua, one of my only friends when the world turned its back on me.

The sting of tears burns at the corners of my eyes, trailing my cheeks and landing on my lips with a salty kiss. The Witch's War hasn't just taken lives, it's seized our humanity, and we haven't done a thing about it.

It all began because of President Malen. He wasn't *just* magic. He was a monster. He wanted one thing, and one thing only: power.

The nation watched him, holding a collective breath. I don't know if they were too terrified, or simply too callous to do anything. All I know is they let him do it.

He evolved from President to something else as he disbanded congress, robbed the U.S. of the constitution, the Bill of Rights. We'd heard of people like this before. Rulers, killers. Still, when history resurfaced... we let it happen.

War occurred. Our country was ravaged. People lost their homes, their loved ones, their lives. We were swept into medieval conditions and a lack of proper medical care. This led to a plague.

By the time Malen was assassinated, most of the country had been wiped out.

Then Vice President Thomas Reed stepped in.

If Malen was the fire, then Reed was the arsonist. Malen was explosive, sloppy, and that was his downfall. But Reed, Reed was smart. He rekindled the flames, controlled the burn. He knew the nation was angry and tired of war. It took a few sparks from the arsonist's match to gain their loyalty.

For years, they've targeted the magic population of the United States.

The lucky ones, such as the Rivers family, end up slaughtered. Others, like my brother, are taken to prisons and internment camps, never to be spoken of again.

I've thought endlessly about where Eli could be—*if* he's still alive. Eli was everything I could never be. He had my father's charisma and his easy smile. He'd flash that dimpled grin and wrinkle his freckled nose and all his mischief would be forgiven. I've always been the complete opposite: shy and serious, always fretting. While Eli took center-stage, I hid in the background.

When the arrest happened, our community was shocked. Friends and neighbors called it a tragedy, a curse. Suddenly, conversations changed and Eli became *that diseased boy*. In their eyes, he became a criminal. People empathized with my mother. They murmured about how difficult it must be for her. Eventually, they stopped talking to us altogether. Prying eyes still watch every time we go to town. They gossip and snicker, watching us as if we're a different species. We're the Coria family, disgraced because of *that boy* and the father that died defending him. Soldiers now visit us monthly. They check us for "the disease", as if magic is bacteria that can easily spread through a cough or an uncovered sneeze. It's been nine years since that day. Nine years of narrowed eyes and cruel words, nightmares and one broken family.

There was only one family in the entire city of Denver that seemed to care. The Rivers stuck with us, even after my family's demise. They helped us when things got tough. Life moved on slowly and painfully, but their friendship always stayed true.

Joshua became my closest friend, so close, in fact, that the adults always teased about our future marriage. We secretly wanted it too. I remember one night where we climbed a tree together and just sat there in silence, fingers intertwined as we stared at the twinkling city lights. It took only a second for the government's planes to arrive, swooping in and dropping their bombs with a deafening scream. We watched for hours as the glimmering city burned and flickered. The smoke and ash drifted to the sky and kissed the constellations as my tears blurred together the colors of a collapsing world.

I kneel beside Joshua's body, which is broken and limp like a rag-doll. He looks so peaceful, tawny eyes winged by long black lashes, staring up at the painted sky above. A shuddering sob escapes me as my fingers trace the copper skin of his cheek, rising to those eyelids and easing them shut. I lean in just slightly, planting a soft kiss to his forehead.

"Kenadee?" My mother's footsteps are light, crunching on the fallen autumn debris.

I don't turn to face her. I don't want her to see my grief. "I'm coming."

She pauses a moment, then replies, her voice its usual matter-of-fact tone, "You can't stay—the soldiers will be coming soon to collect the bodies."

When I say nothing, her feet crunch beside me as she kneels, hazel eyes—*Eli's eye*—calm as they assess the broken remains of a family we loved. "They're gone, Kennie. There's nothing we can do. You know the dangers of loving *them*—you'll only end up dead."

"I-I never knew." I swallow, my words betraying me.

"Me either, but you know that it's in both of our best interests if we stay away. Like it or not, Joshua lied to you. He's magic…. a criminal, Kennie, and that's why he's dead."

I bite my lip, a sudden anger welling inside me. I want to scream, to throw things, to cry like a child, but I know there's no use. The Rivers are all gone. Just like Eli, just like my father, and there's nothing I can do about it.

I nod, wordless, as my mother pats my back and heads down the street. I push myself up to my feet as the wind rises up, toying with my hair. There's a fluttering sound, the tapping of paper, faint among the whispering trees. I turn towards the Rivers' home, Heather Rivers' body strewn across the blood-stained steps, a paper clutched in her fist.

I find myself inching closer, dropping to a crouch beside her lifeless body. My fingers ease the paper from her hands as I let loose a trembling breath. I uncurl the blood-speckled page and let my eyes dart over the messy scrawl of a writer in a hurry.

To hunt or to be hunted, Miss Coria. Survival of the fittest.

2

I CAN'T HELP IT. THE bile rises in my throat and I vomit on the Rivers' front lawn. *I have to get away from here.* Goosebumps riddle my arms as I clamor to my feet and race down the sidewalk, gasping desperately for air.

My mind races. *Who would have done this? Why would they leave a note like that?* Someone had known that I would be there. This wasn't just a raid—this was a message for me.

"What's wrong?" My mother frowns as I come bursting into the house, tears on my face and no air in my lungs.

"I-I-the Rivers..." I gape, bending over my knees as I try to get air to my screaming lungs. In all my haste, I'd left the note back on the scene.

"What are you talking about? What is going on with you? Kenadee?" She follows me through our cramped home as I walk off, making my way to my tiny room and pulling my blinds shut.

"Someone left a message for me," I whisper, trying to control my shaking hands.

"*What?*" she exclaims, alarm taking over her features. Her eyes search my face frantically and for a moment, she doesn't seem to know what to say. She turns towards the window, assessing the situation as the story flies from my lips.

When she doesn't reply, I step towards her, a small child in need of her mother's guidance. "Mom! *Please!* We have to do something."

She doesn't turn from the window. Her knobby, arthritic fingers grab at her cardigan, pulling it tighter around herself. Her voice is cold and quiet, void of the emotion that filled her moments ago, "It was surely just a prank, Kenadee. If you would've left when I asked you to... No good comes from sneaking around like that. You're lucky no soldiers were nearby! Do you know what would've happened?"

I nod, trying to hide the fact that my stomach is twisting itself into knots. My mother stares at me for one long moment, then sticks a hand underneath my chin, tilting it upward so that I meet her gaze. "Your brother and father are dead. You of all people should know the dangers that come with associating with those magic people. Only bad things occur, Kenadee. Keep it up and you'll end up just like them." I sniffle as she strokes the hair from my face. "Now, go wash up for dinner. I don't want to hear about this again."

Knowing better than to argue with her, I make my way to the bathroom, unable to shed the feeling that something wicked lurks ahead.

***

JESSICA PRATHER

I DREAM OF MY BROTHER again tonight. It's so real, that I wake up to the taste of salty tears running across my cracked lips.

We were kids, playing in the woods like we always used to, when all of a sudden, a trap burst from the ground, clamping down on his leg. He couldn't get away. I kept on running, giggling, thinking that it was a prank he was playing on me. He always used to play jokes. What was so different this time? Eli's mischief wouldn't fool me.

Not this time.

Only when he started screaming did I realize it wasn't some joke and that he really did need my help. I turned to run, but my feet were heavy as stones. It was like my body was a statue, suddenly unable to do anything but stand completely still.

I could only watch, frozen by whatever cruel twist of fate held me at bay, as he faded, arms outstretched, reaching for me as the shadows swallowed him whole. I couldn't scream, couldn't move. Once again, he was being taken from me, and then, in a flash, he was gone. I never could rescue him.

To hunt, or to be hunted. Survival of the fittest.

Somewhere nearby, a coyote cries its mournful tune. The others in the pack follow suit, a high-pitched chorus to the midnight skies. I stare at the window, hugging my knees to my chest as the tears fall freely.

The day we discovered Eli had powers, we were playing in the woods that surround our house. It was by pure accident as I swung on the old rope hanging from the tree. We were too young, too reckless to care that the rope was fraying. The next thing I knew, I was falling through the air, a piece of broken rope clutched in each tiny fist. He was too far away to do anything but watch in horror. His hands shot out and I was caught by some unexplainable force in the middle of the air. Floating.

He'd caught me.

When I went bragging to my parents, my mother instantly knew what we had to do. She thought it'd be best to turn him in, to save the family the trouble. If he were caught otherwise, we'd be arrested alongside him. She was looking to spare us. That was the angriest I'd ever seen my father. They screamed at each other all night long, keeping us both awake. We hid in the shadows, fingers plugging our ears. I still could make out fragments, slices of words like *disease* and *monster*. I cried at my father's plea, that deep cry for justice, "Emily, he's our *son*!"

In the end, their fight didn't even matter.

I don't go back to sleep after the nightmare. I stay in that spot, huddled by the window until the dawn paints the sky anew. I like to be awake for the sunrise. It's the melancholy time of the day before the rest of the world wakes and reality hits hardest. I always feel that nothing can really hurt you in the mornings.

Slowly, everything is washed in faded orange light. It's Monday morning, time to prepare for school. I shiver as I throw the covers off and my skin is greeted by the crisp autumn air. I hurry to grab my clothes, putting them on quickly, eager to get warmed up. I tuck my freezing toes into the slippers by my bed and head to the sink, splashing my swollen eyes with water.

"*Focus, Kenadee,*" I whisper, staring at my red-eyed reflection in the mirror. I'd cried all night in silent grief, mourning the boy I once loved, left to the same fate as the family I'd lost.

I can't do this. I can't be afraid. I navigate the best I can through the dark, brushing my teeth and twisting my dark hair back into a tiny ponytail at the nape of my neck. It sticks out in a million different directions, too short to cooperate any way I like. Carefully, I pin back the baby hairs framing my face, which always make me look a bit feral. I definitely don't need that now: My face is still flushed from the tears, my eyes swollen and my head pounding. I look wild enough.

I head to the kitchen, trying to avoid slamming the cabinets as I produce a spoon, the pitcher of milk, and some oats. My mom has already gone to work, and the house sits quiet. It feels forced and unnatural to make any noise at all. Besides, I like the quiet. It helps me think.

When I'm done, I shrug my light jacket over my shoulders and step out into the biting cold of morning, my backpack slung over my shoulder. The sun is just beginning to peek over the jagged summits of the mountains, reflecting the dewy frost that morning brings, which is slowly starting to evaporate.

The forest around me is golden, layered in a copper trio of golds, oranges, and vivid autumn reds, mixed with the deep green of the pine trees. As much as I try to rid it from my brain, all I can think of is the Rivers family, Josh's eyes staring blankly at the sky.

Some joke.

"Well hey there, Speedy-Gonzales!" My friend, Beth, shouts jokingly, running up from the dirt road ahead and playfully squeezing my sides. She laughs evilly as I jump, "I didn't even have to wait five hours for you today! You came early, for once."

My lips tug up in a smile. "Yeah, yeah!" I snicker, ramming my shoulder into her playfully. "Maybe you're just late."

Besides Joshua, Beth is my only other friend. I met her in kindergarten when she'd loudly announced that I was going to be her best friend. Since then, our friendship has stuck. We're two opposites: Beth, wild and outgoing, me, quiet and grounded.

"Nah, I don't think that's it!" She turns and watches me, her expression bearing that maternal-know-it-all-look. "Okay, what's wrong?"

"What? Nothing," I lie, but she narrows her eyes. Beth knows me too well. She's the only person I can cry to about anything. She knows the things that haunt my brain, and doesn't even care that it's illegal.

She watches the trees ahead as she walks, "Is this about *them?*"

I nod, blinking back the tears that threaten to spill. "I'm sorry," she says, her voice a sad whisper, "I know how much they meant to you."

I keep nodding, trying so hard to retain my composure.

JESSICA PRATHER

Not here, not ever. I cannot, I will not think of them.

"It's fine. It's done." I brush it off in a hurry, desperate to change the subject, "So, are you ready for that test today?"

She only laughs, flicking her flowing auburn locks from her shoulder, "Oh, sweetheart. I was born ready. And by that, I mean I forgot all about it until now."

We arrive to class a few minutes early as student's swarm in, engaged in loud conversations. I sit quietly, preferring the solitude as I rifle through my school planner to look busy. Beth sits next to me, talking animatedly with Gentry Davis, the Mayor's daughter, known for rebelling against her strict father by throwing wild parties and sleeping with the poorest boys she can find. In this world, the rich stay among the rich. The poor just die.

Miss Harver, our teacher, paces the room, checking the old watch on her wrist impatiently, waiting for the lesson to begin. Lately, we've been studying the history of the United States. It's my favorite class, imagining what life used to be like when the Constitution existed; when the Presidents had elections and newspapers could print what they wanted. It seems like such a wonderful thing when now all we know is war and death.

The morning bell rings and, all at once, the stray conversations die down. Miss Harver is one of the strictest teachers here. You don't want to be caught talking by her, or you'll immediately be punished. One time, she made two boys scrub the floor with toothbrushes just for asking each other a question about their homework.

She taps a ruler across the board, signaling the beginning of class. But, before she can speak, she's interrupted by the buzz of the intercom.

"Miss Harver?" The secretary's nasally voice fills the tiny classroom.

"Yes?" She purses her lips impatiently. She's grouchy enough as it is, let alone when someone disrupts her class.

"Would you please send Kenadee Coria to the principal's office immediately? It's important."

The entire class' attention turns to me. A few people snicker and whisper, others watch me with large, scared eyes. I'm not a trouble-maker. In fact, I barely even talk. What could I have possibly done to earn this? I stand quickly, gathering my things and attempting to avoid the prying eyes of my snickering class. Could it have been the conversation with Beth earlier? Maybe we were overheard.

What will happen to me now?

Miss Harver's eyes meet mine, blazing with a wicked curiosity. She's never liked me much. Not that I take it personally, she doesn't like anyone. Her gleaming eyes don't move from my face as she replies to the crackling intercom, "She's on her way."

No one speaks as I stand, nervously throwing my backpack over my shoulder. As I move through the desk-cluttered classroom, I can feel every set of eyes tracking me.

My heart beats loudly in my chest as I slowly make my way to the principal's office, dread filling my body. I want to scream. I make up an excuse in my head for talking about *them*. Surely, this is all a big misunderstanding. I can explain it all. I'll do anything to prove my innocence, to stay here with my mom. I'm a coward, trying to stay clear of the law. Lying myself out of arrest.

But what if they don't believe me? What if I am about to end up just like my brother? Arrested for what? Treason? Handcuffed and sent off to die. My name never to be spoken again and my mother, she'll officially be alone—left with nothing but whispers of her stolen family.

I shake my head, scrunching my eyes shut to get the thought out of my mind. That's not going to happen. I did nothing wrong. I won't let myself be another victim of this war.

3

THE SECRETARY, MRS. HAINES, GIVES me a forced, round-faced smile as I enter the large office.

"Hello, dear!" she says briefly, clambering slowly to her feet and rapping her fist on Principal Geartan's door three times.

From behind the shutters, I can see a group of people surrounding his table; men dressed in suits. As Mrs. Haines leads me in, they turn and stare, watching me like predators eyeballing their prey.

When he sees me, Principal Geartan stands quickly, extending a hand to bring me forward. His brown eyes meet mine, seeming just as curious—just as worried—as I am. "Here she is. Gentlemen, Mr. President, Sir, I'd like to introduce you to Miss Kenadee Coria."

I flinch. *President?*

My eyes meet his and I take a step backwards, bumping into Principal Geartan's arm. The Principal doesn't seem to notice. He watches the President nervously, like a mouse before a cat.

President Reed is a much smaller, more fragile looking in person. I watch his smug grin grow wider as he takes in my battered old sweater and my hole-filled jeans. My mouth goes dry with embarrassment. Fingers clasped together on the desk, he leans in.

"Miss Coria, the pleasure is all mine. Take a seat."

I do as he says, keeping my head low as I take the chair closest to the door. The President comes around the front of the desk and lounges against it, folding one leg over the other. "I do hope that you received the gift that was left for you at your friend's home yesterday?"

My blood runs cold. I knew his men were the ones that attacked, but President Reed was behind the note left in Mrs. Rivers' hand? *Why?*

"Well?" He taps his fingers against the desk impatiently, cocking his head to try and see my down-turned face. "Didn't your filthy mother teach you any manners at all? Usually, when you're given a gift, you say thank you." He spits the word *filthy* as if it's a curse word. I suppose it is meant just for the disgusting cockroaches my family must be to him.

"Th-thank you," I whisper, at a loss for any other words.

To my dismay, the President only laughs. He's a lean, middle-aged man with thick gray hair and a salt and pepper beard. His eyes are what scare me most: a dark, nearly pupil-less brown and full of hate.

"Kenadee—may I call you that?" I nod, doubting that I really have a choice in the matter. "Good. Well, Kenadee, we would like for this meeting to be as brief as possible, so let's get started. We are here to talk to you about a very special and confidential project of ours."

Reed's voice is husky and quiet with age, false niceties lingering in his tone.

"What kind of project?" I ask, confused. *How would I be of help to him? I'm nothing but a sixteen-year-old girl.* I frown, glancing up at him. "Wait, so, I'm not in trouble?"

The President and his men begin to chuckle quietly, exchanging condescending glances like it's an inside joke and I'm some ignorant child who doesn't understand. "No, of course not. Unless you have reason to be." He toys with the globe on the edge of Principal Geartan's desk, spinning it with his long fingers. After a moment he says, "You know, I met that brother of yours in my prison. Nice young man… for a wizard anyway. He learned quickly how to behave after a few unfortunate beatings." He stops the globe with his palm and fixes his calculating stare on me. "You probably don't understand the reason for his arrest, do you?"

Rage pulses through my veins at the smirk on the President's lips as he brings up Eli. *How dare he?*

I glower at the man whose smile only grows bigger at my discomfort. "Well? Do you know why your brother was taken?"

"Because he's magic," I fail to hide the shakiness of my words.

The President's dark eyes glisten, "Very good. Yes, that is the reason." His hand claps over my shoulder and I flinch away. He only chuckles, "Sweet, young Kenadee, I'm afraid you might not find this a very enticing task. My fear is that you won't perform to my liking.

Nowadays, it's hard to know who you can and can't trust."

I clamp my jaw shut as he stops in front of me, reaching for a magnifying glass on Geartan's desk and turning back towards me. He holds it up to his eye and watches me through it. After a brief second, he wipes it off on his shirt and neatly sets it back down. "The war is not over. I don't know that it'll ever *truly* be over… As the leader of the nation, that leaves me in a very tight spot. Have you ever heard of the famous dilemma, the *trolley problem*, Kenadee?"

I nod slowly, "There's a runaway trolley, headed straight toward five people that are tied down and unable to move…"

"Exactly!" Reed gives a flash of that cat-like grin. "But, on the other track, there is one person. Now, you're the one next to the lever. You have the power to choose: save one life, or five."

"I'm confused. What's this have to do with me?"

His expression turns serious. "I'm talking about you helping us win this war. Magic has plagued our nation for far too long. You're what? Fourteen?"

"Sixteen," I say sharply.

"Regardless, that's all you've ever known, isn't it? War, bombs, sickness and death… Don't you ever wonder what life was like before the magic took everything from us?"

"I-I-" The truth is, I have. I've always dreamt of a life that Eli and my father were a part of. A life where I could make friends, have a boyfriend, and wouldn't have to worry about them ending up dead.

Reed sees my hesitation and smiles. "What if I told you that you could have him back?"

I inhale sharply. *Him?* As in…

No, it couldn't be.

Hard silence fills the room and out of the corner of my eye, I can see Principal Geartan turn and stare. He wasn't expecting this either. I wonder how much he actually knows about what's happening. Was he lassoed into this last minute like me?

President Reed breaks the stillness with a harsh laugh. "I know what you're thinking, and yes, I am talking about your dear brother, Eli. He's very much alive. I'll even give him back to you—if you do something for me first."

I run a hand over my forehead in disbelief, opening my mouth and clamping it shut again. Tears burn at my eyes, threatening to spill over.

"It's okay, take it all in. Just listen as I explain." Reed says in a low voice, "Your brother is alive. Your mother was taken this morning. We wanted full assurance that you'd cooperate. They will not be harmed, so long as you do as I say."

I gulp, looking at him with teary eyes. "How do I know what you're saying is true? You could be making this all up."

"Ms. Coria, bite your tongue!" snaps Principal Geartan, but the Commander in Chief only waves a dismissive hand.

"Smart girl. Distrust is a wise thing to have in these times. That's why we brought proof." He repositions himself on the desk and nods as his men, standing behind Principal Geartan with grave expressions. One man with a shiny bald head and permanent frown lines cracks his knuckles and wordlessly spreads his hands apart. Geartan and I both gasp as a scene emerges in front of us. Hazy at first, I narrow my eyes to try and see better.

"This was earlier this morning," Reed explains as the image clears. I clap a hand over my mouth as my mother appears. She stands in our tiny kitchen, yellow hair haloed by the stream of morning light in the kitchen window. I can hear the buzz of the radio as she listens, some old song that she hums along with. She pauses for a moment, face turning towards the window. A patch of light illuminates her features—lined with worry.

"Mom?" I breathe, then louder, "Mom!"

She looks so real, as if I could just reach out my hand and touch her. She must see nothing, as she lets out a quiet laugh and mumbles something to herself. Hair cascades over her shoulders as she sticks a finger in her bowl and presses it to her thin lips to sample. Satisfied, she reaches for the bowl, opening the oven and—

The old screen door opening up to the kitchen flings open by the kick of a boot. The bowl goes flying as she lets loose a scream. It takes a matter of seconds for the soldiers to shove her against the wall and press the handcuffs into her wrists.

The picture fades as I bat away a stray tear. I can feel everyone's eyes on me, but I refuse to look away as the image refocuses. This time, I'm in a dark, steely room. There are chains hanging from the ceiling, a limp figure within their confinement. I take in a shuddering breath, this time, not fighting the tears as they cascade down my cheeks.

"Mr. Coria," says Reed's voice as the image begins to focus. He's in full view now, a bat bouncing against his palm as he circles the prisoner. "You haven't actually done anything wrong this time. Think of this as a moment of…motivation."

He drives the bat into his back with a sickening thud as the prisoner—Eli—screams. I feel myself crying out, even though they can't hear me. Eli's figure comes into focus. I barely recognize my brother. Nine years has turned him from a boy into a man. His hair has darkened, his bone structure grown sharp and jagged. Tiny scars seem as common on his face as the freckles that once dusted his nose. His hazel eyes flicker upward at his torturer and his crackled lips part, as if he's about to speak. He doesn't have a chance, as the bat flies into his stomach.

"Stop!" I turn away, feeling sick. The image pauses and Reed's figure is frozen mid-swing. I look at the real Reed in front of me and sniffle. "I'll do it. But, you have to swear that you'll keep them both safe. No more torture!"

Reed nods once at his soldier, who turns off his magic. The image dissolves into thin air and the office is returned to normal. "I'm glad you see things my way. Don't worry. I'm a man of my word. As long as you do as I ask, I promise to let them go free. However, your failure to meet my demands will result in their untimely deaths, do you follow?"

I take a deep breath, wondering how much I'll regret my next words. "Tell me what you want me to do."

Malice glimmers in the President's eyes, "Come with me."

4

BEFORE I CAN EVEN BLINK, Reed's soldiers are at my side, their handcuffs slipping over my wrists. "Just a precaution in case you decide to try something," says Reed, shaking Principal Geartan's hand and murmuring something in a low voice.

I have no choice but let his men tug me down the hall and through the front doors of the school. A black SUV awaits outside in the parking lot, guards with dark suits surrounding it.

"Watch your head, kid!" growls one of the soldiers behind me as he opens the door and pushes me inside. I desperately try to readjust myself, feeling the handcuffs digging into my skin as Reed slips in beside me.

"Now that that's all settled," Reed adjusts his tie and smooths out his impeccable suit as the car comes to a quiet start, "I suppose I can explain why you're here. What do you know of the magic world, Kenadee?"

I gulp. My mind is still reeling from the scene back in the Principal's office. Eli really is alive. After nine years apart, I could finally see my big brother again. I watch the world outside fly by, a sea of copper leaves around us, repeating it again and again in my mind.

THE TRAITOR'S CRUX

Eli is alive.

He's alive, which means I'll do anything to get him back.

"Well?" The President asks, tone clipped with impatience.

I swallow, ashamed that my voice trembles, "Magic? Honestly, I don't know much."

He picks a piece of lint from his sleeve, flicking it before his set of coal-colored eyes come floating back up to my face. "So, you've never practiced the art of magic?"

I feel my blood run cold. Seeing my discomfort only makes Reed's grin widen, "Don't you worry, young Kenadee. I'm sure it's something you've always wondered about. After all, your dear brother Eli is tainted. So was your lover, Joshua. There are so many of you floating around, just beyond our reach…"

"What?" I shake my head at the stupidity of the suggestion. "I'm not—"

"Oh, but you are." His smile sends shivers up my spine. I want to scream, to shout, to get out of this car and away from this man. I can't be magic. Years of blood tests and investigations have proven my innocence. The President is mistaken.

When I say nothing, he leans back in his seat, "I know, this is quite devastating to hear. Let me explain. We've been watching you, Kenadee. Your test results did in fact come out positive, we simply hid that fact from you."

"But…why?" I whisper, drawing in a ragged breath.

"If you knew that you were magic, you might try to use your powers. We wanted to keep you away for as long as we could, let them mature and further our studies. We were always watching—there were cameras installed in your home, spies and teachers assessing your behavior. We knew the risks of having someone magic running free, but we thought that maybe, when the time was right, we could use you."

"This was your plan all along: take my mother, torture Eli, kill the Rivers... all to con me into doing your dirty work?" I breath, recalling Joshua's strewn corpse and the message in his mother's hand.

"Call it what you will," he examines his well-groomed nail beds, looking bored, "but you're here, aren't you?"

"But... why me? Why didn't you just arrest me like you did my brother? Or kill me like you did Josh?"

His eyes flicker back towards my face, a cat-like grin spreading across his lips, "Now that's the interesting part. You see, we studied your bloodwork intensively, as we do any witch or wizard we test. You are no ordinary witch, Kenadee Coria."

"What's that supposed to mean?"

"I have studied magic quite extensively over the years, thanks to the many prisoners I've held, but your magic ability is one of the most powerful I've ever seen. Powers like that... they don't come easily, and that's why I have high hopes for your success."

"So, what?" I frown, "I somehow learn how to use this magic I've had all my life, do whatever it is that you expect me to do, and my family walks free? How do I even know that I can trust you?"

He chuckles, "Oh, yes. You think I may be lying. I'll admit, I would be wary too if I were in your situation. But I can assure you that I am completely serious about this transaction. Eli and your mother won't be harmed as long as you do *exactly* as I say. I don't take kindly to those who try to trick me. Try to run, betray me, and I will personally bring you to the trials, where your mommy and big brother will die horrible, slow deaths. I *will* kill them without hesitation."

Unfortunately, I believe him. I can see the truth of his words written in his smug features. He means it. I sigh, my body uncoordinated with my hands behind my back, swaying as the car hits a large bump. "Fine. What do you want me to do?"

"Well, it goes back to the trolley ordeal. You might think to save the larger number. After all, it's one life for five. But, what if they're the reason for this war in the first place? What if their people are the ones that destroyed everything? Then what? Do you still spare them, regardless of their sins?"

I don't respond as the car slows to a stop at a red light. Reed continues without hesitation, "I'm talking about a group of rebel witches and wizards that took over an abandoned town about three hours west of here. Terrorists, plotting against us from the confines of their sacred little home. Who would you save? Your brother, your mom? Or *them*?"

I furrow my brow, confused. "If they're such a problem, why can't you just send in your military and be done with it? Why do you need me?"

He leans back, staring out the window. "While I have many young magic employees with exceptional powers that happily dedicate themselves to ridding the nation of these radical groups, there's no way for us to actually enter their borders. Their leaders are quite ruthless, you see. They've learned to protect their little hiding spot with the help of their people—barring us from the inside out."

"And you think that *I* can get in?" I almost laugh at the thought. "I know nothing about magic! I just learned that I have powers! What makes you so sure that I can be the one to do this?"

"Your elite powers," he says softly. "They're stronger than any other's. This group can't keep out everyone. They've created this sort of magic barrier. With it, they've managed to barricade themselves in and everyone else out. It's my fault, really. I sent in some of my magic soldiers a few months back, and it didn't end well. Because of that, this group will be suspicious when you arrive. That's why you must feed them a convincing lie, earn their trust so that they'll confide in you, train you. You can learn your trade, you could be my most powerful soldier. No one would stand in your way."

I gnaw on my bottom lip as Reed watches me carefully. Finally, he sighs, breaking eye contact and staring out the window. "The late President Malen was magic, as you know. He destroyed his own kind. He had this vengeance within; a hunger I've yet to see in anyone else. It's the magic; it's evil. It turns people to a darkness which they can never free themselves of. Malen wasn't well practiced in it. He discovered it a mere few years into his quest. If he were at full power and knew what he was capable of, he could've easily destroyed everything." His brow furrows and he looks to me with an expression I almost believe to be genuine. "Contrary to your belief, I'm not a monster. Yes, I did lock up your brother. I have arrested many that were magic before him. I don't enjoy it, but I'll do what's necessary of me. I'm trying to stop a disaster before it occurs—that's why I'm taking on so many young magic soldiers. If I can redirect their powers and make them see the truth, then maybe they'll help us save the world. We can't function in a world like Malen's, full of horrid powers. No matter what you may think of the people you encounter on your mission, they're terrorists, plaguing our lands. By turning them in, by working for me, you're doing your country a great service. I know that it's a lot to take in, but Kenadee, you have all this amazing power. We need you to use it and help us find a way to destroy them."

I watch the buildings turn to autumn-colored trees outside the car window, chewing on my lip. Whether I like it or not, I belong to Reed now. I am his soldier. If I don't do as he asks, I'll be killed right alongside my family. If just one mission is what it takes, then it's the least I can do to save the ones I love.

Reed seems to know what's on my mind. "Think of the trolley situation. Who would you save? A small group of criminals, or innocent Americans that are being targeted by this little rebel group?" He doesn't wait for me to answer as his eyes gleam wickedly, "Turn them in and you'll be an American hero. You'll save your family's lives. Once you're done being of service to me, I will leave you and your family alone. You'll be paid a nice amount of money, a home, and plenty of food. You could live the rest of your life free and happy. Get inside their walls and help me bring them down from the inside. Uncover their secrets. Tell me their weaknesses, wait, as I build my army, make them stronger. Together, we'll take them down in a matter of months and you'll be on your way to freedom."

I let out a sharp breath, considering President Reed's deal. This could be the key to everything. We wouldn't have to worry about the future. I could see Eli again... If turning over a group of criminals is what I have to do, then there's no question. I'll do it.

"So...do we have a deal?"

I nod, letting loose a sharp breath, "Yes, I suppose we do."

5

THE CAR CRINKLES OVER GRAVEL as it pulls into a long driveway. Wherever we're going, it's nestled deep within a cove of trees. I sit up a little straighter, the handcuffs digging into my wrists as I try to see where we are headed. No one says a thing as we stop in front of a large rectangular building, a plain, steely gray with only one window by the heavy metal door.

"What is this place?" I don't struggle as they yank me from the car.

Reed greets us at the front door. "Welcome to the training center. I have them scattered throughout the country for the use of my people. Here you'll prepare for your mission."

I follow them in, looking around with a racing heart. The walls inside are as plain as they are outside, a metallic gray with nothing but maps for decoration. Arms folded across my chest, I walk around the large conference table, feeling their eyes trailing me as I take a closer look at one of the maps. It features the entire U.S.A., tiny red flags in clusters around Colorado, Oregon, Montana, and Wyoming.

I don't hear Reed come up beside me. His voice makes me jump. "Those are the few known locations of witches and wizards in hiding. We conquered the eastern and southern regions of the country."

"Why don't they flee to Canada or Mexico if they know that you're looking for them? Wouldn't that keep them safe?" I ask, then instantly regret my question.

He flashes a wicked smile, "They were just as torn apart by Malen's war as us. You really think they'll take on our magic?" I don't respond, and he continues, "If we can take down the final few here, we'll be much closer to ridding ourselves of magic for good. You're helping with this camp." His finger taps a spot on the map near the border of Colorado and Wyoming, marked with a tiny red flag. "The town formerly known as Steamboat Springs. Now, it's home to the group I mentioned before."

I frown at the teeny red flag, a foggy memory of the town in my mind. It'd once been a ski resort, a tourist destination. They made the mistake of trying to hide the witches in a public building instead of handing them over the government when the raids were going on. Uncle Sam found out and brought in the bombs a few hours later. There were no survivors.

I glance up at Reed. "There shouldn't be anything left of Steamboat... I thought the entire city was practically wiped off the map. Besides... if they're so well protected, how am I supposed to get in?"

"It won't be easy," Reed admits, "This isn't any ordinary group. They know very well what my plans are for them, and they intend to use everything in their power to ensure it doesn't happen." He slips his jacket off his shoulders and deposits it on the back of a chair, "They know my subjects, both magic and non-magic. If they think that you work for me, you'll be in deep trouble and there will be no way for to me to save you. Tread carefully, learn about their camp, and study that barrier."

"And then what? You want me to break it down?"

"Eventually, yes. But first, I only want you to observe and learn your magic. Build it up, Ms. Coria, because the barrier will require an entire wizard army to destroy. If you can establish their weaknesses and train yourself in your craft, we can find a way to destroy them."

"What happens after that?" I gulp, trying to contain my spinning mind. "What will you do with them once it's down?"

Reed's eyes glisten darkly, "You will have backup, of course, when taking down the wall. We'll find a way to disable them. Then, the military will step in. If they don't cooperate, we'll kill them."

I lean against the table, about to respond when a door opens and a harsh-looking boy with a closely-cropped buzz cut comes marching through. He doesn't look my way as he salutes Reed, who waves him off dismissively. "Ah, there you are, finally. Markus, meet Ms. Coria. Kenadee, Markus will be the one to help prepare you for your mission."

Markus gives me a cold look, extending a rigid hand. "Nice to meet you."

THE TRAITOR'S CRUX

"Now," Reed circles around the table so that his back is turned. We both watch as he types in a plethora of numbers and the iron door clicks open, "Let me show you what else you're up against. A more *bothersome* factor."

We follow, stepping down inside a bunker-like room, laden with weapons of all sizes and abilities. A gasp escapes me as Reed plants himself in front of a large screen. "When I told you about the dangers of these people, I wasn't kidding. In fact, there's one in particular that I would like you to always have eyes on. She's an influential member of their ranks, one responsible for various attacks on our people. Markus, if you'd please."

Markus snaps his fingers and the screen flickers on. Reed stares at it with a hatred I've never seen before in my life. A mugshot of a girl just a few years older than me.

"Harlow Creston, age twenty-one. An escaped prisoner of mine," The President growls, "I'm ashamed to admit that Miss Creston got the better of me. At the time, I misjudged her and she used that to her advantage. She's escaped me twice now, and while she's received, well—" he exchanges a smug look with Markus, "—she's been punished. That makes her even more hell-bent on my destruction."

Chills riddle my spine, but I say nothing. Reed plants himself beside me, still staring venomously at the photo of Harlow Creston. "You'll observe her carefully; she's clever as a fox, one of our nation's greatest terrorists—her demise would mean great things for our country. I want you to try and get close to her. Take her in with great measures, stay on her good side. Most of all: be wary of her deceit."

I study her face, determined to memorize each feature. Her image stares back at me, eyes a striking shade of icy blue. In the photo, she sports a black eye and a cut lip like she'd been in a fight.

Harlow Creston, age twenty-one. Highly dangerous.

"Now, on with business," Reed says, opening a drawer and fumbling through it as Markus switches off the screen. "Ms. Creston isn't the only danger there. She's just the only one we know about. Should harm come along, we expect you to use this."

He hands me a small device that lights up with the movement. It's extremely light in my palm, and tiny enough that I can wrap my fingers around it. "It's a communicator. Hold on to it, guard it with your life. The technology will work within the confinements of the barriers, so long as you do not get caught with it. Markus, call Kenadee."

Markus does as he's commanded with a scowl. I gasp as a screen pops up in mid-air, Markus' face an electronic white. "We'll use it to report to one another. In case of an emergency, you can click this—" Reed taps a button on the bottom corner and immediately it begins to flash. The entire device turns red, buzzing maniacally against the hard surface of the table. "We carry it with us always, so someone will always be near if you need them. When you're there, I'll expect you to answer the calls each night at nine o'clock from the safety of your own room. I want you to be a fly on the wall. Take notes, report anything and everything they plan. Keep it some place safe."

I nod, feeling a weight in the pit of my stomach as I tuck the device into the depths of my pocket. All I have to do is this one thing. One thing to earn my family's freedom. One thing to earn my own freedom.

I can do this.

I have to do this.

My hands tremble as my mind races through everything I've learned so far. There are still so many questions left unanswered. Why do I feel like this mission might be the death of me?

I bite my lip as Reed slips on the jacket he'd left dangling on the back of a chair, straightening his collar and nodding to one of his men, who slips out the door and climbs in to start the car. "Now, I have business to attend to. This is where I leave you, Ms. Coria. Markus will work with you to ensure you're prepared for this position. My men will be back to collect you in two days' time, so I suggest you make the most of your time here."

Before I can stop it, I'm calling after him, the question rolling from my lips with embarrassing shakiness. "What happens if I can't do it?"

"We'll kill your family and arrest you. I can promise you a lifetime of torture and rotting in prison. Sweet little thing..." The smile returns, crooked and evil, "You don't want to stand in my way. I'm doing you a favor here. It'd be wise not to forget that."

"Understood," I whisper. My knee bounces nervously as I try to remember all the information I was just given. *Camp in the woods. Harlow Creston. Magic. I'm magic.*

"Glad we have an understanding. Goodbye, Kenadee Coria. I'm sure it won't be long until we see one another again." He slips through the door, as quiet as a mountain cat. I watch the car bounce down the gravel road, spitting up dirt and a cloud of dust as it disappears around the corner. I turn towards Markus and his weapons, ready to begin.

6

"AGAIN!"

At Markus' words I let out an annoyed huff as he rewinds the video and switches the subtitles off. "This is the billionth time I've watched this. Is this really necessary, Markus?"

He doesn't respond, toying with the controls on the remote. I take the opportunity to complain louder, though he doesn't even seem to be listening. "You realize we've been at this all day, right? What's the point of learning to read lips anyway? I just found out I have all these cool powers. I could probably find some trick that tells me everything they're saying!"

He pushes himself off the desk, "Do you want a tiny violin, 'cause I think there's a music store a few miles off."

"I want to learn how to fight and shoot. If they're as dangerous as Reed says—"

"Then a gun won't help you until you have an entire army behind you. They have powers, Coria, dangerous ones. Why do you think Reed keeps pulling witches into his ranks? With our weapons, we don't stand a chance against them."

I think about this for a moment, watching Markus from the corner of my eye. There's something about the way his expression darkened as he said those last few words, as if he realized what I am. A witch, a tainted one...

A monster.

My fingers tap nervously against my leg as Markus brushes past, avoiding my gaze. I pivot slightly in my chair, sticking one bent leg up on the cushion and draping my arm across the back of the chair as a sudden desperation to prove myself washes over me. "Can we at least change the video so I can practice? I've pretty much memorized everything they've said so it's pointless to read their lips."

He's already at the door, pressing his shoulder against it as a small streak of daylight shines through. "If I get back from making us lunch and you can read my lips, then we'll move on."

***

AFTER LUNCH AND A SOMEWHAT unsuccessful attempt at reading Markus' lips, we move on anyway. As he digs through a cabinet, muttering the occasional swear word in frustration, I examine the arsenal of shiny weapons on the wall. When he isn't looking, I reach for a handgun and weigh it in my hands.

"What are you doing? Are you five? Put that down." He snaps, wheeling around and grabbing the gun from my hands. I hold them up in feigned innocence, watching his face turn the color of a tomato. After a few deep breaths he says, "Just don't touch anything, okay?"

I do as he says, leaning against the wall as he turns back to the cabinet and rummages through. "So, how'd you end up here? Alone in the middle of nowhere, training people like me…"

His voice is muffled as he continues to burrow. "I'll do anything to help the cause if it gets magic out of this world."

"Do you really believe it's evil?" I ask after a moment.

His shoulders tense and he appears, a box in his hands. He strides to the counter and sets it down, then turns back towards me with a small voice. "Yes, I do. My dad was magic. We tried to hide him for years until one day he just lost control, went berserk… My mom tried to protect us and got killed in the process. So, yeah… I was glad to be drafted. It meant that I could do my part to end magic. I've seen what it can do."

"I'm so sorry," I whisper as he wipes at his eyes, ducking his head. He does look incredibly young, even for the new draft age. When the war occurred, many of the nation's men died. Each year since, the age of enlistment seems to get younger as Reed gets more desperate for able-bodied soldiers. Markus can't be more than fourteen, and yet, he's already so full of hate.

With his back to me, he collects himself enough to let out an angry bark. "Well? What are you waiting for? Get over here." I do as he says, sensing that right now would not be the time to push Markus any farther than I have already. He folds the tabs of the box shut before I can see what's inside and sticks it on the floor of the closet.

"What are you doing?" I stick my hands on my hips as naturally, he ignores me, sticking a key inside the lock and jiggling it back and forth. Satisfied, he turns to me with a dour expression. "Before you can know what's in the box, you need to successfully pick this lock."

***

FOR TWO DAYS, I SPEND my time watching old videos on mute to try and read their lips, training in basic fight techniques, swearing as I try to pry open locks with bobby pins and learning what information to look for when I get to the camp. Part of my frustration is from Markus and his lackluster training skills. When the soldiers come for me on the last day, I'm feeling only slightly more prepared for what's to come.

"Now, remember," Markus reminds me as the car crawls to a stop, "you stay in the shadows. The things that you learned here are only to be used in extreme cases. You don't fight, you don't engage unless completely necessary. They need to trust you, and trust is earned. You can't get in without them letting you in. That's how the barrier works. They'll be suspicious so you need to make up some convincing lie about how you found them. Always stay in the public point of view, right where they can see you. The more you fit in, the more you'll learn. If you cause trouble—"

"I know, I know." The zipper of my old school bag hisses as I pull it shut. It used to be loaded with notebooks and pens; now it's filled with a first-aid kit, a water bottle, several ready-to-eat meals, the communicator, an army knife, a jacket, matches and a flashlight. "If I mess up, I'll be killed. I promise I'll play it safe. My family's lives depend on it."

"Good, because there's a lot resting on your shoulders. You'll succeed in bringing these people to justice. We'll be with you along the way. Now, we're on a pass called Rabbit Ears, just a few miles from town. You'll walk the rest of the way, just follow the highway. You have the map, just in case?"

I nod, producing the crinkled old paper from my lap. Markus gives a satisfied nod, "Good. Oh, and a fair warning: the state patrol roams this area quite often. Just because you're working for Reed doesn't mean they'll believe it. You're now on the National Wizard Registry, so if they find you, they will arrest you."

"Good to know," I whisper under my breath, assessing the empty streets around me. It used to be a busy part of town, but with time's curse and the war's heavy hand, it's slowly become less and less population.

"Oh!" Markus reaches underneath the seat and digs out the box I'd rescued from the closet. I never got to see inside it. When I clicked open the lock, Markus, in return, confiscated my treasure and told me that he'd get to it later.

I don't hesitate as he places it in my hands, ripping the box open like a child on Christmas day. I produce a tiny, ant-sized object and weigh it in my palm, looking to Markus for some sort of explanation.

"It's the world's tiniest microphone," he says with a sly grin, "but don't let its size fool you. It's been refined through time into one of the best pieces of technology to exist. It'll pick up sound from any room, regardless of vocal tone or background noise. When you get to camp, put it on. Keep it out of plain sight—let no one see that you wear it. It should be pretty simple to hide. President Reed and his team have their own which will connect to yours so that they can hear everything you can. You'll discuss with the President each night during your calls."

I nod, keeping my mouth in a firm line as I deposit the tiny device carefully in the front pocket of my backpack and zip it up. Reed will be listening, no matter what I say and do. The thought hangs over my head like an ominous cloud.

"I suppose that's it then," Markus gives me a final long look before the door opens behind me and Reed's men are grabbing at my arms. "Goodbye, Kenadee. I trust you won't disappoint our nation's leader."

"Wait!" I call, blinking in the broad daylight as the car doors slam shut. Suddenly, everything feels so overwhelming. I'm doing this, I'm really headed into a camp of rogue criminals. I'm a government spy. I'm not ready. I reach for the door handle as the sleek black car purrs to a start, already pulling away.

I stand in the deserted highway, watching, even long after the car disappears around the bend.

7

MY BOOTS CLUNK OBNOXIOUSLY against the pavement as I walk, feeling the thin mountain air taking its toll on my lungs and cursing the brand-new leather on these shoes as they chafe against my skin. A cool breeze laces its way through the aspen trees, sending them into a whispering flurry. I shiver, tilting my head back to examine the graying sky. Sure enough, a single drop of rain lands on my cheek. Moments later, the soft pattering of rain begins to speckle the pavement.

"*C'mon!*" I groan, ducking my head and slipping underneath a tree. I rest my bag against and rock and dig inside, looking for my coat. Once I find it, I slip it over my goosebump-ridden arms and reach back into the bag for the map. I've been walking for what feels like hours—where is this camp?

The rain crashes down harder and a clap of thunder roars, reverberating loudly through the forest. The map crinkles loudly in my hands, already damp and fading despite my efforts to keep it dry. I shut it with a sigh. It's no use. The red pen that Markus had used to mark my path now bleeds across the map in a blur of color.

THE TRAITOR'S CRUX

Tucking the map back into the pocket of my bag, I prepare to make my escape. Whether I like it or not, I have to keep moving. Staying and waiting out the storm is not an option—at this rate, everything in my bag is soiled. If Markus were here, he'd have a fit at my lackluster survival skills. I'm about to grab the bag and head on my way when a flash of silver makes my heart drop in my chest.

A state patrol pulls over on the side of the road, just beyond the trees.

"*Crap,*" I hiss, ducking down. Markus' words taunt my mind; if I get caught by the police, none of Reed's promises will matter. I'll be arrested, sent to die. I'll never get the chance to save my family.

I look to the forest, then back at the highway patrol. There's a chance that I'm hidden well enough in the trees that I won't be seen. I can go deeper and wait for him to leave but—

Another loud crack of thunder ripples through the trees.

If there's a lightning storm, then surrounded by a bunch of trees is the last place I want to be. Do I dare risk going deeper in the forest?

I kneel down beside the trunk of the tree, narrowing my eyes to try and see the officer inside. He takes a big sip out of a mug, then reaches for something in the seat behind him. I hold my breath as another squad car pulls up behind him.

I have to make a move. I can't stay here.

I turn and bolt towards the woods, rushing as fast as I can despite the underbrush threatening to trip me. I don't see the log until it's too late—my ankle lets out a sickening crack and I go colliding with a yelp against the muddy forest floor.

"Who's there?" Comes a man's yell.

I force myself into a sitting position, biting back the scream as I try to move my foot. Red hot pain flashes in my swimming vision as the shouts grow louder.

No, no, no! I have to get out of here.

The rain pelts against my skin as I look around, trying to calm my racing heart. A tree branch hangs a few feet above me—if I can reach it, I can try and get myself up. Slipping my backpack off my shoulders, I throw it into the air, trying to catch the strap against the branch. It snags on the end, bending underneath the weight, and sends the bag flopping to the ground.

Footsteps crack as both officers appear behind me, guns raised. "Hands in the air where we can see them!" one barks.

This can't be happening...

My body shakes, a mixture of pain and cold. I raise my trembling hands into the air as they take a few steps forward. A lanky man with a bushy mustache heads for my backpack, while the other, the heftier man that I saw in the first car, kneels beside my injured foot. I let out a sharp cry as he reaches for my boot. He grimaces and reaches for the buzzing radio on his shirt. "We need a 10-52..."

THE TRAITOR'S CRUX

I search the trees desperately for a way out. I have to do something—I won't just sit here and get arrested. Suddenly, an odd feeling overcomes me; an overwhelming electric sensation, building up—too much to contain. Everything seems to move in slow motion as my body takes complete control.

It's the strike of a match, the electric shimmer of lightning blazing through the sky.

Suddenly I'm not a terrified teenage girl. I'm fear and fire, death incarnate.

"What the—" The lanky policeman is swept off his feet with a lazy flick of my hand, the backpack flying from his grip and landing somewhere in the distance. I deposit him next to the cowering form of the heftier officer. The power continues to ripple through me and I hope for a moment that it never stops. I'm powerful; I'm dangerous.

They've never seen anything like me.

I let out a manic laugh and lift my hands up. Flames rise from the ground, tiny at first, then larger at my command. The rain still falls, the fog still hangs in a thick curtain around us, but the fire continues to dance. It wields itself around them in a circle, trapping the officers within its deadly grasp.

I look from the scene to my hands. My powerful, terrifying hands. They tremble in exhilaration and pain and fear. I draw in a ragged breath, realizing what I've just done.

Magic.

I did magic.

But... *how?*

Everything comes roaring back all at once. My vision swims and my ankle throbs. The rain begins to slow as I look to the cops, now surrounded by a wall of fire.

There's the sound of footsteps behind me, then a slow clapping. Both cops look up in horror, realization dawning over their features.

A low female voice comes from behind me, sending chills up my spine. "Well don't stop screaming on my account, gentlemen."

8 "NOW, NOW, NOT SO FAST. I don't bite," the voice says as I raise my hands, trying to summon the magic that had come so easily before. She emerges from behind me, walking slowly as she takes in my pathetic form. I feel my jaw fly open. I know this girl.

Harlow Creston. The one Reed warned me about.

She regards me curiously, her blonde head cocked slightly to the right, her eyes pale and keen, noticing everything. She looks like a wolf, calculating and fierce. There's something haunting about her, something deadly.

Her voice doesn't fluctuate from its quiet purr. "You have one chance to tell me what you're doing in this forest, or I'll break your other foot and leave you for dead. Your choice."

I gulp. I hate that I feel so small and terrified in her presence. If she learns the truth, she'll probably kill me here and now. Words spill out of my mouth in a nervous cluster, "There's this camp—I was looking for it. It's for people like me..." I make a show of looking to the cops and lowering my voice, "*Magic* people."

THE TRAITOR'S CRUX

In a heartbeat she's at my side, hands poised as some invisible force wraps itself around my neck. My lungs cry desperately for air.

"What do you know about the camp?" she hisses. When I don't answer, her hands twist, the magic clenching me tighter. My hands fly to my throat, trying to claw free.

I finally manage to croak out a lie, "Just that it's for witches and wizards. I'm magic. I wanted to find it—my mom kicked me out!"

She doesn't say anything, but releases her hold and I'm sent falling backwards. Everything hurts as the world goes momentarily blurry. I fight through the pain, watching as Harlow lets down the wall of fire and talks to the cop in a low voice. After a moment, they just nod then head calmly in the direction of their cars, not looking back.

"What'd you—what'd you do to them?" My voice is jumbled and hoarse. My body hurts...

Harlow crouches beside me, a cruel smile on her lips. "You're in luck. You get to come back with me."

Before I can react, her hands do their dance and everything begins to dissolve. She says something that I can't understand as the world around me fades to ash.

9

MY MIND BUZZES AS THE world comes rushing back at me. My thoughts and memories are next. The woods, the police, the fire. Harlow. Camp.

What did she do to me?

My eyes flutter open and I wince at the too-bright light staring back at me. Ignoring the bile rising in my throat, I force myself up into a sitting position. My heart beats anxiously, the deep tenor of a drum in my chest as I look around.

I'm in a hospital room. I'm lying in an old bed, my wrists shackled, and clothed in a white and blue speckled hospital robe. The gentle beeps of machines are the only sound in the room besides my shaky breathing.

The door clicks open and a dark-haired girl peeks through. She seems around my age, with beautiful dark skin and a long, graceful neck. "Well, good morning, sunshine!"

"Wha—where am I?" My voice is groggy and faint.

The girl ignores me and grabs a chair from the far corner, scooting it next to the bed. She plops down and uses a stethoscope to listen to my heart. "Just breathe normally."

I do as she says, trying to hold back the million questions I'd like to ask.

Satisfied, she removes the stethoscope and places it on the counter behind her, the chair rolling loudly against the tile. "You had a broken foot. Luckily, it was a clean break, so it was an easy mend. The spell cast on you was the real doozy—knocked you out for a few days."

Well, that explains it. My mind replays the scene in the forest. Harlow must have knocked me out so that she could bring me back to the camp.

I turn towards the girl, prying further. I have to make sure that this is really it. For all I know, Harlow could have sent me off somewhere and been on her way. "So, where am I, exactly?"

She gives me a small, sad smile. "I don't think I'm allowed to answer that. You scared lots of people with your arrival here. I think the leaders would like to talk to you first."

So, it is true. I'm here—I'm at the camp.

The girl chuckles at my wide-eyed gaze, "No worries, you're not in trouble. They're just curious mainly. You have to admit that it's strange that a girl like you was walking through the forest alone. You are looking much better, though. No offense, but when Harlow brought you in, you weren't looking too hot."

I play stupid. "Harlow? The one that threatened me back there?"

The girl laughs brightly. "In her defense, she thought you were trouble. She didn't expect to find someone capable of magic wandering through the woods. What were you thinking?" Using a flashlight, she shines a light into each of my eyes, one hand gently on my forehead.

"I-I don't really know..." I mumble, wondering how much of the story Harlow told them.

"Well, it was stupid of you! It's not safe anywhere for us."

I say nothing, bowing my head like a child as she scolds me.

She scribbles on a clipboard and places it at the end of the bed. "Alright, well, I'm gonna warn you now. The leaders will be stopping by later to chat. They're not quite convinced of your intentions." She disposes of her gloves and flings them over her shoulders. I blink in surprise as they disappear in mid-air. The girl doesn't seem to notice, "I'm Delia by the way. It's nice to finally meet you! Now that you're awake, I mean."

I sigh, leaning back into my pillow, stomach queasy with anxiety as Delia gives me a warm smile and disappears in the hall. So much has happened in the past few days. So much is at stake—I could've blown everything. As my mind drifts to Reed, a terrible thought comes over me.

My backpack is still in the woods.

The communicator, the bug... any way I could have communicated with Reed. They're all gone.

Horror fogs my mind. I can't get past the overwhelming thought of Reed as he realizes that I'm not around to answer his calls. What does he think right now? My heart races for my mother, left alone at the killer's home. She's probably at the White House with the president, being threatened and tortured. And Eli. It's been years of imprisonment. If he's alive, my guess is that it won't be for much longer.

I just ruined everything.

***

A FEW HOURS LATER, A gentle knock comes at my door. Delia pokes her head in again, a happy-go-lucky grin lighting her face. "You have visitors…" she says in a sing-song tone. She opens the door wider to reveal a dark-haired young man with beautiful deep green eyes followed by Harlow.

I barely recognize her after being so disoriented in the woods. She's cleaned up, blonde hair fastened back by a clip and wearing a collared blouse tucked neatly into her trousers. I can't help but think that she looks different from the girl in the mugshot. Devoid of dirt, mud, and bruises, she's one of the prettiest girls I've ever seen. The only signs of her once being a prisoner are the two faint scars, ghost-like on her cheekbones.

Harlow doesn't wait an instant to brush past the boy, a scowl on her face as she plants herself in a chair. "Delia, if you could give us a moment, please?" The blonde's icy gaze doesn't leave my face.

Delia purses her lips, stuffing her hands into her pockets, but complies. "It was nice to meet you, Kenadee. You two don't wear her out!"

Harlow waits for Delia to leave as the boy yanks up a chair beside her. There's something boyish and polite in his all-American looks as he inspects me with a shy sort of curiosity.

Harlow, on the other hand, scowls as she throws her head in the boy's direction. "This is Bryce Coughlin. We're the leaders that run this place."

"Nice to meet you." Bryce flashes me a deferential smile, extending a tanned hand.

I look to his outstretched hand to the cuffs on my wrists with a frown. Realizing the dilemma, he pulls away, dropping a sheepish gaze to the floor. Harlow smirks.

"Look," I say quickly, hoping that the embarrassment I feel isn't reaching my face. "I know what you're thinking, but I'm here for the same reason you are. I want protection from Reed."

A lie, but I continue with the same half-truth that I told Harlow. I'd been kicked out for my magic and I was worried about being caught. They listen in silence, watching me carefully as I tell my tale.

After a moment, Bryce's eyes meet mine again, brimming with questions, "How did you know about this camp? It's meant to be a secret. Only certain people know about it."

I maintain eye contact, determined to make this lie believable, "A friend told me the rumors that there was a camp full of witches in an old abandoned town. I didn't know if it was true, but I had nothing else to lose..."

"Oh, please—cut the crap," Harlow sneers, "We take extra precaution to ensure that this camp stays safe. No one knows about it unless they work for a certain slime bag, so why don't you stop wasting my time with lies and tell us the real reason why you're here."

"Har!" Bryce snaps, glaring at his partner. "Stop trying to scare the girl!" They exchange dark looks before Bryce turns back to me with a kinder expression. "Look, we'll protect you, we just want to know that you're telling us the truth. Did President Reed put you up to this?"

An image of Eli, limp, bloodied, and chained, pops up in my head.

I swallow and shake my head no.

"Well," Bryce says after a moment, "I guess that's it then. Welcome to our home."

"What?" Harlow snarls, bolting upright in her chair. "Absolutely not! She's lying through her teeth."

"*Harlow!*"

She shakes her head, "I'm putting my foot down, Bryce. We are not letting her just roam about, free to do as she pleases. People's lives are at risk!"

"Can I talk with you outside, please?" Bryce's voice is a low growl.

Harlow's to her feet an instant, "I thought you'd never ask."

Bryce throws me an apologetic smile over his shoulder as they hurry out the door. I watch through the little window as Bryce throws his hands in the air, each word getting more coated with frustration. Harlow, on the other hand, maintains control. Her tone is quiet and steady, too low to be heard through the walls.

She says something and Bryce scoffs. "Not everyone is out to get us, Har. Some people genuinely need help! She was looking for a safe place where she wouldn't be caught!"

Harlow says something that I can't make out.

"What do you suggest then?" asks Bryce, "Throw her out? Give her to the government? You of all people should know how that works out."

She shushes him, loudly. "Do you want the entire camp to hear you?" Her voice drops again, and I lean in to try and hear. "Look, I don't want her here. No one should know about this camp unless they work for Reed. We have lives we're trying to protect, Bryce."

He says something I can't hear. I turn away, feeling nauseous. She's right—I shouldn't be here. All I'm going to do is cause destruction and pain.

The door flings open and they file in. My heart races. While Harlow's face is a careful mask, Bryce wears the frustration visibly across his features.

Does that mean that Harlow won? Will I be kicked out, left to go back to the President with my tail between my legs?

Bryce tousles his chestnut hair with his hand, defeat radiating from his slumped shoulders. "Okay, Kenadee. You're free to stay, *but* we will be checking on you often."

That's it?

"Of course," I try to hide the relief that floods my body, "Thank you so much!"

"This is your only warning. Step out of line, and punishment will be rewarded," Bryce continues, "We won't be forgiving if you endanger the lives of our people."

I nod quickly, forcing a smile to my face.

"Excellent." Bryce stands, apparently satisfied with our meeting, "Then it's settled. I'll come back for you tonight or tomorrow, whenever Delia decides it's time for your discharge. We'll get everything prepared for you in the meantime. I'm sure you're ready to get out of here."

"I am *so* ready."

"Good." Bryce smiles, one hand already on the doorknob. "C'mon Har—we have a meeting to get to."

Harlow throws me a final wolfish glare before following Bryce. I hear her, just as the door sweeps closed, voice a low growl, "Whatever she does, Bryce, just know—it's on your shoulders. Not mine."

10

DELIA RETURNS SEVERAL agonizing hours later, doing a happy dance in the doorway. "You're about to be released! I know, I know, waiting is the absolute worst, but Bryce is on his way over right now to find you. You need anything before I discharge you from here?"

"No—I'm fine, really," I promise eagerly. I wiggle my toes for good measure. "My foot doesn't even hurt."

She brushes her dark corkscrew curls from her shoulder, clearly pleased. "Well, I sure hope not. I've worked as a healer for years and I like to think that I do a good job."

I smile politely, watching as her palms turn towards the ceiling and all the tubes and the machines follow her magic guidance. With a shove-like motion, she flicks her hands to the right, and any signs of medical equipment are gone. She smiles to herself and claps her hands together, ridding them of imaginary dust.

From there she turns back to me, fumbling with something.

"Sorry, secret spell. I'm not supposed to let anyone see. Let me just unlock your restraints." She swivels back around with a shiny brass key in her palm. I rub my wrists as the locks click open, wincing as my fingers trace the tender spot where the cuffs chaffed my skin.

"Sorry about that. Looks like they were a bit tight..." Delia winces, giving me a remorseful look. "I'll give you an ice pack to take with you to your room. Let me just go grab Bryce and tell him that you're ready. While you're waiting, why don't you change into these?"

She produces a bright pink t-shirt, jeans, and some slip-on shoes for me to wear. They look too big, but I'm just excited to get out of the awful hospital gown. It takes some extra effort from my weary body, but I ease on my new clothes and wait, taking advantage of the quiet room to think. I have to come up with a new plan, and fast. Somehow, I'm going to have to find a way to communicate with Reed without earning any more suspicions from the leaders. I'm not out of the woods yet with Harlow. It's clear she doesn't believe anything I said. I'm going to have to tread very carefully until I can earn her trust.

The door scrapes across the floor as it opens, loud and heavy. I jump at the sight of Bryce, so happy to get out of this stuffy room that I think I could kiss him. He laughs at my reaction. "I see someone is suffering from the hospital blues!"

"Get me out of here!" I joke back.

I wave him off as he tries to help me from the bed, eager to get out of the dark gray room with its depressing décor. I move too quickly, though, and have to lean back into the bed to regain my bearings. Bryce offers a steadying hand, concern written into the knit of his brows.

"I'm fine," I breathe, "I've just been lying down too long, is all."

"I'll show you to your room, that way you can get some rest if you'd like," he says as I slowly pull myself back into a standing position. The door pops open and Delia waltzes into the room, an ice pack in one hand, a white bag in the other.

The contents of the little bag rattle as she holds it up. "Here's a little something for your pain, if it comes back. It's pretty common to feel some aches and pains for a while—magic can cure a lot, but it does have its limits. Only take the medicine if you need to. Make sure you eat something with it! If you have any questions, I'll be around."

"Thanks Delia," I say, taking the ice pack and wrapping it around my throbbing wrist. Delia hands the prescription bag off to Bryce to hold as we wave goodbye and head out.

"So, now that we're alone, I wanted to apologize for our first little meeting," Bryce says, matching my slow stride as I try to weave through the throngs of people and wheelchairs clogging up the halls. "Harlow is…"

"Intense?" I say, only half-joking. I don't want to admit how much Harlow Creston actually terrifies me.

"That's one word for it," he replies. "Trust is a really hard concept for her sometimes. She's been getting better about it, there are just certain things that seem to set her off."

THE TRAITOR'S CRUX

We make one last right turn through the winding halls before two large glass doors appear. A bright ray of sunlight shines into my eyes as fresh air floods my senses.

"This feels like heaven!" I gasp, throwing my head back to gaze lovingly at the pale blue sky. Bryce lets out a good-natured laugh. There's something different about him, in the warm summer light. His square shoulders are loose and relaxed, short hair rumpled from the muggy afternoon. When he smiles at me, it's an easy, genuine smile.

"If you want," he offers, "I can show you your place so you can get some rest before dinner."

I shake my head. Maybe it's the radiance of the afternoon or just the relief of getting out of the hospital, but I'm not ready to be cooped up indoors quite yet. Tonight, I'll worry about calling Reed and getting on Harlow's good side.

But first, I say, "Can you show me around?"

"Of course," he looks to my injured foot then back to me, "but we should probably do a spell. It's kind of a long walk otherwise."

Trying to get over how odd that sentence sounded, I let him reach for my hand. With one hand still free, he digs around in his pocket and pulls out a small device with intricate carvings on its face. He holds it up for me to see. "We use these to get around. It'll take you to wherever you need to go—just do the spell and it'll put in the latitude and longitude of whatever location you desire. I stuck one in your welcome basket at your place. Everyone around here uses one."

"Anywhere?"

He nods, "Well, I'm assuming. I haven't tried the moon or anything, but if that's your thing then who knows?"

"*Cool!*" I whisper, as Bryce laughs and closes his eyes. His fingers tighten around mine as a sudden haze appears around my feet. Slowly, it creeps up towards my knees, then my hips. Panicked, I look to Bryce, who doesn't even budge.

The fog moves faster and faster, now at my torso. I look down to see that the lower half of my body has vanished within the heavy blanket of magic haze. It crawls faster rising up to my neck, my mouth, and the top of my head.

The fog takes over, a world of pure white. I feel like I'm in a never-ending tunnel, no sign of light, no way to escape. The next thing I know, I'm crumpled on the floor gasping for air and Bryce's hand is reaching to help me up. I let him pull me from my knees into a standing position, where I stagger like the alcoholic man who used to live next door.

"Sorry," Bryce says remorsefully, "It's kind of a doozy the first few times you do it. You'll get used to it!"

I'm about to respond, but then I glance around. We're in what looks like downtown Steamboat. There's no sign that there were ever any bombs that destroyed anything here. People of all ages mill through the streets, chatting happily, as there's no President trying to kill them and no war that once turned this town into rubble. Restaurants line the sidewalks, people sitting outside and sipping leisurely at their drinks. Signs on the street boast about summer clearance sales, or new-in autumn clothing. The mountains sit proudly in the background, the sun lowering itself to their peaks.

I feel myself let loose a sharp breath as I turn towards Bryce. "It's like... nothing even happened here."

The sun hits him in the eyes, making the emerald green more pronounced as he squints towards me, "We were desperate a few years back. Reed was on our tails and we had no place left to go. So, we came here, we protected the borders, and we enlisted everyone in rebuilding this place. It's become a home for a lot of us. We all work together to make it run."

"There are a lot more people than I expected..."

He shrugs, following my gaze towards the life buzzing around us. "Harlow and I... we started a few years back with saving prisoners from different internment camps. Then Reed responded by building this magic army, and honestly, they're tough. They got ahold of some of our people and made a big show of their deaths. We just couldn't risk sending anyone else out there."

"That's awful," I feel my heart sink in my chest. For a moment, I want to tell Bryce everything. But I can't. The truth is, they're all criminals here. From what Reed said, they're planning an attack. I can either turn them in and get my family back, or I can side with them, probably ending in innocent American's deaths as they seek their revenge.

I have to pick Reed.

As Bryce gives me a sad little smile, hands in his pockets, I change the subject. "So, is there training for people like me that are new at magic?"

He takes to the subject change with a grateful smile and spins on his heels, all-business, "C'mon. Let me show you something!"

Bryce doesn't stop his long-legged march until we're walking into a tall, glass building that looks out at the bluish mountainscape.

When we step inside, my jaw drops. We're in the biggest library I've ever seen in my life. I gape at the spiraling staircase that disappears into the level above. Bryce doesn't hesitate to climb them, clutching the railing with one hand and pointing eagerly with the other. "One of my favorite things we've built here. We do have books just for entertainment, but what you're wanting is actually here on the second floor."

We come unto the landing and he leads through the shelves, weaving in and out of their dark cherry wood. He comes to a sudden halt in front a section crowded with ancient covers and broken spines. The smell of musty pages fills my nostrils as I gape at all of the beautiful books.

Bryce reaches towards the top shelf and tips the top of a book so that it falls into his hands. "These are grimoires. Magic is a bit different for each person. We all might have different ways to do a spell, whether it's verbal, or physical, that depends on the person. Then there's healers, like Delia. They can't just fix an injury—

they usually create potions for different ailments. Grimoires are to help us document our spells so we know what works and what doesn't." He flicks off the coat of dust on the cover and opens the old, leather-bound book in his hands. The pages are yellowed with age and the handwriting is barely clear enough to read.

I lean in close to see as he continues. "The grimoires you'll find here are the finished ones. It usually takes years to fill one out completely. We like to keep documentation of everyone's work here in the library for new arrivals like you to study and practice. You never know what will work for you and what won't."

"This is amazing!" I say, flipping through the pages.

"Grab as many as you'd like. Take them with you to study."

I look at him excitedly. "I can do that?"

"It's a library, isn't it?"

I don't need any other encouragement. I stand on my tiptoes and reach for covers of varying states of decay and age. When both of our arms are full and I'm inhaling musty book dust, I decide that's probably enough.

"Okay, here's the thing," Bryce cranes his neck to see past the large pile in his arms. "I said take as many as you'd like, I really should've emphasized the importance of not taking the entire library. There's no way you'll read all of these before they're due back."

"Look," I laugh, taking extra precaution not to trip down the stairs considering I can't see where I'm going, "I'm eager to learn my magic, okay? If this is what it takes, then so be it!"

He presses his back against the door to open it and we step into the daylight, "I said study them, I didn't say they'd be your only method of training."

"What do you mean?"

He stops, trying to balance the tower of grimoires as he fishes in his pocket for the transportation device. When he finds it moments later, he looks back towards me with a blasé shrug, "Harlow trains the new arrivals. You'll be working with her mostly when it comes to magic. Studying is just a great idea so you can practice."

I almost respond, but he's already reaching for my hand, the cold metal of the device in his palm. We're swept away by the fog.

11

I FIND MYSELF SPRAWLED ACROSS a lawn, pinned down by the grimoires in a complete ironic twist.

"I've got to learn how to land on my feet," I grunt, clambering up as Bryce reaches for the fallen books. Learning that Harlow Creston, of all people, is going to be my magic instructor caught me completely off-guard.

Maybe it's a good thing. After all, Reed made it very clear that he wants me to get close to her. But on the other hand—it's Harlow. Which means life is going to get very difficult.

"Well? What do you think?"

My eyes move from the neatly-trimmed lawn I'd just been laying across to the little blue house that Bryce gestures towards with raised brows.

"I love it... whose is it?"

"Yours, of course."

"Mine?" I repeat, following him up the wooden steps to the door. Two wicker chairs, a tiny table, and a large potted plant decorate the porch as Bryce turns to me.

"Now, like pretty much everything in this town, this house runs on magic. We signed your name on the owner list this morning, so now only you can unlock it. It's simple, don't worry. All you have to do is press your hand against the door."

I nod, putting the books on one of the wicker chairs and pressing my palm against the dark wooden door.

There's a mechanical click and the door creaks open.

I let out an excited laugh, stepping aside to let Bryce in.

The house is tidy and bright inside, light washing in through the pale curtains. We step into the living room where there's a brown leather couch, a TV on the wall, a coffee table, and two comfy-looking chairs.

Bryce puts the grimoires on the table and turns towards me, running a hand through his brown hair. "So, we stocked the house up for you to get by a few days, but if you don't feel like making dinner tonight, there's a mess hall just downtown there. Honestly, you're only about a block away. I'll be there at six if you want to come. I'm just meeting up with some friends."

I nod politely, unsure if I really feel like being social tonight. Now that Bryce is about to leave and I'm about to be all alone, the reality sinks in. I'm going to have to figure out what to do about meeting with Reed.

Bryce uses his head to motion towards a hall, "The kitchen is that way. Harlow and I left some money earlier, in case you need supplies. I will also set up a training schedule for you to work with Harlow on your magic. If you need anything, there's a town map and a list of emergency contacts on the fridge. You can press our names on the paper and Harlow and I will know that you need us."

"Got it," I say, throwing him a short smile. He stands there awkwardly, rubbing the back of his head. I reach for his arm, squeezing it gently. "Hey, thanks for everything, really."

"Of course," he shrugs it off like it's no big deal, "Welcome to camp! We're glad you're here."

As he shuts the front door behind him, I abandon the stack of books and drift down the hallway. Sure enough, a small kitchen opens up to my left. There's a coffee pot beside the stove, an oven, a small pantry, a fridge and microwave. A table sits against the far dining room wall, painted a cheery yellow.

I go back through the hall until I enter the bedroom. A bed bigger than my old one sits between two night stands. I realize as I open the door to the closet and flick on the light, that I don't have any extra clothes. It looks like the leaders were prepared though, as a jacket, a few t-shirts, two pairs of jeans, and my dusty old hiking boots sit in the back. I turn the light off and head straight for the bathroom.

It's the first time I've actually seen myself in I don't know how long, and I'm terrified by my reflection. I'm a ragged mess of unruly hair and caked dirt. Violet bags hang underneath my dark eyes as if I'm more zombie than girl.

I decide to take a shower, watching the blood, leaves, and dirt empty down the drain as I press my head against the tile, letting everything soak away. What will Reed do when he realizes I'm not answering the communicator, or wearing the mic?

A sobering picture of Eli getting tortured clouds my mind.

Hurriedly, I switch off the shower, shivering as I wrap a towel around my cold body. I dress myself in a purple t-shirt and jeans, run a comb through my knotted hair, then make my way to the living room. I plop down on the couch, selecting a grimoire and opening it across my lap.

Surely somewhere in one of these, there's a communication spell I could cast. There has to be a way I can get a message to Reed, somehow.

I trace each line with my finger, skimming the pages in hopes of finding what I need. When I don't find anything in the first book, I toss it aside with a groan and reach for another. Two loud raps on the door pull me from my concentration.

"Who's there?" I jump to my feet, expecting to find Bryce on the other side of the door, but there's no one there.

Only a small box sits on the welcome mat, taped neatly shut. Confused, I grab it, scanning the streets for any sign of the person that left this. There's no one. I close the door behind me and race towards the kitchen, sliding a knife across the tape.

My fingers reach inside, tentative to what they might find. They land on something cool and sleek as I pull out the communicator. *My* communicator—dusty and encrusted with dirt, as if it'd been found in the woods.

My heart freezes. I don't breathe.

A small, crumpled piece of paper skitters across the counter. My hands tremble as I open the note.

Thought you might need this back.

12

I HAVE TO GET OUT of this house.

Someone in this camp knows who I am and what my purpose is. But *who*?

I look to the bright green clock on the microwave, which reads 5:45. Reed won't call until nine; I have roughly three hours.

I take a few calming breaths. The President will know what to do, how to handle this. For now, I need to take Markus' advice and stay well in the public eye. I have to pretend that things are alright, even if they're not.

I go to the closet and slip my jacket over my shoulders. The late afternoon thunderstorm is just beginning to rumble in the distance. Judging from the gray skies, the rain isn't too far off.

I head towards the opening in the road, eyeing a few buildings in the distance. Bryce said the mess hall was just a block away but coming across the busy street from before, I'm not sure which way to go. Luckily, a voice behind me saves the day.

"So, she decided to come, huh?"

"Hey Bryce!" I toss him a sheepish grin, "I'm glad you're here. I think I'm lost."

He chuckles, stuffing his hands in the pockets of his leather jacket. "Well, you're in luck, then. Right this way, ma'am."

We hurry towards the sidewalk, ducking underneath the various awnings of the building as the rain begins to pour. He finally stops in front of a bright red door and holds it open.

"Kenadee! Bryce!" Delia calls, standing to wave us over.

The mess hall has several brightly colored tables with mismatched chairs around them. I look around for the food line, giving Bryce a confused glance. "Where do we get the food?"

"All you have to do is find your spot at the table, and we'll explain from there," Bryce half-yells over the crash of silverware and voices.

"Oh, my goodness, finally! I thought you two got lost!" Delia says, looking impatiently at me and Bryce. The table is crammed with a large group of people around my age, who, as Delia talks, turn and stare at me with the expressions of people who just got caught gossiping.

I cross my arms self-consciously across my chest, giving a tiny nod to the suspicious looking crowd in front of me.

Ignoring the dirty looks, Bryce introduces me. "Hey guys, I'd like you all to meet our newest member. This is Kenadee!"

"Hi," I say nervously as several sets of eyes stare me down. No one responds, making the situation that much more awkward. Luckily, it only takes a single beat for Delia to step in.

"Kenadee, this is Benson, Kenzie, and Tess." She gestures towards a boy with chocolate colored hair and sharp cheekbones. He barely looks at me, too busy pretending to be immersed in his meal. Beside him is Kenzie, her long brunette waves flowing loosely down her back. She says nothing, but meets my gaze with a snicker before turning to Benson and whispering something.

Tess, a redhead with freckles spotting her entire face, is the only one that smiles. She scoots over on the bench and pats the seat, "Here, come sit by me!"

Grateful, I quickly go to take it, ducking my head to avoid everyone else's judgmental gazes. Bryce scoots in next to me, throwing me an apologetic look.

"So, how does this work?" I ask, desperate to change the subject, "You just sit down and food comes?"

"Wait for it..." Delia says, stabbing a piece of broccoli with her fork.

Seconds later, a tiny pop of orange appears in mid-air, transforming into a menu that floats light as a feather into my open hands.

"See? Tap your finger on whatever you want to eat and it'll appear when it's done cooking," she explains.

"Magic. It's great, right?" Tess adds eagerly.

After perusing the menu, I decide on a big, juicy hamburger, tapping on the picture as I was instructed. It evaporates a moment after my touch, leaving me staring in awe at the table before me.

"So, Kenadee, what's your story?" Tess inquires biting into a carrot that's nearly the same color of her hair.

Crap. What do I tell them?

I debate lying. Whatever I do, I need to keep away from the suspicions that they already have about me.

I decide to play dumb. "Uh, what do you mean?"

"You know, how you ended up at our camp? Bryce and Harlow have been really tight-lipped about it! Everyone's been making up their own versions of why you're here and how you found us." She peers slyly over to Bryce, who ignores us, talking animatedly with Benson and Kenzie.

"Well, it's a really long story…" I shrug it off, tracing my finger across the patterns in the table, "You probably don't want to h—"

"Ah, here she is! We were wondering where you were!" Bryce catches all of our attention as he gets up to greet someone. I catch a glimpse of sandy blonde hair.

Harlow.

She doesn't seem to see me, laughing as Bryce says something I can't quite make out. All I know is that Harlow Creston is the last person I feel like dealing with.

Unfortunately for me, Delia waves to get the blonde's attention. "Hey! Har, look who's here!"

The girl's ice-colored eyes drift towards me, her smile faltering at the sight. Her gaze turns cruel and cold, taking me in like I'm a measly little bug she's about to smash.

"Hi," I say in a small voice, giving her a meager wave.

She looks me up and down silently before turning back towards the other leader, "I thought we agreed that she was supposed to be under surveillance, Bryce."

"Har—" Bryce says, giving her a warning look. "Can we not do this here?" The entire table is quiet as they watch.

"Fine. We'll talk later," Harlow says calmly, her voice dangerously low.

The weight of the silence at the table hits hard. She hates me. They all do. How am I supposed to earn their trust when they already dislike me so much? And surveillance? What if I need to meet with the President? How will I warn him if they're right there listening?

Delia leans in as Bryce and Harlow debate quietly on the other side of the table. "Ignore her. She can be a bit hard to handle at first, but she'll come around."

I don't believe her, but I'm grateful for the attempt to make me feel better.

"Alright, well, if you don't want to talk about the camp, can I at least ask where you're from?" Tess licks a spoon clean before dipping it back into some soup, watching me with warm brown eyes, the freckles speckling her cheeks turning up with her smile.

My plate appears, piece by piece, dropping before my eyes. It's crammed with delicious food I haven't had in ages. I immediately dig in, practically drooling from the hunger.

"Oh, um, I'm from Denver," I say, clearing my throat. I have to restrain myself from clearing the entire plate of food before me. I was much hungrier than I thought.

Tess leans in on her elbows, "So, you aren't too far from home! That's not the case for me. I'm from Minnesota. I can't say that I miss it that much, though. It's too cold."

I'm too focused in on my food to muster any response but a polite smile.

"Well, we're glad you're staying. It's fun getting new people here. There's lots of people, but most keep to themselves. Not many young people our ages. I actually don't know how the leaders handle it. They're younger than most of the members here, but they got elected as leaders because they basically created this entire camp. Everyone just loves them!"

I almost snort. *Harlow?* For some reason, she seems pretty hard to love.

"Oh, speaking of which, you are coming to the bonfire, aren't you?" Delia adds looking at me expectantly.

"What's that?" I ask, taking a sip of my water.

"What, the gracious host didn't tell you? It's this huge event we have a few times a year. Most of the camp shows up. There's games, rides, prizes—kind of like the carnivals. Do you remember those from when we were kids? I love 'em!" Tess reminds me of an eager child, exclaiming loudly with excitement.

"You should come," Bryce agrees, butting back into our conversation. "It's tomorrow. You can hang with me if you'd like."

I resist the smile that threatens to rise. It's been so long since I've had friends, people that care enough to invite me to things. Not to mention, this is the perfect opportunity to see people, to take notes on the kinds of people that live here at this camp.

"Yeah, that sounds like fun." Deep down, my mind stings at the pain I'm bringing down upon these people.

I'm on my way to destroy their lives. How can I just smile and go along?

I guess we all have a bit of a monster in us.

***

I WAKE THE NEXT MORNING to wet drool stains on my pillow and streaks of sun washing in through the closed blinds of my window. I yawn, and as I roll over, a grimoire slides off my stomach and onto the bed. I rub my eyes before swiveling the alarm clock towards me.

2:12 in the afternoon. I definitely overslept.

When I got back from dinner last night, I waited and waited in nervous anticipation for Reed to call. When the clock struck midnight and I realized that Reed was probably fast asleep in his mansion, I nestled under the covers to read a grimoire and tried to calm my racing mind.

I cast aside my covers and pull my sore body into a sitting position. Today, I need to focus on Reed and his mission. Whoever left the communicator at my doorstep needs to see that I'm not afraid. If I act like I'm doing something wrong, I might blow the entire operation. It'd be just what Harlow is looking for. I could only imagine her delight then.

THE TRAITOR'S CRUX

Kicking my legs from the bed, I go straight to the kitchen to make coffee. As the coffee pot begins to rumble, I find a mug the color of the sun and a spoon from the drawer. Somewhere outside a lawn mower roars to life, and I consider how strange this little town is. How safe it feels. This would be my life if there was never a war.

Once the pot is full and steam billows from the top, I mix my coffee with some milk from the fridge, stirring as the metal clang of the spoon meets ceramic. I wash my face with some raspberry-smelling soap from the cabinet and run a comb through my messy hair.

Satisfied, I throw on the first clothes I can find—a maroon t-shirt and some faded blue jeans, and pad barefoot to the porch, coffee in one hand, a map of the town in the other. A group of kids giggles as they race through the streets in front of me as I take a seat in one of the wicker chairs. Technically, I could try and use my magic to transport myself around instead of trying to memorize a map. After all, my powers worked that day Harlow found me in the forest. The "how" part is what I can't figure out.

I chew on the inside of my lip, a sudden idea coming to me. Looking around to make sure no one is watching, I lift my hand above the map.

Nothing happens.

I swallow in frustration, trying again. Not that I expect anything grand to happen—I don't even know the spell that I'm trying to make work—I just want to see if my powers will come back. That day in the forest they were so strong, so terrifying. It's like they controlled *me*. Is that what magic is really like, or was it the heat of the moment, the fear I felt so deeply?

"Trying your powers, are you? Don't worry, magic is finicky. The more you practice the better it'll be." My head pops up to find an elegant woman with golden-brown skin and a presidential smile steps onto the porch. She's dressed in a white sundress and sandals, one hand on her pregnant stomach and the other clutching a plate of cookies. "I'm Nadine, your next-door neighbor. I thought I'd stop by, introduce myself, and bring you some goodies."

"I'm Kenadee," I say sheepishly, taking the cookies. "Thank you for this! Would you like to come in?"

"Oh no, honey, I'd better not. I'm part of the town's advisory board and the leaders called together a last-minute meeting. Can't be late!"

"Oh?" I ask, trying to act much less curious than I actually feel. Maybe Nadine is the key to finding out new information for Reed.

"Yeah. Reed's apparently up to something again." She rolls her eyes to emphasize how annoying she finds this fact.

I feel my breath hitch in my throat. This meeting couldn't be about me, could it? Is Harlow finally convincing people that I'm up to something?

Nadine sighs deeply, turning to go, "But what can you do, right? Anyway, do you need anything before I go? It's probably pretty confusing around here without magic."

"Actually, yeah..." I admit, "Where can I find the leaders? Bryce said something yesterday about a schedule and job hunting."

"Their offices are at the town hall. Here," she holds out her hand for the map, which I surrender. She chants something foreign under her breath, and a bright red pin pops up on the top of a building. She hands it back to me with a smile, "There. The spell will show you the way. The meeting should only last half an hour and then they should be back."

I thank her again with a genuine smile as Nadine pulls a transportation device similar to Bryce's from her bag. In a flash, she's gone.

I turn towards the door, a plateful of cookies in my hand, reminding myself that I'm not here to make friends.

13

AN HOUR LATER, I ROAM downtown, frowning at the map in my hands as a bright red arrow tells me to take a left.

I follow its directions until, in bright flashing letters, the map reads YOU'VE ARRIVED. I tilt my head back, squinting against the beaming sun at an old red and orange bricked building about three stories tall. Inside, its halls are quiet and still, darkened by the lack of windows. A directory floats in mid-air, names in bold letters and arrows pointing at which direction to go.

Finding the leaders names, I'm pointed to the right. Sure enough, I come to a door with HARLOW CRESTON AND BRYCE COUGHLIN, CAMP LEADERS on a gold plaque.

The offices are as quiet as the hallway. I'm the only person besides the receptionist, who talks animatedly to a floating image that sits in the air. Curiously, I can't hear it making any noise. Is that a phone? I wait impatiently, leaning my elbows on her desk as I look around the room. Windows face outward, the first I've seen in the building, and I can see the tall aspen trees outside as a few groups of people occasionally stroll by, enjoying the afternoon sun.

The secretary still ignores me for her floating head conversation. Growing impatient, I rotate so I'm straight in her point of view. "Excuse me, ma'am. I'm looking for Bryce."

She glowers at me and rolls her eyes to whoever she's talking to. "Give me a second, there's a person who clearly can't wait."

She extends her palm, using her fingers in a pinching motion, freezing the screen of the photo. I smile politely, ignoring the dirty look I receive in exchange.

"What do you want?" She asks coldly.

"Is Bryce here? I need to talk to him," I repeat, trying to make my voice pleasant.

"Mr. Coughlin isn't here right now," she responds matter-of-factly.

"Will he be back soon?" I ask. "The door thing said he's supposed to be here right now. His hours are nine to four, right?"

She huffs, her gaze unflinching from mine, "I said he isn't here, *didn't I?* He had to step out for some emergency. I didn't get any more information. I'm not his babysitter, believe it or not. Miss Creston is here, would you like to speak to her instead?"

"Uh, well—"

If I wanted to leave, I'm too late. Harlow emerges from one of the rooms, dressed in black pants and a lacy top that looks much too delicate considering Harlow's personality. "Alright, Julie, I'm leaving," she says, her back turned to us as she locks her door.

The receptionist, Julie, betrays me. "Do you know when Bryce will be back? This new girl insists on speaking with him." She pops her gum, attention back on the computer screen.

Harlow turns towards me, a mocking pout on her lips. "Aww, Bryce actually let go of your hand? Whatever will you do?"

I blush, shaking my head as I turn towards the door. "I'll just come back later."

Harlow's voice stops me, "He had an emergency. No one knows when he'll be back. Unfortunately, it's my job to help you and be accommodating in these kinds of scenarios. What do you need?"

I face her again, sighing. "He mentioned a training schedule. I was only following up."

She clicks her tongue. "Luckily for you, you're talking to the person in charge of training. Meet me tomorrow at the gym, six A.M. sharp. Don't be late."

I nod slowly, turning to leave when the anger churns in my stomach. I spin to face her, the words spilling out before I can stop them, "What's your problem? I did absolutely nothing to you! I just wanted to find the camp."

The blonde chuckles quietly, arms crossed over her chest as she takes a few steps forward. Her glare is so full of hatred, part of me wishes I could crawl under the covers and hide. "Do you think I was born yesterday? People don't just show up like that unless they're up to something. We work hard to keep this camp a secret. Want to know why?" I say nothing as she comes towards me, as dangerous as a predator. "Reed and his soldiers try to get into this camp. They want all of us dead. The last time they nearly succeeded, so forgive me if I see past your little sweet-girl act. Why don't you tell me what you're up to? Hmm?"

"I want to talk with Bryce," I restate, trying to stop the shakiness from taking over my voice. I can't let her know how afraid I really am.

She sneers, "Of course, you do. Just keep your head down, new girl. Keep on kissing Bryce's ass. He may think that you're innocent, but I don't. I've had my share of snitches before and I know people like you. If you hurt anyone, I swear to God, I will ruin you."

"I'm not," I spit, lying through my teeth. "Looks like you have nothing to worry about."

She knows. She's onto me.

She hits me on the shoulder as she leaves, not bothering to say another word to me. The door slams behind her, no more words left to say.

Julie and I look on in awkward silence, unsure of where to go from here. She unmutes the phone as if suddenly remembering the conversation she held before I so rudely interrupted.

I see myself out, trying to calm the panic that threatens to spill over.

14

"MORE BOOKS ALREADY? DIDN'T you bleed them dry yesterday?"

When Bryce finds me a few hours later, I'm in the library, searching through the massive number of ancient books, taking comfort in the familiar mildew scent of paper that's served a long life.

"Ha. *Ha*," I say pointedly, biting down on my lip to keep the smile at bay. I turn my attention back to the books. I can't do this. I can't like a person I'm going to betray.

"But really. What are you doing? You may be magic, but there's no way you could have read all those grimoires already!" He leans against the shelf with his shoulder, watching me with those vivid green eyes. He's so close, only inches away. I catch his scent of coffee and aftershave and swallow.

"I want to be prepared. I start training tomorrow."

What I don't say is that I don't want to give Harlow any leverage by not being able to perform to her liking.

"Oh, yeah, Harlow said you came by the office. Sorry I wasn't there, I had an unexpected emergency. A kid's powers went awry by accident and, long story short, I had to disconnect his hand from his forehead."

"What? No! That's horrible," I gasp, forgetting that I'm not supposed to be looking at Bryce as he suppresses a laugh. I shove him teasingly in the shoulder, "Don't laugh. That sounds like something that would happen to me."

"Then you're lucky you live in a place filled with magic—we can always fix it. Well, ninety-five percent of the time at least…"

"Just ninety-five? That's comforting." I snicker, "Dare I ask about the other five percent?"

He laughs, waving a hand as if it's nothing, "Well, they're screwed, to put it kindly. Anyway, Harlow made you a schedule for the rest of the month." He pulls some papers from his pocket and offers them to me.

"Thanks." I unfold them, pressing out the crease with my fingers and looking over the training schedule. "Wow, every single day? Harlow doesn't mess around."

"But she's the best trainer you'll ever have." He studies me for a moment, then says, "If you don't mind me asking… what happened between you two? Harlow was all pissy like she'd been in a fight, and I like her, I do, but I know how she can be. Did she say something to you?"

"Um, I mean, she answered some of my questions for me." I don't look him in the eyes, Harlow's blunt words replaying in my head. She knows and she's going to kill me the moment she realizes the truth. I lied to her face and she knows it.

"Just tell me what she said. Trust me, it happens a lot. She isn't one to filter her words. It always seems to cause hurt feelings. How did she offend you?" His tone rings with exasperation, clearly used to Harlow's method of dealing with people.

"Just that she doesn't trust me and she'll ruin me if I quote unquote *try anything.*"

Bryce sighs, shaking his head. "She certainly doesn't beat around the bush, I'll give her that. I'm so sorry she did that. I promise I'll talk with her about it. She'll get used to you soon enough and leave you alone. She's just nervous about something that's been going on lately."

"What do you mean?" I pry.

His eyes meet mine, the thin streaks of sunlight making one eye appear the color of celery. "I'm really not supposed to tell you. It's a confidential subject. You really shouldn't worry about it, anyways. We're prepared to handle it."

I bite at my lip, hearing the news that I dreaded most. What do I say when I'm the danger, the thief lurking in the shadows, waiting to strike? "Well, surely, if we're in danger, there's something we could do, right?"

What kind of danger, exactly, is he talking about?

He does his best to smile, but it doesn't quite reach his eyes. "No, don't you worry about a thing. You're safe. I shouldn't have even brought it up."

I nod, unsure of what else to say. I'm going to have to report this to the president when he calls.

"On a happier note, the bonfire is tonight. You are still coming, right? It would be good for you to get out and meet everyone. This is the one event that people actually show up to," Bryce says, his tone getting brighter at the subject change. His smile makes my heart skip a beat.

"Yeah, I'll probably stop by for a bit." I really don't want to go, but it would be good. I can work on earning people's trust and seeing how the camp works.

He throws a crooked grin my way. "Yes! I'm glad. You might even get to hear me ruin a song with my terrible guitar playing."

"It's all I've ever dreamed of."

He checks his watch. "Well, I have another meeting that I'm late for, so Harlow might murder me, but if not, I'll see you tonight?"

As he walks off, my hopes die. I can never have him. After all, I'm the one seeing to his destruction. Harlow's spot on about me. Part of me wishes that he could see it too, that I wouldn't have to live in a world filled with lies. Reed's note from the forest replays in my brain. *Survival of the fittest.*

They need to learn that too, before it's too late.

***

I CAN HEAR TESS AND Delia bickering on my front porch before I even open the door.

"If you freeze tonight, it's your fault," says Delia, gesturing towards Tess' sandaled feet.

"Delia, it's August!"

I pull the door closed behind me as Delia scoffs, "Practically September. The fall weather is coming. You know, you do this every time, T!" she mimics her with a melodramatically high-pitched voice, "*I'm from Minnesota! I don't get cold like you do*! Then, it gets dark and you realize there's no hot sun on you anymore, then the whining begins! Kenadee, would you tell her, please?"

They both turn on me as I throw my hands in the air. "I'm only here for the bonfire."

"Whatever. What do I care? It's not like I'm your mom," Delia exclaims. Tess sticks out her tongue as Delia holds out the transportation device. "Now, let's go! It's already started."

We land somewhere on the edge of town. The darkness is setting around us, the sun sneaking lower and lower beneath the mountains. The air is crisp and thin; the fresh smell of the forest reminds me of home.

People are everywhere, voices drunk with excitement. Tess asks me question that I don't hear because I'm scanning the crowd for familiar faces. "Sorry… what?"

"Where's your head tonight? Definitely not here," Delia asks, watching me with concern, "You okay?"

"Yeah, fine," I say quickly, "It's just a lot take in."

"You sure?" Tess watches me carefully, as if she can see right through me. I nod briefly, avoiding her eyes. I can tell she doesn't believe me, but she lets it drop.

"You know what I think?" she asks, shivering as she walks, "I think you need to let loose a little. Have some fun. We'll introduce you around!"

"Yeah, but you gotta come out of your shell. C'mon now!" Delia trots forward, grabbing my hand and dragging me ahead of Tess. I can't help but laugh, even as they practically rip my arm from its socket. We top the hill and I can see the orange flicker of fire licking at the darkening sky. Giant benches center around the bonfire area, where lots of people mill about. As we near, my ears tune into the calm strumming of an acoustic guitar and a sweet, low voice crooning away.

"Oh, yeah, should've warned ya. There's always music. You'll get used to it. It's like a freakin' concert all the time. Especially with Bryce."

"*That's* Bryce?" I ask, surprised, listening as he plays some Elvis song. My dad used to listen to Elvis, rocking one of us on his hip as he'd dance while making dinner. I close my eyes at the sweet memory.

"Yeah, Bryce is always singing something. You'll be able to detect him from a mile away. After a few days, you'll be sick of it!" Tess and Delia exchange a look with raised brows.

As we head closer, I can begin to make him out. He's hunched over a guitar surrounded by a group of people as he strums animatedly. He looks happy and carefree, lost in the music.

We find spots closest to the fire, right across from Bryce. Nearby, I spot Kenzie, the girl from the mess hall. She's immersed in conversation, joking and giggling in a sea of girls, clearly the center of entertainment. Harlow sits on the other end a few feet away, appearing lost in thought as she stares expressionlessly into the fire.

I hear my name and look up just as Kenzie and the group of girls burst into fits of laughter. I blush, digging my tip of my shoe into the dirt.

"Knock it off, Kenz," Tess says, her voice surprisingly vicious. The girl only scoffs back, clearly not used to being stood up to. She stands up and leaves, her group of admirers trailing behind her like a flock of ducks. "Ignore them," Delia says, turning towards me and blocking Kenzie from sight, "They're jealous. Kenz can be a real bitch when she wants to. It's really just a show to try to get Har's attention. Kenzie's always kissing her ass because she's a leader. I can tell it drives Harlow crazy."

"I'm used to mean girls," I say, brushing it off. I've had my fair share at school since my brother and father were found as guilty criminals.

"That doesn't make it okay. I promise they'll get better. Give them time." Tess smiles kindly, but I don't believe her. Something tells me Kenzie won't be changing any time soon.

"So, how do you like camp so far?" Delia leans in closer, trying to talk over the noise of the guitar and the crowd. The breeze picks up, making the leaves around us rustle in the now -dark skies.

"It's been great so far. Most everyone has been nice. I start training tomorrow."

Tess groans, "I remember those training days. Not fun."

"You get to work with Har, right?" Delia asks, pulling the edge of her blanket to her shoulders.

THE TRAITOR'S CRUX

I nod. "Unforunately. Which means you might find me dead somewhere."

"Yikes. I remember training with her. They were some of the most intense times of my life," Tess says loudly, then looks across the fire. Fortunately, Harlow doesn't seem to have heard. "I used to hate going to class with her because she's so tough. But, she's the best magic teacher we have here. Everyone that's ever trained with her can prove it."

"I don't know... She really hates me, you guys."

"Oh please, she doesn't hate you," snorts Delia, "You've got to take her with a grain of salt. She takes a long time to warm up to people. She was locked up for years with Reed. Got arrested twice. She won't ever talk about it, but everyone knows that he did something awful to her."

I consider asking more, but the music stops and Bryce's eyes land on me. My heart skips a beat. He waves happily as Delia and Tess begin whispering about something else. Bryce stands and sets down the guitar, saying something to Harlow who tears her distant gaze away from the fire for the first time since we arrived. She watches him disappear into the shadows, then must feel me looking. Blue eyes lock on mine, and for the first time, they're not hate-filled and cold. They're... haunted, confused, like she's been somewhere else entirely.

There's a popping, the crash of fireworks, and she jumps, looking towards the source of the noise.

"Ooh, look!" Tess jumps up from her seat, distracting me as she points to the air. "The fireworks show! This is the coolest part. No one can see or hear it from outside the camp. Isn't that awesome? I hope they have the singing ones this year! Have you ever heard of those, Kenadee? No, never mind—I guess you wouldn't. Wait until they come! You'll love them!" She hurries forward, shoving herself through the crowd trying to get a better view.

The fireworks burst vividly straight into the sky, framed by a backdrop of speckled bright white stars. Delia groans, "I better go find her. I swear, Tess is the biggest child I've ever met at times. She probably shouldn't be left alone. You wanna come with?"

I shake my head no, feeling content in front of the warm fire. "Nah, I think I'll stay. Catch up with you later?"

"Yeah, of course! We'll come find you after. Tess and I are having a good ole fashioned sleepover tonight, if you want to join us!" She winks before disappearing into the large mass of bodies.

Most everyone has rotated that way now, clearing out the ring of fire. I sit by myself for a moment, grateful for the second of silence to myself. This might be the perfect opportunity to take some notes for Reed.

I pull out the notepad I shoved in my pocket before I came to the bonfire. It's a faded navy color and so small that I'm forced to write in tiny letters. I glance around. No one's watching, which makes the timing perfect.

I jot down notes of what Bryce mentioned before, about danger in the camps. I don't know that Reed will be that interested, but it's a topic at least to cover. I also write down everyone's name so far that I've met.

> HARLOW — SUSPICIOUS LEADER OF CAMP. MY MAGIC TEACHER
> BRYCE — ALSO A LEADER. LOTS OF MEETINGS. SAYS THERE'S DANGER
> DELIA — NURSE
> NADINE —

My pen pauses in mid-air as loud screams sound from the firework show followed by a gigantic white flash. I look up just in time as a huge flame shoots straight into the air, a massive firework unfolding from its depths. It morphs into a bird, then an elephant, too big and too bright. The people are nervous, slowly backing up. It doesn't vanish like other fireworks. Instead, it only grows bigger and brighter.

Intrigued, I stare at the transforming flame as it soars through the sky. Just when it seems to fill the entire sky, it begins barreling towards the crowd of campers.

I stand, tumbling backwards over the log as I watch in horror. Somewhere in the dust and dirt, I lose track of my notebook. People are scattered everywhere, pushing, shoving, trying to get out.

The ball of fire hits the ground, making it shake as it explodes amongst the trees, throwing people backwards off their feet.

More and more flamed fireworks fly into the air, taking only a second before they explode, one by one, falling from the sky. I'm lost in a world of smoke, chaos, and confusion. The crowd of people is too heavy for me to get through or spot anyone I may know.

What's happening? Is this an attack?

"*Hey!*" someone slams into me with full force, shoving me backwards. They don't stop, but disappear once again in the trees. Lying on my back, the disorientation hits hardest. I stare at the sky, now covered in a heavy blanket of haze and smoke.

"Are you stupid?" someone yells over the roar of the people. Harlow comes into view, standing over me with panic in her eyes. She reaches for my hand to help me up. "Go inside!" she orders once I'm on my feet. She begins to turn away as I grab her arm.

"What's happening?" I ask loudly, feeling the smoke in my throat.

"I don't have time for this!" she yells back, yanking her arm from my grip. I follow, grabbing her shoulder this time. She swings around, her eyes wild with fear.

"Harlow, what's happening?" I repeat, holding onto her firmly. For a brief second, her frightened eyes meet mine.

"I don't know. Go inside, get people in and we'll talk."

I do as she says, letting go of her shoulder and turn to join the crowd, taking one last glance as her blonde head disappears into the madness and fog.

15

EVERYONE HEADS FOR THE closest building, which is a raging storm of panic and tears when I enter. I'm forced to shove through, making my way slowly around the throngs of people clumped tightly together. So far, I don't see any familiar faces. Standing on my tiptoes, I do my best to peer over the sea of swarming bodies and people taller than me, anxiety forming a tight knot in my gut. How will I find them in all of this mess? How do I know they're okay?

The sweat, the sounds, the smell of fire still stuck in my nostrils is unbearable. Bile rises in my throat as I clasp a hand to my lips, barely making it in time to the trash can. I clutch its plastic edges, vomit plummeting into its depths. All I want to know is what happened. Is this the danger that Bryce was talking about? Or was it something else? Immediately, an image of Reed appears in my head. I shake it off.

No, it can't be. How would it?

I throw up again into the trash can, wiping my face weakly as my white knuckles clasp the handles. I'm thrown aside as someone slams into me with massive force.

"Ow! Careful!" I groan. Despite her tiny size, Tess is strong and her hug is even stronger. She hangs onto me tightly, her red braids messy with hairs sticking out every which way, her clothes reeking of smoke.

"Oh, my god, I was trying to find you but you were gone! Don't you ever scare me like that again!" she scolds once she finally lets me go to breathe again. She looks to the trash can, taking in my vomit-covered chin. "Are you okay?"

"Me? Yeah, I'm fine. Just a bit shaken. I'm glad you're here, though. Where's Delia?" I ask, looking around. Usually, the pair are inseparable.

"She's a doctor so she had to stay behind at the scene, see who she could find. Help the people that got hurt."

"Oh, do you know what happened?" I ask, wiping at my chin.

She shrugs just as lost as I am. "I don't know, it was crazy. I mean, it looked like this one spell... but the weird thing is that they're illegal here at camp. If they find you doing it, you get kicked out. It's *that* bad," she says nervously, biting at her lip as she looks around the room.

The thumping of a mic immediately captures the crowd's attention. We all turn to the front where Bryce and Harlow stand with weary looks on their faces, waiting for the conversations to die down. Slowly, the voices begin to quiet as all eyes turn to the leaders. I can tell right away from looking at them that whatever this was—it was unexpected.

"Hey everyone, settle down please," Bryce starts politely, the usual cheer gone from his tone, "We were all there to witness, and we all know what happened, so I'm going to get right to it. There was an attack on us tonight from unknown sources. As of right now, we have no fatalities from the explosion and only a few are injured. Those that were hurt have already been taken to the hospital and remain under intensive care. We have specially trained forces out searching the grounds as we speak, looking for evidence. We don't have much information at this moment, but we can assure you that we are doing everything in our power to find the guilty party. Once we do, we promise that they will pay a heavy price for the danger they brought us all tonight."

The crowd begins to shout, talking over one another in voices filled with anger and desperation. "Everybody needs to calm down so I can—" Bryce begins, but everyone is too panicked. He's drowned out by the roar of the crowd.

Harlow steps up to the plate, grabbing the microphone impatiently from Bryce. "How about you all shut up and listen?" Her voice is low, almost eerily calm, but the people listen immediately, passing around several obnoxious *shh* as the noise once again dies down.

"Thanks, Har," Bryce says, his voice dripping with gratitude as he continues, "Anyway. Since we don't know who did this or why, we'd like to offer free lessons for all campers in defensive magic. We believe acts like this can be stopped if we stay strong. Come see us for a sign-up sheet if you are interested. We're adding in a new rule to ensure everyone's safety here—"

He's once again interrupted, his voice drowned by the frightened cries and angry yells of people searching for reason. He begins to talk louder, his voice still lost in all of the confusion, "It's just for our safety. Just in case!"

"Hey, people!" Harlow says a little more intensely this time, steering the microphone to her face, "Do you wanna hear this, or not?"

Once again, the buzz of the crowd dies down, this time, as people glower at the two leaders standing in front of them.

Bryce continues nervously, his voice unnaturally loud and his green eyes betraying his worry, "Starting tomorrow, we will be having a mandatory curfew. You are all to be inside by nine P.M. You must have special permission from one of us if you have any exceptions or unique circumstances. I'm sorry it has to come to this, but we believe that it's in everyone's best interest…"

This time when the angry crowd picks up, he doesn't try to fight it. He mumbles something meekly into the microphone before turning to Harlow, worry written in his features.

I can see how tense they are from here. Like they're arguing. As if feeling my eyes on them, Harlow turns my way, glowering straight at me. Something in her expression tells me that she believes I'm the one to blame for this. Feeling anxious, I look away, grabbing Tess's shoulder. "Should we get out of here?"

I may not have caused this tonight, but I am a spy. I'm causing terror in private as I meet with the president, telling him all of their secrets so he can find them. I'm going to kill them all.

Reed is a monster, that's clear. He may not have done this, but I'm sure he has a lot more planned for them. I wish so badly I could tell them everything. The guilt is eating at me, a burden I feel I can't bear. I'm already falling apart, taking them with me, deeper and deeper to the pits of despair.

With no place to hide from myself, the tears threaten to spill.

I nearly let them.

"Bryce!" I yell, trying to elbow my way through the crowd, "*Bryce*!"

After the speech, everyone left in a mass group, making it hard to breathe. I can see him ahead of me, his head of thick dark hair. I can even hear him, trying to explain the reasons for the new rules to some furious people. I can hear their shouts, wondering why the leaders aren't sharing more information, accusing them of keeping information from their own people.

Part of me wonders that too. There was something in the way they seemed to argue after the speech, their tense body language, and Bryce's nervousness. Were they only frightened from the attacks, or is there more to the story? I remember Bryce saying that there was danger. *I shouldn't even tell you this…*

"Bryce!" My voices strains as I do my best to get his attention. Hearing his name, he turns around, confused.

When his eyes meet mine, he gives a weak smile, one that doesn't reach his eyes.

"We'll talk tomorrow once everything calms down a bit. Come see me in my office and I'll explain!" he offers to the angry woman who he was arguing with. She rolls her eyes, but turns and heads out the door.

"Hey," he says making his way to me, exhaustion making his voice husky.

"What *really* happened back there?" I ask, not bothering with the niceties. I know something's up, and I want to know what it is.

"Well aren't you just the sweetest little thing?" Harlow appears from behind, sneering as she looks me up and down, "You think you can waltz up here and demand an answer? Who do you think you are?"

"Har—" warns Bryce, but I don't back down. Not tonight. I want to know.

Ignoring her, I turn to Bryce, "I want answers. So does everyone else. We know something's up. You can't just lie to us. These are the people that you're supposed to be protecting, not keeping secrets from."

The panic subsides a little. If they were thinking that I was behind it, there's no doubt that Harlow would be interrogating me right now. They must have other reasons, and I want to know exactly what's on their minds.

"You know what, new girl? You just got here and I'm already sick of your attitude. How about you go to bed with everyone else and let us worry about the problems?"

Harlow's up for the fight. We're both too stubborn for our own good.

"Will you two please just stop?" Bryce asks, exhaustion betraying his annoyance.

I ignore him, my temper flaring, "Well, shouldn't you be telling the people what's happening? If people are in danger, you should be getting them out of here. They have a right to know if they're at risk."

Because of me. You should get them out because of me.

"Maybe we should just resign and let you take over," Harlow spits. She comes closer, a full head taller than me, welcoming me to a fight.

"Maybe I should," I snarl back.

"Stop!" Bryce yells this time, shoving between us. "This is ridiculous. We're all on the same team here. No offense, Kenadee, but we're handling it. You're new here anyways. You know nothing of this camp or the problems we have. I've told you several times to drop it."

I try not to hit Harlow as a smirk forms on her lips. This is what she's been waiting for. Me to press too far, to prove to her that I'm not innocent. Now, she definitely won't back down.

"Fine." I spin on my heel to leave, frustration screaming inside me.

I don't stop until someone grabs me from behind, forcing me to spin around, "*Hey!*" Harlow growls.

"What?" I shout louder than I planned. I'm furious, mainly at myself. How could I be so stupid? She's onto me, even more now. I was supposed to be getting on her good side, not making enemies.

Her face is only inches from mine, ice-colored eyes boring into mine. "I warned you, new girl. You're really that stupid? I'm sure that you're behind this, and the moment I find out any information about your attack, you're done. You don't even know the lengths that I'll go to."

"I'm not afraid of your threats. I've done nothing wrong." I spit back, feigning the confidence I lack.

Not another word is spoken as I rip my arm from her grip and walk away. I can feel the cool chill of Harlow's gaze following me, making me tense. My brain sings the same song over and over again, taunting me with the phantoms that I'm about to create. I can't deny what she said, I can't hate her for it; it's the truth.

I'm the monster that's about to destroy them.

16

MY HEART RACES AS I slam the door behind me. Flinging my jacket across the living room in a sudden surge of emotion, I let the hot tears roll freely down my cheeks.

How will I ever pull this off and get away with it? I'll either be caught by the people here, or I'll be arrested and forced to watch my family die. I have nowhere to turn.

A loud bang makes me yelp in surprise, tripping backwards as the communication device Reed gave me bursts open, unfolding into a large screen before my eyes. A woman appears, typing rapidly on a computer, her eyes hidden behind a pair of square-framed glasses.

"Miss Coria?" She says briefly, giving me a quick once-over as her fingers fly over the keyboard.

"Uh, yes?" With tear stains on my cheeks and hair mussed from the ash and smoke, I must look like a complete disaster.

"Good, I'll transfer you over to the president," she says, leaning over to push a button on her desk. I open my mouth to protest, but the woman is already gone. Static waves taking over the image as the screen reappears, revealing the president, another glass of alcohol in hand. He takes in my wild appearance, a slow, cat-like smile spreading across his lips.

"You look like you've been through the ringer," he says dryly.

I fume, "Well, if you would've seen—"

He begins to laugh, a shrewd, drunk-induced chuckle, "You don't have to explain what happened tonight. They were my plans, after all."

"What? *How?*" The president told me that he couldn't enter the camp.

He snorts, "Really, Kenadee? You didn't think I'd be trusting only you for this job, did you? You're not the only spy there. Who do you think brought you the communicator? I sent them looking after Ms. Creston got the better of you. They tried to find the bug too, but you must have lost it somewhere in that godforsaken forest."

I gape. If there's another spy around here, I have to work extra hard to prove my loyalty. If Reed even believes for a second that I could be taking their side, he won't hesitate to make me pay.

"Close your mouth, Miss Coria. You underestimated me. Didn't think I would do something like this? Need I remind you that this is war? I don't stop until I get what I want."

I shake, whether with fear or anger, I'm not quite sure. "There were children there. You-you… They could've died! They haven't done anything—"

"You think I care, Miss Coria? They will not stand in the way this time. Justice will be served. I will not cease until they are given to me, do you understand?" The humor is gone from his voice as he challenges me to disobey him. "War isn't pretty. People die, and that includes children. You can be angry with me, but it doesn't change anything. The entire population of magic users *will be* handed over to be at some point. Will you stand with me, or against me? Do remember what I'm capable of; your family's fragile lives are in my hands."

I sniff, remembering Eli getting tortured and trying to control the rage that threatens to come loose. "I'm on your side."

"Good, good." Once again, a slow smile spreads to his lips, "Then tell what you've learned so far."

I take a few deep breaths. I have to do this. It's not about me, it's about Eli and my mom. I have to look out for them. "Not much. One of the leaders, Bryce, mentioned that there was danger."

"Danger?" The president cocks an eyebrow, rocking in his chair as he listens.

"Mhm. That's all he said."

He leans forward. "Interesting. I want you to find out more. Do whatever you must do to get inside, to find out more about this magic. See what they're doing with it."

I nod in reply, looking down at my feet.

"Oh, and Kenadee, do try to be happier. Soon, you'll have everything you've ever wanted."

Without another word, the screen turns black and Reed is gone, his words haunting me.

THE TRAITOR'S CRUX

***

"AREN'T YOU GOING TO EAT?" Tess looks over at me with visible worry in her puppy dog eyes. She looks miserable. We all are. The entire mess hall seems as if a deep, dark spell has been cast upon it. The threat has scared all of us. No one seems to know what danger lurks beyond the walls of the barrier. Well, expect for me and Reed's other puppet.

"No, I'm not hungry," I mumble into my coffee, slowly churning in a packet of sugar. I expect a fight, or at least a big lecture, but she must decide to spare me today. We're all in a mood, too tired and scared to hassle each other. Even Tess and Delia, usually so full of conversation and animation, can't seem to bring themselves to care.

"So, you begin training today?" Delia asks, trying her best to lighten the mood at the table.

I nod wretchedly, "In fifteen minutes, actually."

"Yikes." Tess grimaces, "I'm sorry. I'd tell you it was okay, but we all know that it's not a good thing to be on Harlow's bad side. People were talking about that argument you two had. Sounded pretty ba—*Ouch! Delia!*" she sulks and rubs the spot where Delia elbowed her, glaring at her best friend.

I raise my brows, "She thinks I did the spell. I don't even know how to use my magic, let alone do *that*." My mind drifts to the notebook I'd lost in the disaster. Who knows where it could be now or who could possess it? I make a mental note to search the grounds after training tonight.

"Look, we were all a bit off-kilter last night. I'm sure she didn't mean it. Just go do your thing, learn the magic, and get out. Do a good job and she'll see how hard you're working. I'm sure this will blow over and she'll forget all about it."

"I sure hope you're right," I say doubtfully.

"You'll be fine," Delia affirms, but I can sense she's lying.

***

A FEW HOURS LATER, I can definitely see that things aren't going to get better with Harlow. We're in the huge gym, painted a deep gray, with mats covering the concrete floors.

"Go again," she instructs as I struggle through my last push-up.

I groan loudly, dropping to my knees, "Harlow, please, can we do something else? I don't know… magic?"

She paces around me like a prowling wildcat. "Magic? Is that why we're here?" she answers, sarcasm seeping in her tone.

"My point is," I pant, "I just don't see what this has to do with magic training."

She says nothing, turning her back to me and snapping her fingers.

"What are you doing?" I pull myself up to my feet, watching in amazement as her hands dance in tiny little movements. The room begins to swirl, slowly transforming itself before our eyes. In a heartbeat, the cave-like training area is filled with equipment: weapons, knickknacks, and a wall of books. I feel an awed breath come loose.

"Alright, listen up. I'm only going to explain this once. Magic works differently for every person, but you can count on a few key ingredients. The first and most important is physicality," Harlow begins, her expression unreadable as she turns back towards me, "You have to want it. You need to be aware of your own strength, be in tune with your mind and your muscles. It's all relative."

"Okay—"

"I wasn't done. Rule number one: listen. Do not interrupt me, you understand? I'm the teacher here, you're the student. That means your job is to sit down and shut up. You don't want to do it? Then you're out, got it?"

I say nothing.

"Good." Her ice blue eyes drill into mine, "We're going to be doing physical training every day to get you where you should be. Mediocrity is unacceptable in my eyes. I hate failure, stupidity, and laziness. You will learn magic. You will train. You will listen."

I bite my lip nervously as she pulls a chair up across from me.

"Now let me explain the kind of things we do in here. Every day you'll train to become a stronger fighter. If you're weak, your magic will be too. Plain and simple." She props her elbows on her knees, leaning in, "Before we can go in-depth on magic, I want you studying magic. You need to know its history, its laws."

"Magic has laws?"

"Yes, just like anything else in this world, it has limitations. Magic needs something to feed off of. You can't just conjure up something out of the blue. That requires a... rare form of magic."

I think of the magic that came from me that day in the store. Reed had said I had a special kind of power... is this what he was talking about?

"What do you mean by rare magic?" I wipe my sweaty hands on my pants, watching Harlow's face carefully. Her lips twists into a crooked smile, "A rare form of magic that only a small percentage of the magic population possesses. It's the kind of magic that built the barrier and made the camp what it is. It's also the magic most easily drawn to the darkness." I swallow as she gets to her feet and leans on the back of the chair. "But, we'll save the heavy stuff for another day. We're nearly out of time already."

I stand and follow her to the middle of the mat as she explains, "Magic is physicality, but it's also control. You have to be able to control yourself, your desires and needs. It can go dangerous, and fast, if you're not careful. So, let's start with the fun stuff." Harlow removes the faded baseball cap from her head and throws it to the ground. "You're going to make this thing move."

I watch her hands move up and down as she commands, "*Levitate!*"

The hat follows her hand, spinning in circles as if flies, mimicking her hand movements.

"See? It's simple. Now, your turn," she says, dropping the hat and stepping aside to watch. It seems easy enough, so I follow her example.

I raise my hands clear into the air and yell, "*Levitate!*"

Nothing happens.

"Again," Harlow demands.

I take a deep breath, focusing on what I have to do.

I did magic before; I can do it again. I know I can.

My hands quake, unsteady, *unsure* of their own strength. All this power hiding within me. A soft breath escapes my parted lips as my nerves seem to ignite.

The power wells within me, a timid, fearful thing.

I thrash it forward with all my might, and—

Nothing happens.

Harlow's smile is a wicked one. "Again."

17

A FEW HOURS LATER I sit on my porch, angrily trying to find a levitation spell in one of these grimoires.

Practice this morning came to a painstaking halt as my magic finally did appear, but in a strange twist of events managed to destroy everything in the room and not even touch the hat.

Harlow didn't have to say a word as she silently produced a broom from mid-air and shoved it in my direction. As if it were the best moment of her life, she ran the one-sided commentary the entire time while eating potato chips. Things like, "Missed a spot" or "Look on the bright side. At this rate, you probably can't embarrass yourself any more than you already have."

When I asked the stupid question of why she wouldn't use her magic, she only laughed and said, "My schedule's free until lunch. I have the whole morning to fill."

Needless to say, training isn't going the way I want it to.

I take a sip of my coffee, trying to rid myself of the memory.

"There she is, our newest witch!" Bryce appears out of nowhere, courtesy of the transportation device, and strides towards the porch. He looks exhausted, but cheery nonetheless. "I just came to drop these books off for you. Harlow chose them for you to study before your next lesson. I didn't think you'd mind that I offered to take them while she's in a meeting."

"Aren't the grimoires enough?" I ask, frowning as he sets them down on the little patio table.

He gives me a sympathetic look. "It's Harlow. Sometimes it's better not to argue."

"True," I admit, then a terrible thought comes over me. "Did she uh—did she tell you what happened?"

"Oh, did she ever." He laughs, then, as I slam my hand into my forehead, adds hurriedly, "But don't worry about it. It takes everyone a while to get used to it. I think Har sometimes forgets that we were all beginners at one point."

I don't look up. "Well I took bad to a whole new level. I'm pretty sure I made the biggest fool of myself ever."

"I'm sure it wasn't *that* bad."

"Oh, trust me, it was bad. I'm embarrassed she even had to see it." I let out a mortified laugh, then point towards the house. "Hey—you want some coffee or tea?"

Surprisingly, he nods, "Sounds great. Herbal tea, if you have it."

He follows me inside, kicking off his shoes at the door and revealing his mismatched socks. I put the tea kettle on the stove while he looks around. He seems to take in every detail of the house, a faint smile on his lips as he glimpses out the window to the backyard. I watch him for a moment, trying to fight the grin that wants so badly to come.

Somewhere in the past few days he's let down that leader persona around me. He's not just the friendly face around camp, greeting everyone by name and asking about their families. He's given away another hint of the person underneath. And as he turns my way with a happy smile, those eyes shining and bright, my heart skips in my chest.

I jump at the scream of the tea kettle, thankful for the direction. With my back turned towards Bryce, I remind myself why I'm here.

Don't get close. He's going to be arrested. Him and everyone else here—

"You okay?" He comes up behind me.

"Of course!" I lie, reaching for a mug and pouring the hot water inside. He holds it up as if to say thank you, then drops the tea packet in to steep.

"You want to know something?" he asks, now eye-level as I wiggle my way up to sit on the counter.

"What?" I take a sip, watching him over the brim.

"I think you're going to be just fine here… and that comes from the heart," he says with false seriousness, patting his chest.

"I'm not so sure about that. I might be the magicless witch here. Then what will become of me?" I ask, only half-joking.

THE TRAITOR'S CRUX

He clicks his tongue, "Well, I don't know, Miss Kenadee. I guess we'll have to keep you, regardless."

For a second our eyes meet, and I want nothing but to kiss his lips. *I can't do this. Ever.* I clear my throat and we both look away, suddenly immersed in everything but each other.

Every part of me wishes I could tell him everything. Admit it all right here, right now. But the second that I do, Reed will know. I'm sure of it. Then, there'd be no way to save my family. They'd be gone within minutes.

"So, uh, how are things in the command center?" I ask softly, breaking the heavy silence, "After last night's attack, I mean."

He grimaces, taking a sip of his tea and wincing at the heat, "Not so good. Everyone's pretty shaken by it. And the thing is, we can't figure out how it even happened. You can't even do those spells under the barrier. It should be physically impossible unless..." He stops himself. Once again, he's said too much.

"Unless what?" I push, curious.

"Never mind. It couldn't be. Anyway, I'm sure we'll get to the bottom of it and things will go back to normal."

"Mhm. You mean this perfect life in this perfect town that you built? No bombs, no Reed... All sunshine and rainbows."

He snickers, "On the contrary. We don't even have resident unicorns here."

I punch him teasingly, "You know what I mean. The rest of the country's torn apart and then there's this little camp, pretty much left unfazed."

He toys with his mug, spinning it with his hands. The ceramic pangs against the countertop and I worry that I offended him. He gives me a solemn glance. "It's our job to protect everywhere here, Kenadee. We're so lucky to live comfortably, but if it weren't for the war in the first place, we wouldn't be here."

"I wasn't saying—"

"I know," he says quickly, "Just hear me out. Our people come first. Reed's tried to kill us for years, he's done horrible things. The rest of the country hates us. They want us dead. What other options do we have?"

"Of course, I'm sorry." I shake my head, "Ignore what I say, I'm flustered after training this morning. So, tell me, how do you get all this stuff here? All the food and what not?"

He takes a drink and smiles mischievously, "*Well...* of some of the not-so-glorious moments, we've had to utilize whatever we can. It usually involves mind spells on truck drivers, getting them here instead of Denver..."

I gape teasingly, "Bryce Coughlin!"

He holds up his hands, "If you want to get technical, it's Harlow that does it. I can't do mind spells!"

"Why's that?"

Just as he's about to answer, something in his pocket begins to chirp loudly. He sighs deeply and extracts it, a small device that looks almost like my communicator. "Duty calls. Thanks for the tea, but I better take this."

"Yeah, go." I say, though I'm suddenly brimming with curiosity. Why can't Bryce do this so-called mind spell? I watch him from the corner as he stops, a final thought on his face.

"Oh, and Kenadee?"

"Hmm?"

"Go show Harlow that you can kick butt. I believe in you!" He gives me a roguish wink before disappearing, and I can't help but laugh.

For a small beat of a second, the worry fades from my mind, replaced by pure, absolute happiness; like an idiot, I sit and smile to myself.

18

A WEEK LATER, I RACE through the forest, panting as I try to match Harlow's long-legged strides. The crisp morning air sets fire to my lungs as I leap over a fallen log, watching hopelessly as the blonde disappears over the hillside. I stop to catch my breath, hands on my knees, and think of how disappointed Markus would be in my performance.

Footsteps crunch over the leaves that have scattered all over our running trail as Harlow reappears, throwing her hands up in the air. "Tell me, do you try to be this pathetic, or does it come naturally?"

I laugh humorlessly, "Do you try to be such a bitch all the time, or is that just your personality?"

To my surprise, she lets out a low chuckle, "Alert the media: she jokes. Now, hurry up if you want to get any training done today. If you beat me back, I won't even make you do push-ups."

"Deal!"

With a burst of energy, I'm off, leaving a surprised Harlow in the dust. Moments later, I hear her behind me. She's at my side in an instant, jogging at an easy pace.

"I'm impressed—that's better. Now, go harder; if this is your best, it's not good enough."

I fight to match her pace as camp comes back into my line of vision. Golden light shines through the trees like spilled honey, and except for the two of us, there's not a single sound in the forest. The trail comes to an end, opening up in the grassy open meadow where the building lies. I push myself further, not quite ready to let the blonde win.

She sprints into the building with me fresh on her heels. With the training room in sight, I shove forward with a final surge of energy, just barely touching the door first.

My heart races in my chest with adrenaline as she places her hands on her hips, panting. Her cheeks and the tip of her nose are blushed pink from the cold air as she smiles slightly, "Look at you, new girl. No push-ups today. You finally did something noteworthy."

The warm layers I had originally put on for the morning chill now make sweat pour down my back. I take a long sip from my water bottle as she reaches for the baseball cap on her head and waves me forward. "You know what to do."

I close my eyes, taking deep, calming breaths. I can hear her quiet footsteps behind me as she paces, observing.

You've got this.

I collect my thoughts and raise my hand slowly in the air, trying to find the force behind it. When I think I'm ready, I let out a firm, "*Levitate!*"

I open one eye. The hat hasn't budged. Behind me, Harlow snorts.

"Oh, come on. You need to mean it, new girl. You have to want to move the hat. Every part of you. Again."

Frustration bubbles in my chest. *Go, Kenadee. Do it.*

I begin again, focusing on the hat, on movement. I try to relax, taking deep breaths and I slowly elevate my hands towards the ceiling.

Just make it move. That's all you need to do.

"Levitate!" I yell, forcing my energy forward towards the hat.

A shudder goes through the cap, making it pop up a few feet in the air, then spiral back down to the floor, sliding to Harlow's feet.

Harlow remains unimpressed. "That was better, but you're too tense. You don't want it enough. Relax and go again."

"I'm *trying*!" I complain, "Maybe something's wrong with it…"

"Don't kid yourself. *Levitate*." She steps in front of me, and in a swift movement, lifts the hat into the air. It spins in circles, following the flow of her hands.

She drops her hands to her side, making the hat go cluttering along with them. "Don't try to give me those bullshit excuses. You know how I feel about them."

"*Levitate!*" I shove my hands into the air, but this time, I don't get a single movement from the cap. Nothing but stillness.

"C'mon, new girl, you aren't that incompetent. All you have to do is pick up the hat. Use your powers.

THE TRAITOR'S CRUX

They're screaming to get out of you. I can tell by just looking at you right now. Getting mad? Getting frustrated? Well, do something about it," Harlow digs.

"I'm trying!" I don't turn to watch her as she paces around me. My heart races and my fingers tick with a sudden anger I can't seem to calm.

"Really? Doesn't look like it. All I see is failure. Do you *want* to fail?"

"You're not helping! You're supposed to be my teacher!"

"Don't try to blame me for your own failures." She comes closer, this time, by my ear. Taunting, laughing. "*You're* the one who isn't doing it. You're stopping yourself. You have to want it. So, show me. Show me what you're going to do to make it happen."

I fume, "It's only been two days. I'm trying my hardest."

She laughs, planting herself straight across from me, arms folded across her chest. "Oh, yeah? You know what? I think you are full of it. I think you know it too. You're not trying—"

"Not true—"

"You beat me today, which tells me that it's not incompetence. Are you lazy? Is that it?"

"Shut up," I say through gritted teeth, my fists clenched.

"You gonna make me? How about I shut up if you show me you can lift that stupid little hat, huh?" She raises a brow, extending a hand towards the hat. Waiting. Slowly, the mocking smile spreads to her lips. "That's right. You're too afraid. What is it, newbie? Afraid that you're a failure? That you'll fail the mission you were sent here for?"

She catches me by surprise. I drop my hands, spinning towards her in alarm, "Wh-what are you talking about?"

I watch in horror as she produces my missing notebook from her bag, dangling it in front of me with an arched eyebrow.

My silence is her answer. "I've been tracking you since you first arrived. I wasn't about to let Bryce win and put the camp in danger. What did Reed offer you, new girl? It must be pretty good if you're willing to sacrifice an entire camp of people. Too bad he won't give you what he promised. He never does. What, he told you that he'll give you back your brother?"

Eli? She knows?

"How do you know about Eli?" Alarm rings in my ears. She's known all along.

Harlow leans over, picking up her hat from the floor and dusting it off before placing it on her head. "I know lots of things. I've been watching Reed just like he sent you here to do to me. The thing is—we're always several steps ahead. We have magic. We have power. He's not going to beat that unless we mess up big time. As for your big brother, let's just say he and I are good pals."

She holds up her hand for me to see. Across the back is a series of numbers and letters, reading *HD476804*. "My prison I.D. The 'HD' stands for highly dangerous. I was under intensive security, just like your brother. We had lots of great conversations when we weren't being tortured."

"How are you here?" I ask stupidly.

"I escaped. I'm not planning on going back there either, so you should find a new plan." She pulls her ponytail through the hole in her hat, "I really hope you aren't dumb enough to think that Reed's going to give you what he promised. We both know he's not that type of guy. He's playing you. He's been playing you ever since you were born. It's what he does."

I say nothing, folding my arms defensively across my chest. Harlow regards me with a level stare, then sighs, softening just a bit. "As much as I hate to say it, I know the situation you're in, and I'm giving you one final chance. I won't tell your secret if you help us. You're one of us now."

Tears well in the corners of my eyes, the fear suddenly taking the place of the anger I held moments ago. "But how? He has my family, Harlow. He took my mother, too."

"And we'll get to them. But you need to understand that doing his dirty work, turning us over to him, won't do you any favors. I guarantee you he has a prison cell with your name on it. You can help us. We can go get your brother and mom, free them. We can beat Reed. He's not a good person." She watches me carefully, looking for my reaction.

"What if he finds out? He'll kill them…"

"He's going to kill them no matter what unless we can help it. That's why we have to step up."

I throw around the idea for a second. Harlow knows, and she'll blow my cover if I disagree to it. I'm going to have to convince someone here that I'm on their side. But who? Who can I trust?

She hands the notebook to me, throwing her bag over her shoulder and sliding her hat back onto her head. Her hand is already on the doorknob as she turns back one last time. "Think about it. I'll give you tonight. But think about it if he calls. Think of the lives you're destroying. And for what?"

The door slams behind her, leaving me in the dark. Suddenly, it's too much to bear. I don't bother to grab my things from the room—a stupid mistake since it will disappear immediately after we leave. The rooms always leave unless they're scheduled for use. Magic is wonderful and somewhat annoying that way. It doesn't even cross my mind.

Instead, I just run.

I flee the scene, running from myself, from Reed, from the constant cycle of games and war. I can't breathe; I can't focus. I can't live this way any longer. I have to get the fresh air, go outside and see the sunlight. I have to get away from these walls, inching closer and closer, crushing me inside them.

People stare as I breeze by them, too enraptured in the fear and anger streaming out of me. Someone reaches for me—Bryce, the happy grin on his face. I brush past him, ignoring his shouts. I don't stop until I'm beyond the buildings, a shadow between the trees. Within their asylum, I sink down onto a log and cry, the tears boiling from within me, everything too much for me to handle.

"Kenadee?" I hear Bryce before I see him appear through the aspen trees. I try my best to wipe my tears away even though it's useless. I'm a wreck. I don't look up as Bryce comes and sits next to me on the log, only inches apart. "What's wrong?"

"Nothing. Just needed a second," I lie, wiping at my nose with my sleeve and avoiding his eyes, trying to make my voice sound stronger.

"Mmm, I see." We sit in silence for a second as I sniffle. "You know, when I first was learning how to use my powers, I set my instructor's hair on fire," he says, matter-of-factly, twisting his face into an amused smirk.

"Oh, yikes!"

"Mhm. He ended up shaving it all off to hide it. Pretty intense stuff."

"I can tell."

"But that's probably enough about me already. What's going on? Why are you so upset?"

"Nothing...just a stressful training," I lie again through a ragged breath, watching my hands.

"You sure it's just that? Most people don't cry over stressful trainings. You seem like you have something else going on."

I almost tell him. If I don't take Harlow's side in this, she'll break the news first. And if that happens, Reed will know immediately.

"Sorry, I'm just missing home a bit."

So many lies.

He chuckles quietly, "You're going to be fine. Right now, things are tense and everyone is up in arms, but we'll get through it. I promise. Things will die down in the next few days and it will be like nothing happened. Just a small scare, nothing we can't handle. And the magic thing will come easier. It's just difficult right now. It always is for beginners."

I say nothing, feeling neither comforted or inclined to talking at the moment. No matter what I do, people will get hurt. I don't know what else to say to Bryce when all I can offer him is lies.

"Hey." He nudges me, eyes suddenly gleaming with mischief, "Wanna see something?"

I just barely nod and let my hand slip over his. Call it reckless or stupid, but all I need is to get away. Lost in the woods with Bryce, forgetting everything else.

He takes me down a winding trail, weaving in and out of the trees, his large hand resting over my smaller one. They fit together so well.

We stop in a clearing, where tiny, delicate wildflowers blossom from the ground in brilliant colors. Around us, the trees form a gigantic circle far enough apart to allow sun in, which shines brightly on the debris-filled forest floor.

"Look!" whispers Bryce, holding out one hand to tell me to be still, and using the other to point at a fawn staring lazily back at us from a few feet away.

I lean back against a shady tree, watching Bryce attempt to get closer, feeling the sleepiness that the afternoon sun always brings. It reminds me of my childhood, playing in the forest with Eli. We'd run for hours, just two kids with no worries about the future. We'd leave with full tummies and berry stained fingers, happy and young, our minds vivid and our responsibilities nonexistent.

Bryce wheels on me, eyes bright with excitement. He's only inches away. "Come here!" he whispers gently.

I creep slowly so as not to spook the deer. Crouching down beside Bryce, I watch the deer give us an indifferent look and return to her grazing.

"Here, girl!" he says softly, clicking his tongue. His fingertips graze mine as he outstretches my hand, turning it towards the sky. She takes interest, nose twitching as she scours my palm for food. It tickles, and as I laugh, she bolts, bounding off into the safety of the multicolored trees.

Neither of us move. Bryce's voice is low, and yet, so loud among the quiet and rows of trees. "It's a really bad habit, but people do it anyway. The deer are pretty tame because we all spoil them by feeding them."

A moment passes as I glance up at him, his shoulder against mine, his hand still on my hand. He gulps and his Adam's apple throbs. I'm paralyzed in place, unable to glance away from his set of warm summer eyes.

I can't do this. I shouldn't do this.

I'm not meant to fall for him. I'm meant to kill him.

His lips part as if he's about to say something but decides against it. Instead, he leans forward, hands brushing against my cheeks. Our kiss is electric, wonderful, and slow. A shiver runs through me, even though there's no breeze, no chill to the air.

Reality hits with the force of a crashing wave. I shove him away, my fingers flying to my lips, tracing the place where his had been.

His face twists in embarrassment. "Oh, my God. I'm so sorry. I—"

"I can't do this," I whisper, and I swear that nothing hurts worse than those four words.

He nods slowly, understanding. "I shouldn't have— I'm a leader. I—I, uh, I have to go." Before I can stop him, he disappears back into the trees.

19

"WAIT... HE KISSED YOU?!" SQUEALS Tess, drumming her hand excitedly on the library table and earning a death glare from the librarian. All the heads in the room turn to look at us, but Tess doesn't mind. She squirms in her chair like an over-excited puppy.

I shush her. "Yell a little louder next time, why don't you? I don't think they heard you in Canada."

"Tell me everything!" she insists.

I shake my head, "Look, I'm trying to study for one of Harlow's stupid tests, so if you don't mind—"

"Don't worry, you're not bothering me!" she props her bright pink shoes on the table and rocks in her seat, "Here, I'll even help you!"

"You would do that?"

"Sure! I've survived a few of Harlow's tests in my time. What are you stuck on?"

"Well..." I flip through the dusty pages of the text book until I find the beginning of the chapter. I'm supposed to be studying the origins of magic, but maybe I can find out something more from Tess—something to give to Reed. "What do you know about protection spells? Like the barrier here at camp?"

"Easy," she chirps, her freckle-dusted cheeks rising up in a grin, "Our camp security team created it. Any normal person walking through the woods only sees forest—and if they're non-magic, they'll literally walk right through it without actually stepping inside. They did it after a security breach a few months ago. Some of Reed's soldiers had tried to enter the camp, that's why Harlow was so suspicious about you."

"They tried to enter? What happened?" I play along.

She grimaces, "At the time, the barrier protection wasn't what it is now. They got in, caught a bunch of us off-guard and killed people. Luckily, Harlow got to them before they did too much damage."

I knit my brows together, thinking of Reed's fear. "If we're magic and we have all this power, then why are we hiding? Why don't we just kill Reed?"

Tess sighs sadly, "Reed pretends that the country is in danger because of us, but in truth, he's a much bigger threat than we could ever be. He's been recruiting magic soldiers for a while now, training them in spells much darker than anything we can ever pull off."

"But, Harlow said that kind of magic is rare…" I whisper, thinking of my own powers. Reed called them elite. Hearing it now, it all makes sense. Reed is recruiting only those with dark magic. If it's as powerful as Harlow says, then it won't take long for Reed to kill off the magic population for good.

"It is, but Reed's tracking them. There aren't many, but what they lack in numbers, they make up for in power. Their powers aren't like ours—there aren't lots of physical limits where they're involved. If they want to randomly create something out of thin air, they can. The only thing working against them is that most of Reed's soldiers are brand new, which means they have a pretty limited arsenal. That kind of magic is darker, so it weakens them. Unpracticed ones tire somewhat easy if they use too much at once. Still, their powers are stronger—their basic spells could kill us. It'd take a lot to defeat even a new one."

Shivers rise up my spine. Reed said he had wanted me for my powerful magic, but he hadn't mentioned this. All this time, he's recruited only those that are like me. The rest of the magic population ends up dead or in prison, but the ones that are like me… they become soldiers. Killers. That kind of magic could rule the world.

"I didn't mean to scare you," says Tess, reaching over and squeezing my hand. "I guess it's good to know the truth. We have to do whatever we can to assure it doesn't happen."

"Yeah. No, of course. I agree." I meet her doe-eyed gaze and force a smile.

"How about I go get us some coffee and then I'll help you study more?" She jumps to her feet and tucks in her chair. "Oh, and Kenadee? You don't get to blow off this whole Bryce topic forever. I have a feeling you two are a match made in heaven!"

"Sure," I snort, "Considering the fact that he's avoided me for the past few days? We're off to a great start."

She gives me a knowing smile. "Be patient. Good things are yet to come, my friend!"

I don't respond as she skips off into the distance, humming to herself and nearly colliding into a passerby. For the first time since I've arrived, the gravity of the situation hits the hardest: I'm going to betray her. I'm going to betray them all.

***

I LEAVE THE LIBRARY LATE, partially because Tess doesn't know how to stop talking—which is probably due to the fact that she sprinkled about ten packets of sugar in her coffee—and because Harlow gives tests even more difficult than her training sessions. Tess yawns, stretching out like a cat, "That was *exhausting*. No offense, but I'm never helping you with a test again!"

"Aww darn." I pretend to be disappointed, when in all reality, Tess did anything *but* help me. After she got coffee, she painted her nails, complained that I was taking too long, then went and got more coffee. I wonder how she sleeps at night.

She follows me to Harlow's office, not taking a single breath between her sentences. It's ten o'clock and the office is quiet. Harlow isn't here, and neither is Julie, the rude secretary. Only a golden strip of light shines under

Bryce's officer door. Even with it closed, I can hear him singing softly to himself. I smile at the thought, but back into reality as Tess says, "Kenadee—it's your chance!"

"What? No. Let's just hurry up and get out of here," I say quickly. We've been avoiding each other for days. I don't even know what to say to Bryce, let alone how to get back to where we were before. I miss him, but I don't know that I can ever talk to him without wondering what could have been. There are so many possibilities, and in a world full of Reed, I can't determine what they might be.

"Kenadee!" Tess tries to whisper, but whispering for Tess is practically a soft yell. "You have to talk to him!"

"Shh!" I hiss, pressing the paper against Harlow's door. The wood crackles and groans under my magic, swallowing it until the paper is gone completely, now somewhere in the depths of Harlow's office.

I'm reaching for Tess and trying to push her towards the exit when there's a soft pop, and another door creaks open. Bryce's head pops out, squinting at first as he tries to decipher what's behind the noise, then widening when he realizes who it is. We both freeze, paralyzed as Tess tries, and fails, to contain her excitement. She looks back and forth with a cocky smile, then pretends to yawn. "Well, I've had enough excitement for tonight. Bye you two!"

"Tess!" I hiss, reaching for her, but her wiry arm slips free. She's out the door in a heartbeat, leaving me to silently curse at her. I turn back to Bryce slowly, wondering what on earth I could possibly say to make things right between us.

THE TRAITOR'S CRUX

My heart flutters like a bird in my chest as I say, "Look, Bryce—"

"No," he says, cutting me off, "I know what you're going to say. I shouldn't have kissed you. I'm a leader here, I-I just shouldn't have done it."

"Oh…" I whisper, feeling the sting of his words. He's right, it couldn't have worked. It shouldn't have happened. I'm not here to fall in love. And yet…

The magic word: yet.

When he says nothing, I wrap my arms across my chest, suddenly desperate for that small, vain comfort. "You know what? I'm actually mad that you kissed me! Not because I didn't like it, but because now what are we going to do? Hmm? Ignore each other? Pretend that things never happened?"

His brows draw together and he takes this in for a long moment, "Isn't that what you want?"

"What I want?" I scoff. It's a valid question because I don't really know anymore. All I know is that I shouldn't. I can't. "What I want is my friend back! What I want is… is…"

"See? You don't even know!" he throws his hands in the air. "What am I to you, Kenadee? This person you can tug along?"

I take a few dangerous steps closer, lowering my voice in a way that would make Harlow proud. "Are you really suggesting what I think you're suggesting?"

He looks down at me with a glare. "I don't know. I never thought so, but I've been wrong about people before."

I let out a sharp breath, anger rising like flames inside me, then it hits me. He's right, and he doesn't even know it. I'm playing him, I'm playing everyone here. My shoulders sag as I meet his green stare. I don't feel angry anymore. I just feel awful.

"I'll make it easy on us then." His eyes soften as I begin to turn. The space in front of him where I'd stood seconds ago sits empty and void. If this was another world, another situation, I could have Bryce Coughlin as mine. I could be free to kiss him, to love him. "Goodbye, Bryce."

Tears blur my vision as I walk to the door and he lets me. I let the door fall behind me, all the sadness and the rage swimming upward. A muffled sob escapes my lips as I press my hand to my mouth, mourning what could have been.

I hear the door behind me, but I refuse to look back. A hand reaches for my shoulder, brushing it with the lightest of touches. "Ken?"

I gulp, hating that I'm crying, that I'm feeling this way; hating Reed for making me do this. "Go away."

"No." One word, one syllable, and it makes all the difference in the world.

I turn on him, not sure how to even react to that. All I can muster is, "*What?*"

"Give me this moment," his voice pleads, and I lose every ounce of fight within me. "Give *us* this moment before you just walk away. We'll be the ones, who determine whether or not this was all for nothing. Let us decide, Ken. No one else."

I kiss him, with all the meaning in the world. He's everything all wrapped into one: the morning sky bathed in a million different colors, the blank pages of an unwritten story, the stilled sea after a raging storm. His hands in my hair, the fire within my blood. He's something untouchable, a treasure not meant for me.

He's not mine to keep. He's mine to kill.

And yet.

The word sinks itself into my bones, leaving me breathless.

Yet. Yet. Yet…

20

"YOU REALIZE THAT STARING AT a closed grimoire won't actually help you memorize it? Trust me, back in my magic-learning days, I tried." Bryce scoots out a chair, making it squeal against the concrete, and sits down, sliding my coffee towards me.

"Oh, just give me my coffee, would you?" I pretend glare, shoving the grimoire out of the way.

"Sheesh, someone's not a morning person. I was merely pointing out that my younger, more unmotivated and angst-filled self would have found a way to get out of studying magic. I was not a go-getter," Bryce teases, checking the time. "When do you have to be at training again?"

"Six, on the dot. Any later and Harlow finds a new way to torture me. It's like a game of see how Kenadee will humiliate herself next."

He frowns, emptying a sugar packet into his coffee, then pressing the lid back down. "I thought practices were going better."

"They're getting there…" I take a sip, wincing as the hot drink scalds my tongue and thinking of the last training session I had with Harlow. Sure, my magic is doing great. After a bunch of practice with the grimoires and finding what works, I've managed to pick up the hat and so much more. Harlow's been challenging me with plenty of new spells, making them harder and harder each time. I can feel myself getting stronger each day—but that's not the problem.

The real trouble lies in what Harlow knows. I'll be expected to make a choice, to choose a side. I want to trust her. I want to tell her everything. I want to be at hers and Bryce's side as they defeat Reed, but he has the one thing that's holding me back: my family.

I can't let them die because of me.

Reed hasn't mentioned anything yet, but I also worry about this other spy. Whoever is in the camp with me knows who I am. They've been to my house, they've openly attacked within camp walls. I can't associate with Harlow, make plans to screw over Reed, without the possibility of them finding out.

Then there's the other problem. The biggest problem: Bryce Coughlin. I can't let it go on, but I also can't bear the thought of stopping it. Sure, it started with me just trying to get information, but it quickly turned into something else. Bryce is the one thing I can't seem to let go of, no matter how hard I try.

He looks at the time once more then pushes out his chair, "Dang it, I'm late. I gotta go—I have a pre-meeting meeting with the security team." He clutches his coffee with one hand and leans in to kiss my forehead.

My heart skips a beat as he pulls away. "How about I cook you dinner tonight?"

"I can't. I'm babysitting for Nadine and Jay. You know, because they're going to your post-meeting meeting." I stand too, reaching for my backpack. It's nearly training time and I don't want to be late.

He pretends to pout, pulling me in close. "Well it shouldn't be too late. You could come over after."

"I have another test tomorrow," I fib, "I have to study."

I don't want to say that I have to be home to catch the phone call with Reed.

"Fine," he huffs, "Then tomorrow?"

"Tomorrow night," I affirm, "It's a date."

He kisses me once more before pulling away, biting his lower lip to hide the smile. I grin back until he turns away and the guilt takes over.

***

TODAY, I'M GOING TO LIE to Harlow Creston's face.

I say it again and again in my mind as I enter the training room, but I still can't believe it. It's stupider than screwing over Reed! *Harlow*, who could kill me in an instant and would probably do so happily.

Am I really going to do this? Am I really this stupid?

The door to the training room is propped open when I arrive, and I can see Harlow's back as she flips through a book. She looks up as I enter, coffee in hand, and

THE TRAITOR'S CRUX

slams the book closed with the signature presumptuousness I've yet to see Harlow lack. "Finally, you're here. Glad I didn't disrupt your little coffee date, but I told you to be on time or not come at all, remember? Since you like to waste my time, how about I waste yours? I'm adding twenty more pushups, two rounds for every ten minutes you missed. Go."

Expecting a larger punishment than added push-ups, I don't argue. I finish the set and crawl to my knees, a heap of sweat and labored breathing, without her noticing.

Taking a large swig from my water bottle, I watch her magic emit bright silvery sparks as two bright red chairs fly down from the ceiling and land neatly on the ground. She dusts off the imaginary dirt, pleased, and spins around to face me. "Alright, we're doing some mental stuff today. It's a bit harder than what you're used to, but I think you're ready."

"Great," I say, trying to sound optimistic though my stomach feels like a rock. I toss the water bottle onto the top of my bag and take the seat opposite of her. We face each other, so close our knees nearly touch. I smile, channeling my inner Tess. I have a show to perform.

"First, and most importantly, I need you to wipe that stupid grin off your face," Harlow says, rolling her eyes. I glower, but obey, sitting up neatly and mimicking her solemn expression. "Today, we're going to explore the mind."

"What's that even mean?" I ask, wrinkling my brow. My head spins anxiously. If she reads my thoughts, then she can know exactly what I've been up to with Reed.

"It *means* that you're going to enter my thoughts. This is a really good spell to use if you need to do mind control. It should only be used in an emergency, but it's highly useful. You can use it on anyone to manipulate their thoughts, see their memories, and more. Plus, they won't even realize that you were in there. You can erase any trace of it."

"Is this even legal?"

She gives me a wry look, "If you use it around camp, obviously not. But Reed's army is growing. They know spells that would give you nightmares for the rest of your life. If we have to fight back, we have to fight dirty."

"Why are you teaching me this?" I shake my head, "I thought you didn't trust me?"

Her wolfish gaze assesses me. "Because I trust that you'll do the right thing. If not, I'll kill you myself. You're caught, whether you like it or not. The fact that you're here tells me that you don't want Reed to win either. Now, are we done playing twenty questions? Can we begin?"

Panic makes my palms sweaty and I nod, trying to focus.

"Alright. I want you to enter mine first. That way you can get practice. Don't worry, I did a protective spell so you can't mess up my brain," she says, catching my worried expression. "All you need to do is concentrate, to think of me. *Be me* to get inside my mind and see my memories. I won't teach you the control part for obvious reasons. Easy enough?"

"What do I say?" I ask, biting my lip.

"Nothing. This is a silent spell. A physical one. Not even the grimoires have substitutes that you can use. You have to want it, you have to go for it. That's all."

I nod, taking in her words with a giant gulp.

I close my eyes, willing myself to focus. Taking a deep breath, I think of Harlow. I've got to get into her head. I have to be her.

Get inside her mind. That's all you have to do.

Harboring the energy inside me, I clench my eyes tighter and mentally throw myself forward.

It's like a tunnel, some sort of cloudy-like vision. Is this what it's like to be in someone's head? I'm speeding through, a mere spectator viewing this strange new thing. I can see the world spinning, but it's like I'm going too fast. *Memories. You have to get her memories.* Something begins to appear before me, a scene, but it's blurry. I can't see a thing. It's too–

Without a warning, everything goes black. I feel myself getting slammed back into my chair, my head pounding. I look up at Harlow, who just snickers, leaning back in her chair casually, like it was the easiest thing in the world to throw me from her head.

"Ow! That hurt!" I say, rubbing my head.

"Whatever," she sneers, "Do it again. You did alright for your first time, but you have to mean it." She leans back even farther, eyebrow raised, mocking me.

Okay, focus. You can do this. Get in her brain, that's all you have to do.

I feel myself break through her barriers once again, floating in that limbo-liked vastness of the in-between stage. I'm halfway through the spell, I just have to get to her memories. I feel my body tense up, focused on the outcome.

Get to her memories.

I feel something, some sort of power as it rushes forward, grabbing onto something. It must be Harlow. It has to be. A glimpse of something flashes by too fast to see. I can't latch on…With a rush, and a huge amount of force, I'm sent backwards.

"Ow!" I curse, glaring at Harlow, who laughs from her seat.

"Not so easy, is it? You can't let people kick you out like that. You need to try harder to get inside or you're not gonna get anywhere at all. Try again, and this time, mean it. You want inside my head, don't you? Try harder, think harder. Be a better me than me."

I sigh, taking a deep breath and letting it out slowly.

Do not let the frustration get to you. You have this. You were in. Do better. Harlow. Be Harlow.

Images of her flow through my brain, the halo of blonde hair and blue eyes, the scars barely visible on her cheeks, the faded New York accent, sometimes appearing in her vowels…

With a final big effort, I push my powers forward, thinking of getting inside Harlow's mind. *Do this, do it. I know you can!* With a burst, a sudden white light, I find myself lost in her mind.

The white is gone. Instead, a scene is in front of me. I'm in her memories, finally.

Suddenly, my—no, her—world begins to slow, fading out, then in.

I'm Harlow, but a much younger, noticeably less grouchy, version. She can't be more than four or five. The house around us is cramped and cluttered with dim lighting. Beside us is a baby, barely old enough to walk, a bright red crayon clutched in its hands. *Harlow has siblings?*

I watch as younger Harlow hums cheerfully, her feet sprawled in front of her, and not a single worry in the world.

Inside her mind, I can feel the real-life Harlow tense up, nervous as someone in her memory comes around the corner.

"Harlow, knock it off! I can't stand that sound!" A woman stands in the kitchen, a cigarette nestled between her fingers, which are clutched around a bottle of beer. Even from far away, I can see how much she resembles Harlow. She has the same pale colored hair, the same small frame.

"Mommy, look! It's for you!" Mini Harlow picks herself up, running to her mom, picture in tow.

Her mom doesn't turn around, rolling her eyes as Harlow pulls at her leg for attention, "Get out of my face, Harlie!" the woman yells, her anger boiling over. "God, I'm sick of tripping over you stupid kids. Always needin' this and that. Can't ya leave me alone for one goddamn second?"

The door opens, surprising them both.

"Daddy!" cries Mini-Harlow, running to him. He looks nothing like her except for the pale eyes. I can feel goosebumps form on my skin as he gives her a cold once-over, then shoves past her roughly.

Harlow's mother smothers her cigarette and puts the beer on the counter as if trying to hide it, her back rigid with fear. He's tall, towering over her as he leans forward, grabbing her.

"Is that one of mine?" the man growls. It's barely distinguishable from where Harlow sits.

Suddenly, I fear for this woman. I can still feel the real-life Harlow across from me, her sadness, fear and rage clouding her memories.

"Are you stupid? What did I just ask you?" the man demands, his voice threatening, ready to explode.

Her syllables are sloppier than Harlow's faint New York accent. "I'm sorry, honey." She gives him a shaky smile, "I had a stressful day, that's all. Those damn kids make me want to rip my hair out. Lo-look, I'm makin' steak just for you! I-I sold lots today and thought I'd make it up to you for makin' you so mad yesterday."

He grunts, clearly satisfied at the promise of steak. "Just don't drink any more of my stuff, got it? What's mine is mine. You know how I feel 'bout sharin'."

The picture around me blurs slowly, fading from that memory in the living room. It reappears, transforming before my eyes. Now I'm in an older Harlow's memories, probably twelve or thirteen-years-old.

Her friends talk loudly as their shoes clunk against the pavement. I don't think she's listening though. I can feel the dread inside. She doesn't want to go home.

She parts with a wave goodbye as they come upon a brick brownstone, pausing with her fingers on the door before heading inside.

"Harlie!" The shrill voice rings through the house. Her mother's in the kitchen again, this time rocking a new baby on her hip. It wails loudly.

"Hey, ma—" Harlow's voice is much higher, younger.

"Be of good use, will ya, and take this thing away from me? I'm sick of it." Her mom comes forward, shoving the baby towards Harlow, who takes it and starts bouncing it on her hip.

"She's hungry. Did you feed her today?" Harlow asks, a bit of familiar annoyance creeping in her voice. Her mother's already around the corner, not listening. "Ma?"

She follows her mother's lead, the baby now quiet on her hip as it clings to her shirt. It's used to Harlow. It's clear that she's more of a mother than their actual mom is.

She comes around the corner to her mom on the bed, which is piled with dirty clothes and beer bottles.

"What do you want now?" her mom screeches, trying to hide a packet of something behind her back, "Go feed the kids!"

Harlow obeys. I can feel the disappointment she has, her feelings as I see her past. The embarrassment, fear...

the sadness. She grabs a pan in the sink, buzzing with flies. Once it's washed, she gathers up some bread, slabbing on some butter and cheese and making two grilled cheese sandwiches.

"Harlow!" A boy comes running up, only a few years younger than her. The baby from the first memory. He grabs her waist, and she hugs him just as tightly.

"Hey, buddy," She says softly. It's strange hearing her this way. Gentle is not the word I'd use to describe Harlow, but here, it's like she's a different person. "Whoa, what happened?" Her brother's face is bloody and bruised. She examines it, worried.

"Um, some kids at school," the boy mutters sheepishly, "It's nothing."

"Yes, it is! Did you show ma?"

He nods, "She told me she was too busy to look."

She examines the gash on his forehead, the most worrisome of his cuts. It's deep enough to be dangerous if not taken care of. He needs stitches.

She sighs, looking around her nervously. "Okay, don't tell anybody about this. Got it? I'll be in big trouble." She kneels, eye-level with his forehead. "*Sano*," she says softly. She's confident. She's done this before.

His forehead immediately begins to patch itself back up, healing the bend in the nose and the fat lip. The bruise around his eye fades, all new. The magic makes everything all better. Like nothing ever happened. He smiles up at her, clearly excited.

"What the hell was that?!" Harlow hadn't seen her father come around the corner. She didn't even know he was home. Now, he stares at her with his bloodshot eyes, nostrils flaring.

She cowers naturally as he comes forward, preparing to take the hit.

"You're one of them!" he bellows, grabbing her arm and sending her flying backwards against the wall. The baby, still on Harlow's hip, begins to wail from the fall. Harlow grabs him instinctively, holding him as he cries, protecting him from the wrath of her father.

"Call the cops!" her father yells to no one in particular, "And get the damned kids away from her!"

My world fades once again as the memory heads away, flashing into a new one. Harlow's legs are strapped down; she's laying on some table. She instinctively tries to fight, but can barely move. She's trapped.

"Don't fight it, Miss Creston. It'll only make it worse." A voice seeps into the room from an intercom placed above her. Several cameras are placed around the room, taking in every move, everything that Harlow does.

"Please, don't do this!" she wails, her fists clenches as she struggles pointlessly against the bonds. This isn't the cool, collected Harlow that I know. This is someone completely different, scared, alone.

She's ignored by the intercom, instead, the door buzzes open as a team of bodyguards swarm in, surrounding the president himself. Although a younger version, Reed looks almost exactly the same.

Even in memory form, the sight of Reed sends chills down my spine.

"Hello, Miss Creston, I'm sure you know who I am. President Malen couldn't be here today, so I thought I'd welcome you personally to the Center for Magic Control."

"What're you going to do with me?" she cries, fear dripping from her voice. The president only laughs.

"Why, my dear, don't worry. We aren't about to kill you, if that's what you were wondering. You are very useful to our cause, Miss Creston. I can promise you that if you join us, you will be honored as a hero. We will be powerful, have the world at our fingertips. We can rule, but we need your help. We need your magic," he says simply.

"Screw you! I want no part in this." The Harlow I know rises in her. She spits at him, making him flinch back. His happy facade vanishes immediately, his glower growing deeper as he stares her in the eyes.

"Ah, you are a spirited young thing, aren't you? What you don't realize is that as of your arrest, you are ours. You have no choice in the matter. We can make it easy, or we can make it difficult. Which would you prefer, young lady?" Despite his angry words, the president looks shaken. It's like he's frightened of her, defenseless in her presence. He should. If she wasn't chained down, she could easily destroy him.

"I said—"

Reed interrupts her, clearly knowing what obscenities are about to be thrown his way. "Gentlemen, let's lock her up for a bit. No food, no water. Whatever beatings are necessary. Maybe she'll think twice about the things she's about to say."

The men behind Reed nod obediently, holding her head down as one of them injects medicine into a long syringe, its needle glinting off the lights above.

Harlow screams, but they're too strong. She can't win this, and she knows it.

The memories betray her panic as the cold needle meets her skin and slowly, her world goes black.

I'm ripped from Harlow's head, gasping as I'm thrown back into my chair by magic's fading hands. Slowly, the real world comes back around. We sit in the training room, chairs in the same exact places. Harlow watches me, panting. There's something different in her face, that same haunted look in her eyes that I saw during the bonfire. It's gone in an instant as the usual sneer takes its place.

"And to think: I used to be a cuddly little kitten just like you."

21

"THAT WAS PRESIDENT REED," I stutter stupidly, scanning Harlow's face for an explanation.

She rolls her eyes, lounging back in her chair, "Wow, nothing gets past you."

Her memories race through my mind. Malen and Reed had her and wanted to use her for something. *But... what?*

"Harlow, what was he talking about when he said he needed your help?"

"Reed and Malen had special plans for me because, what can I say? I'm just a lucky girl." I can still see the desperation in her eyes, like a person whose memories burden her day and night. Her hands shake, even though she tries to hide them. She's scared. "There are different types of magic, I guess you could say. Some are more powerful than others, and some are... purer. Do you remember how I told you about dark magic?"

I nod and she continues, "I'm one of those witches. So are you—though, I think Reed's let that one slip, hasn't he?"

THE TRAITOR'S CRUX

Let her think that you're on her side. "Yeah, he did…" I admit.

"I figured as much. Practically any witch that he recruits has it. And it's the obvious choice—our magic is darker than the rest. More powerful and deadly. It's also influenced by intentions: the more we do dark magic, the more it affects our soul. Malen had the same types of powers—he let it turn him evil."

"It could shut off our humanity? That… actually explains a lot in Malen's case."

She nods, "He figured it all out too. Hit the soul-sucker jack-pot, if you will. He knew if he could find enough people like us, he'd have an entire, easily-influenced army at his disposal. In all reality, Reed is just following along in his footsteps."

Goosebumps cover my arms. "But surely he couldn't do that. People don't just listen—"

She raises a brow, "Oh yeah? Explain the war then. Explain how he got so many on his side. It's easier than you think. People are dumbasses. It wouldn't be hard for him at all to influence the darker side of our powers. You know how they operate. Torture, threats, blackmail—they play dirty to get their way. That's what Reed did with you, isn't it?"

"Harlow…" I whisper, thinking of the past few weeks. All the magic, the lies, the betrayal. She has to believe I'm on her side. "Reed… he told me that he picked me because of my powers."

To my surprise, Harlow only smirks. "Of course, he has. Your powers are extraordinary. I can see why he wanted you."

Harlow frowns, rubbing the tattoo on the back of her hand absentmindedly. After a moment, she jumps to her feet, a thought bright in her eyes.

"What are you doing?" I follow her, watching in confusion as she lets out a sharp breath, running a hand through her hair as she pauses, eyes distant.

"Of course," she whispers, but I'm not sure if it's to me, or herself. "It all make sense."

"What makes sense?"

She turns on me, excitement in her eyes. It's a new look for her. "I thought you did it on purpose that night, but you didn't, did you?"

"What?" I scoff. "I don't know what you're talking about. Did I mess up your brain after all?"

She twists her hands in a spell similar to the one done in Reed's office, where they'd shown me firsthand the torture my brother was going through. She doesn't look at me as she explains. "I've been tracking you since you came here. That night it was you that set off those fireworks."

"Okay, I think you need to lie down."

Harlow shakes her head, "You had your guard down. Reed stepped in with one of his own and took control of you. You didn't even know it was happening."

"That's not possible. I was with Tess and Delia all night. Except…" I pause, the realization dawning over me. I was with them most of the night, but they left to go see the fireworks. "No... there's no way! I remember just sitting there..."

That night comes to life in the tiny training room, everyone seated just as they had been around the bonfire. The fireworks begin to pop in the distance. Tess and Delia stand and leave and I remain, scribbling in my notebook. I gesture towards the scene, "See? I was right there!"

"Look!" she points, just as I stand, almost robotically, and tuck away the notebook I'd been writing in. The orange flames dance towards the sky, and I'm nothing but a silhouetted shadow. My hands dance with the makings of a spell, a stream of bronze sparks fly from my fingertips. In the distance, the fireworks begin to mold. Shivers tingle up my spine as moments later, the screams begin.

Harlow waves the spell off and turns towards me, watching in her wolf-like manner. "The weird thing is... at that time you were brand new, unskilled and untrained. There was no way you were capable unless someone was taking advantage of those powers. They were controlling you, Kenadee."

"But-but how come I don't remember any of it?" My hand clutches the wall, desperate for something to hold on to as my head spins.

"Brainwashing spells are easier than you think. He probably just wiped your memory after, or turned it to what he wanted you to see. I don't know why I didn't put two and two together. I was trying to figure out how you did, but it wasn't you at all..."

Chills run up my spine, my heart beating too fast for my chest. I can't seem to catch my breath. I did this to them. It's my fault. What else could Reed have done with me without my knowledge?

"Look," Harlow leans forward, an unusual kindness in her deep blue eyes, "We'll find out how he did this, but know that it wasn't your doing."

"Harlow…" my mind races, I don't know what I'm doing. Suddenly, I'm not pretending anymore. I draw in a ragged breath and say, "He has my brother and my mom. Harlow, he'll kill them."

"Trust me, I know how Reed works. You've got to buck up, because you and I—we're the ones with the magic to stop him. Now, we both know deep down that he's not going to give your family up. He'll throw you away, too, right after you're done with us. But here, at this camp, innocent people are in danger. Are you really going to kill everyone over a man we both know is a monster?" Her voice is low, but gives me chills on my arms.

"But how? He has eyes all around the camp. He told me. And if he has people working for him that can—that can do *that*..." I shiver at the thought of them possessing me. They were inside me and I didn't even know…

"Easy. We keep practicing your magic, building it up. You're getting stronger every day. We'll teach you how to not be vulnerable, how to keep them from influencing you. And we'll fight—if he wants war, we'll give him a hell of a war. I've got some beef with him anyways."

"What if he catches us?" My voice is soft, nearly a whimper. "He made me watch a video of him torturing my brother. Harlow, I can't let it happen again."

Harlow shrugs on her sweatshirt and sticks one hand on the door handle, "I won't lie to you. It's definitely not rainbows and unicorns. I've seen what that man can do and I still have nightmares from it. But it's worth the fight if we get to destroy him. I think I'm willing to risk myself for the cause. I really don't like the idea of him having power over the world. He's a bad dude. Do you really want all our deaths on your hands?"

She gives me a faint smile before she's out the door.

***

I JUMP AS A FAMILIAR voice calls my name, too lost in thought to notice Tess running to catch up behind me. "Hey!" I say, surprised.

"Just got done with training, I see," Tess observes as she catches sight of my sweat-stained clothes and messy hair. "How's that going?"

"Good, it's getting better," I say a little too quickly. "Anyway, I was just headed back to my place. See you later?"

Tess grabs my arm, pulling me to a stop. "Um, actually, I was just wondering if you wanted to take a walk with me for a second?"

I look towards the direction of my house, considering this. Even though a walk is the last thing on earth I want to do right now, something in Tess' expression compels me to agree. "Sure, a quick one, okay? I have to get ready to babysit tonight."

"Great, thanks. I just—I don't know. I feel a bit weird today and need someone to talk to…" She drifts off, looking around anxiously.

"No worries. I'm here." I watch the redhead anxiously. Something is definitely bothering her. Her usual cheer is gone, replaced by nail-biting and beads of sweat dusting her forehead.

We walk through the busy downtown as people brush by. There are lots of people that are out, walking around, talking loudly, and enjoying the short span of time before fall ends. It won't be long. This week already, we've had a few snowfalls. Luckily, it hasn't stuck. Yet.

"So, what's up?" I ask, nudging her with my shoulder. "You're worrying me."

"I don't know. I just have this really weird feeling that I can't shake today. It's stupid. I just can't quite get over the feeling that something bad is about to happen."

Her words chill me to the core, I look around to make sure there's no one listening and pull her gently to the edge of the sidewalk, dropping my voice. "What do you mean? Like… *death?*"

Just like Harlow and I talked about. Are they about to do something again?

"Like I said, it's stupid. Just ignore me, I'm being a total buzzkill today." She shakes her head, brushing it off completely. But just as she says it, yelling comes from behind us. We both turn just in time to see people scatter, a large crowd disrupted as they stumble over themselves.

A girl stands in the middle, young with her long ponytail reaching to her lower back. Tears run down her face as she gasps, weeping, "I'm sorry, I can't con—"

As if something snaps, the girl's tears immediately stop, her expression growing glassy. One of the boys shakily steps forward as her hands lower from their defensive position. "Alex?" he asks timidly.

The girl erupts into manic laughter, her eyes far off, glassy and strange, "You're dead and you're dead and so are you."

All she needs is a water bottle and, lifting her hand, she summons the liquid. It spirals around her, a shimmering arc, then hardens, crystallized, becomes ice.

In a second, chunks of ice fly in every direction. Someone to my left screams in pain as it lands its target. I duck just in time as a particularly sharp icicle sinks into the tree behind my head.

I look around in a rush of adrenaline. Do I dare try the mind spell? End this now? But I just learned it and what if—

We hear a yell as everyone on the court momentarily freezes with hope. Benson, the grumpy boy from the first day, comes around the corner, Bryce in tow.

They hold up their hands in the air as a sign of surrender. She sends a flurry of knife-like icicles in their direction, landing one in Bryce's arm. He clutches it, falling back with surprise.

"Don't you come any closer!" she warns in a mocking sing-song tone. Her eyes look so hard all of a sudden, so.... demented. "Or one of these will end up in your heart."

"Don't worry, we're going to stand right here, Alex. But you need to listen very carefully. This isn't you," Bryce says, his voice calm and careful, even as he rips the bloody shard of ice from his arm with a wince.

Alex lets out a horrible, wicked laugh. "You're right, it isn't. She's gone. And so are you and you and you. Dead, dead, dead!"

Bryce opens his mouth to speak again, this time the horror visible in his eyes. "Al—"

He doesn't finish his sentence before the girl shudders and the Alex from before comes back to herself. Almost robotically, a piece of ice raises in her hands. Alex whimpers, unable to stop herself. "I'm sorry," she sobs as she drives it into her chest.

I'm vaguely aware of the screams that fill the air as the girl spews blood, crumpling to her knees.

Reed. He knows. He knows and he did this.

I stumble backwards, taken over by fear. I ignore the ugly tears that stream off my nose and onto my neck, a horrible wail emerging from my throat.

The light dwindles in Alex's eyes as the sacrifice surrenders herself to the arsonist's sparks.

22

I SIT CROSS-LEGGED ON Mia's—one of Nadine and Jay's daughters—bed, reading her a bedtime story in a ridiculously high-pitched voice that makes her giggle. Unfortunately, I can't pretend to be as happy—thoughts of Alex keep drifting into my mind. Right in broad daylight with people everywhere. The attacker was clearly not worried about being caught.

"Please? Read it again!" Mia says, ripping me from my thoughts as I finish the story and fold the book closed. She wrinkles her button-like nose in the cutest of fashions as I shake my head. "I've read it three times. *And* it's past your bedtime."

"But—"

"No buts! Your mom and dad will be back when you wake up. Plus, you have to be up bright and early for school tomorrow. Good night!"

I close the door, ignoring her protests, and wait for a moment to make sure that she's not climbing out of bed. When she doesn't emerge, I tiptoe upstairs to clean the kitchen—ravaged by uneaten pizza crusts, spilled sauce, and crumbs like dust on the seats. My eyes ache, swollen from crying, my mind still completely numb from today's events.

Alex... I'd never met her, but always saw her around the camp. She was sweet and kind, if not a bit shy. She was the type of person that everyone loves automatically, someone genuine. And now she's dead because of me.

I look up as the door opens and Nadine appears, husband right behind her.

"Kenadee, I'm so sorry we're late. That meeting took a little longer considering, well... you know." She clears her throat, then in a swift change of subject says, "This is my husband Jay. Have you two met?"

"No, we haven't met! I'd shake your hand, but uh—" I hold mine up to show him the remainders of our pizza night.

He laughs, a deep, booming laugh, "Ah yes, cleaning up is always an adventure. Were they good at least?"

Just as he asks, a little voice appears. Mia runs to mom and nestles her head in her neck, "I can't sleep."

Nadine throws me an apologetic smile, "Thank you Kenadee! Jay, pay the poor girl please. I'm off to tuck in this little one." Mia's giggles echo as they disappear down the stairs.

Jay reaches for his wallet, plopping into a chair. He's a middle-aged man with laugh lines and graying hair. He seems the type of person that always wears a grin. He hands me a large bill. "Here's a little extra, considering you stayed late. So sorry again."

"Did you find anything out about the attack?" I pry, watching him as I stuff the money into my pocket.

He shakes his head sadly, "Nadine and I might be needing you here a lot, if you're interested. I have to train my entire security team on some new defense spells—there's been talk of the raid again and I want to make sure that they're prepared to try and take on Reed's soldiers."

"Wait... raid?" I swallow, remembering Reed telling me that they were planning something. I thought it was all a lie...

"Oh, that's right, I forget you're new to this camp," Jay sighs, "Before the real danger started with Reed and all his magic soldiers, we'd raid his prisons. Get out who we could, you know? Harlow's been somehow watching everything that he's doing and found out that he's getting most of his magic soldiers from the prisons. So, if we raid, and take away the opportunity, he'll lack the army he needs to attack."

My mind instantly goes to Eli and my mother. They're going to be saved! I won't have to worry about Reed anymore, I can just have them back.

I smile stupidly to myself. "That's—that's wonderful!" Then a terrible thought comes. There's another spy who will surely tell Reed everything. His army will know, they'll fight. I push my bangs back with my hand and look at Jay. "But how do we keep it from Reed? All these attacks are by someone that reports to him."

"Well, we'd have to provide some sort of distraction. Unfortunately, that's the part we'd have to figure out." His mouth straightens into a line, "Who knows that it'll even happen? It all really depends on our people. They're not too intent on leaving the safety of these walls or putting our camp at risk. Who knows if we'll even find the numbers to go through with it, you know?"

"Yeah," I reply, thinking for a long moment. This is the most excited I've felt since I've arrived. The idea of getting them free, of separating ourselves from Reed once and for all. I could live a happy life here with my family.

As foolish as it might be, I say goodbye to Jay and transport to Harlow's office. She's still there, door cracked open and light seeping through. Her head pops up from her paperwork as I knock, eyes widening with surprise. "What are you doing here?"

I look to make sure it's just us, then close the door behind me, feeling as if this is the stupidest thing I've ever done. And yet, the words roll off my tongue so easily, "I want in."

She watches me for a second like she's trying to decide whether or not I'm joking, then must decide against it as she flicks a finger and the blinds rattle shut. She comes to the edge of her desk and leans against it, motioning towards the chair. "Take a seat, and let's talk."

"I can't stay," I lick my lips nervously and glance at the clock. Reed will be calling any minute. "And I can't let him know, either. He'll kill them Harlow, and I won't let that happen. All I know is I want them back. We *have* to get them back."

"We will," she promises, and I know that she means it. "I'll do everything in my power to ensure it. You just keep telling Reed what he wants to hear for now. Give him no reason to cause them harm. I'll take care of everything else."

Hope swells in my chest and I nod eagerly, giving her a small smile. "Thank you, Harlow. For this."

Her crooked grin seems almost warmer when it appears. "No, thank *you* for helping me kick some presidential ass."

I reach for my transportation device and disappear from the room, her smile the last thing I see.

***

I ARRIVE HOME JUST AS the communicator lights up, flicking on the lights as the secretary gives a very dramatic sigh. "Took you long enough, Ms. Coria we called three times," she scolds bitterly as I plop myself on the couch in front of her.

"I think you'll get over it," I snap. She glares, but doesn't say another word as she automatically transfers me to the president.

"Oh, so you *are* alive." He sneers, checking his watch for emphasis. "My secretary was about to have a fit."

"I was... gone," I reply, pulling my cold feet on the couch and covering them in a striped blanket.

"Well I am an impatient man, Miss Coria, you understand that, don't you?"

I nod, chewing on the inside of my cheek.

"Good. I am glad we're on the same page. And I hope that you understand why I was forced to kill that girl?"

"No, I don't." It comes out before I can stop myself. I stare at him hopelessly, wondering if I even want the answer.

He chuckles wickedly, making me want to rip his throat out. "Well, it's simple. I've had eyes on you, just to make sure that you've been doing your job. Some of these spells are so tricky—they even got past Ms. Creston. Impressive. Although, it seems your loyalties are a little mixed-up lately."

Panic floods me as I let out a lie, "I was only lying to Harlow. Trying to get her to believe me."

"She made herself a part of it a long time ago, Miss Coria. When she escaped my prison with many others, freeing them. I don't take too kindly to that."

"What?" She mentioned being locked up with my brother. Why didn't she take him too?

"Of course, she did. She's clever like a fox, I'll give her that. But Miss Creston and I aren't through. She will pay the price for what she did."

"What does that mean?"

He guffaws again, amused by his own cruelty, "You'll see when you hand her over to me."

I begin to stammer, trying to find some excuse. "I—"

"The point is, I know *everything* you've been up to, Kenadee. I know of your little romance with Bryce Coughlin, about your conversations with Ms. Creston, and your newest source of information—the attack. Were you planning on telling me?"

"I-I was, I promise! I just found out minutes ago—they might not even be able to go through with it."

A smile sprawls across his face, "Oh, I'm ensuring that they won't. We're taking away their chance. Tomorrow at the funeral for that girl, you're going to hand Ms. Creston over to me."

"W-what?"

He wants Harlow.

Tomorrow.

"You heard me, dear girl. My soldiers and I are already prepared. We know that it will be no problem for you. You've had all this time, surely you know how to breach the barrier by now? I only need a few minutes."

"It's not that easy—"

He holds up a hand, "I thought it might come to this. Your brother is with guards as we speak. One word can end in his death so if you want him to live, you will do exactly as I ask," I swallow, nodding with tears in my eyes.

"Yes, okay! Don't hurt him!"

"What you must do is simple. Let us in the camp, and we'll take it from there. If you do as I ask, your family will be spared for now. If you try to cross me, they will be dead, you understand?"

"What will you do to Harlow?" I ask hopelessly. I think I already know the answer. He's already proven himself a monster. His vendetta against Harlow is clear—the girl has made a fool of him too many times. Whatever he does to make her pay, it won't be pretty.

To my demise, the president laughs his horrible laugh, his smile cruel. "I don't see how that's any of your business, Kenadee. Keep in mind, Harlow has tried relentlessly to endanger our mission. She's lucky I don't off her the moment I get my hands on her."

Fear knots my stomach. I have to come up with a plan. He's going to hurt Eli if I don't give her to him. There's no possible way to get them both out of this. I only have one option. "How do I know you won't harm anyone else in the camp?"

"I am not a liar. It isn't their time... not yet." He takes a sip of his alcohol and clears his throat, "Consider this a lesson: I am watching you, Kenadee Coria, and I will do everything in my power to make sure that I win. After you hand us Ms. Creston, you'll find out how to increase your power enough to keep that barrier down for good. Get in my way, and Eli will pay."

I nod quickly, "I understand."

23

I RAP MY KNUCKLES ON the door of the security building, telling myself for the zillionth time that this is for my family, and that we can save Harlow if the camp goes through with the raid. I can't save my brother if he's dead.

Before I can break down the barrier for Reed, I have to take care of the security system. I had originally hoped that I could use a mind spell to get the guards to take it down, but unfortunately, the spell requires more than their basic magic. It requires dark powers, like mine.

So, first things first, I need to make sure that the security team won't be a threat.

The doorknob jiggles and a guard appears, giving me an annoyed glance-over as he steps out into the hall. "What do you want?"

"Can I come in?" I bat my eyes for effect.

His dark brows furrow, "Sorry—I'm the only one on duty, I need to be working, not—"

He's too late. I throw my powers forward with all my might. Harlow had taught me only the basics of the mind spell, not the actual aspect of control. I grit my teeth, feeling my magic catch something.

THE TRAITOR'S CRUX

Caught off-guard, his mind is open. I slip inside, watching as his thoughts and memories go flashing by.

I nearly laugh with excitement. *I did it!*

Smiling sweetly at the guard, I test out my control, "Now, move aside and let me through."

He does as I ask, sloth-like movements as I keep a tight reign over his mind. Kicking off my black high heels designated for the funeral, I slam the door behind me. He stands still, too caught up in my magic web to be let free. "You will reset the security spell tonight. No sooner, no later."

He gives another obedient nod and moves aside while I turn my attention on undoing the spell around the town. It's almost like the alarm systems that we used to have in the non-magical world—certain spells or actions can trigger it. I hover my hands over its keyhole and begin to chant. There's a slight rustling throughout the room, then my magic explodes, coursing through me with raging intensity. I smile to myself as there's a loud crack and the everything goes still again. Something heavy and cool to the touch lands in my hands.

A key.

I focus once again on the keyhole, trying to remember the spell from the grimoire. It was an old one I found at the bottom of my library pile, dusted and grimy, but with a noticeable amount of dark magic spells.

It had anything a person could imagine, from basic defense spells, to security spells, such as this one, and mind control. I stayed up reading it all night, unable to sleep. Whoever donated it to the library clearly forgot that this spell was in there. I wonder to myself why this is as the key slips inside and the spell comes undone with a dying electric buzz.

I turn just in time for a door behind me to swing open, a surprised guard gaping at me. I don't wait a second, putting a defense spell to the test. I pin him against the wall, but he realizes what's happening. He squirms, making my magic's grip falter slightly.

I make my move, dropping him and replacing the former spell with mind control. He sees it coming and raises a hand. The light crackles above as the guard pulls it from the fixture, bright sparks emitting from above. I barely have time to leap out of the way as it strikes the wall behind me with a horrific bang.

I don't wait. The mind spell rages from me once more, catching on a single memory.

I watch it unfold—this guard, a girl, staring back at him with wide-eyes. She smiles coyly, as the guard leans in.

As I force this memory to replay, the guard's control lessens. "That's right," I whisper, "Just let go."

"Let go..." he repeats, letting his hands fall limp at his sides. I move slowly, as if he's an animal I'm trying not to spook. I sigh, feeling my hands shake with the intensity of controlling both guards at once. "Now. You both will forget all about this. You do not know anything about the camp being raided. It's a normal, safe day, and you were only doing maintenance on the border. Go back to your work, forget my face."

THE TRAITOR'S CRUX

I look back and forth between the guards. They gawk back at me, mouths open. Together, they nod. I clench my jaw, yanking myself away from their minds.

As they fall to the ground, I reach for my heels and escape into the hall. The funeral preparations have begun.

***

I MAKE SURE NO ONE is watching before I take the running trail through the forest, where Harlow and I usually go for our runs. People are already filing into the church where the funeral service will be held… I can't be late.

I come to a stop at an oddly-shaped tree. Harlow would never go past this point, declaring that it was at the edge of camp boundaries. Only leaders are allowed outside the barrier, and she was never willing to let me step through.

I creep forward until my hands bang against the smooth invisible wall. I take a step back, prying a hair tie off my wrist and tucking my hair back into a ponytail. Once I'm done, I set the book down in front of me.

This isn't just any spell. It's a rare, ancient one. In one of Harlow's many books that I was required to read for training, I learned that most ancient magic has been replaced. Most modern magic only requires a flick of the hand, the training of the mind, the will to make it obey. Some ancient spells, however, were not changed. Some were simply too powerful to be dealt with, and were cast aside for centuries. Some, for dark magic like ours, are rarely practiced and widely feared because of their brutality, strength, and darkness.

I flip through the grimoire's pages until I land on the dog-eared corner that I'd pressed down last night. Standing and shaking my limbs loose, my hands find the invisible wall. The words of the spell begin to roll from my tongue, melodic and foreign.

Muros frangere.
Muros frangere.
Muros...

I falter for a moment as the barrier seems to quake underneath my fingertips, gentle at first, then growing in its rage. I let out a sigh of relief and continue chanting, angling my head back to watch as the wall begins to light up.

I'm actually breaking down the camp walls.

24

I STEP BACK TO EXAMINE my handiwork, nothing but a stretch of highway and forest beyond the city limits. The borders are open. Now, Reed can enter the camp walls.

Right on cue, my communicator buzzes in the pocket of my dress, the code from Reed telling me that he's on the trail.

Giving one final look around, I turn and stumble back to camp, my dress dusty, pantyhose torn, and a new ache in my bones from using so much power. I shouldn't have risked pushing myself as far as I did, and yet... it worked. I can't believe that I pulled this off. It's like the feeling when I surrounded the police officers in the ring of fire. I never knew how intoxicating magic could be, how strong I could feel with these powers at hand.

The chapel doesn't sit far from the entrance of the camp. Outside its doors is a sea of black as people mill about, a few heads staring at my ragged appearance. I ignore them, silently thanking the height that my heels give me as my eyes scan the crowd for Harlow.

"Kenadee! Hey! Over here!" I wince at the sound of Delia's voice behind me. Before I can slip away, she's

THE TRAITOR'S CRUX

beside me, long neck craned like a swan, long earrings dangling against her bronze skin. "This is so awful, isn't it?"

I nod as Tess pops up beside her, giving me a sad smile hello.

"We should probably go find a seat. It'll be starting in just a few minutes," Delia says, then knits her brows together, "Hey, Ken—you okay?"

"What? Yeah…" I say distantly, "Have either of you seen Harlow? I want to talk to her before it all begins."

"You two are buddies now? Consider me impressed." Delia snickers, "And yeah, she's right there."

Sure enough, Harlow leans in the chapel doorway next to Bryce, shaking hands and passing out programs. She's dressed up, wearing a lacy black dress and heels, her long blonde curls draping her shoulders. Beside her, Bryce wears a black sweater over a collared shirt, dark hair gelled back neatly. His eyes glance up, but I refuse to meet them.

"Kenadee?" Tess turns her doe-like eyes on me, "We're headed inside. Are you coming?"

I gulp, glancing at my friends, "I'll be there in a second, okay? Save me a seat?"

"Harlow?"

As Bryce ducks around the corner, I reach for her shoulder, catching her by surprise. She jumps, pulling away. When she sees that it's me, she sighs, "Sorry. I just—I need to get some air. Will you excuse me?" Her voice quivers, just barely as she brushes past, making her way out the door.

My hand reaches for the communicator in my pocket. They linger for a moment on the button as guilt makes my stomach churn.

It's for my family. I have to.

I click the buttons twice to tell them she's outside, and stick it back into my pocket before slipping through the front doors. Now, I only need to distract her.

I follow her out, seeing her blonde head disappear around the corner into the trees. My heel crunches loudly on a leaf, breaking the stillness of the forest. If she hears, she doesn't reveal it, a cigarette held neatly between two fingers.

"Harlow?" I call, stepping around to see her face. She doesn't look at me, but brings the cigarette to her lips, inhaling deeply.

"Please don't say anything. I just… I had to get out." Her voice is a shaky whisper, which scares me. I've never seen this side of her, even after invading her head and seeing the memories within. Harlow doesn't break down. She doesn't cry. Harlow fights.

"You wanna walk?" I ask, using my head to point towards the trail. I need to get her away from the building, just in case someone happens to see. She says nothing, but folds her arms over herself and walks in suit beside me.

"Did you know Alex well?" I ask after a moment.

Ignoring my question, she catches my gaze on her cigarette and gives a short, humorless laugh. "I know, judge me all you want. It was the only thing able to help me after I escaped. Reed did me in real good. Never knew what a panic attack was until one day I was in a meeting with Bryce. Something triggered me and I lost it. Crying, screaming—all of it. Luckily it was Bryce, but uh—I just couldn't handle daily life anymore." She trails off, taking another tearful drag, and exhaling slowly. "I don't do it a lot, except when I need really it. Tess caught me once and yelled at me about getting cancer for three days straight. I told her I didn't care. Why should I?"

I shake my head, "What's that supposed to mean?"

Her blue eyes meet my gaze before she drops them, smothering her cigarette with her foot and snapping her fingers to make its remains disappear. "He got his revenge already. The first time I refused him, he branded me. See this?" She turns around, shrugging off the sleeve of her dress. A large tattoo decorates her shoulder blade, spreading down towards her back. I realize that it moves, a sand timer, full of motion. The bottom is nearly filled, with only about a quarter of sand left in the top.

"What—" I stammer, confused.

"It's my death sentence." She kicks a rock angrily with her foot, "Isn't Reed just a peach? He chose it because it shuts my body down slowly. Makes it all the more fun to die. It was your brother, actually, who did it. Reed tortured him, got in his mind, made him give me the tattoo. Reed told me he'll take it off me if I help him. Since that'll never happen, I guess I'm a time bomb."

"How did you escape?"

"The first time wasn't me, but some other powerful wizard that got us all out. Unfortunately, we were all caught and given these beauties for disobedience. Reed has a surprising amount of magic people working for him, thinking that it'll get them the easy way out. It's supposed to be a horrible death," she says, tugging the shoulder of her dress back up.

The communicator buzzes three times in my pocket: they have eyes on us.

I pry deeper, keeping her attention on me. "Well, then, how did you escape the second time?" I kick the dirt with my heel, ignoring how dusty they're getting as I try my best to shove my emotions out of the way.

The new, more vulnerable Harlow answers quietly, surprisingly going along with all my questions. "It was a day that I knew they were having limited security. The president has temper tantrums and had just fired a bunch of guards. I, uh, killed the distracted guard and stole the keys. A few of us got out before Reed realized what was happening."

"God, I didn't realize…" I shake my head, sickened by it all. She's about to go back, and there's nothing I can do about it. I'm the one handing her over to the devil himself.

"Don't feel sorry for me." A spark of the original Harlow rises up from the sorrow of the moment, "It's over and done. He pulled my head from the clouds and I thank him for that. Humanity doesn't exist, and that's why the war does. He made me see it."

There's a movement in the corner of my eye.

"Harlow," I whisper, turning the girl towards me as, suddenly, a guard appears around a tree. "I'm *so* sorry!"

THE TRAITOR'S CRUX

A guard steps from the trees. Then another, and another.

Harlow looks at me with raw terror in her eyes.

The first one fires his magic at her, but it doesn't take Harlow long to send him screaming, flying through the air. More and more soldiers appear, streaming out of the aspens. She's surrounded, a bird in a cage. A spell flies toward her and with a swipe of her hand, she reflects it back on its owner. Another round of bright blue sparks emits from someone's hands. She sees it, but she isn't quick enough. A second person joins in, combining their powers. Then a third, and a fourth, and—

Harlow doubles over, clutching her head and crying out in pain. Someone else adds to her pain, sending a flurry of red jolting into her stomach. She's struggling, trying to climb back up, but I can see her shaking limbs from here.

Hot tears burn my eyes as I force myself to watch Harlow's undoing. I did this to her, I ruined her life.

She makes one last feeble attempt to use her powers. I can see her hands raise, but the sparks only spiral to the ground, burning out with her strength. There's nothing left for her to give.

A slow clap comes from my right, making my spine crawl. The president appears beside me, his gait slow and leisurely, sunglasses sheltering his eyes, hiding them from both the sun and me. "Good work, Miss Coria, I must say that I'm impressed. You are a great actress!"

I stand firmly and say nothing. All I can think is that this is it. There's no turning back now. Out of my peripheral vision, the soldiers yank Harlow to her feet. There's another flash of light, a buzz of electricity, and she screams in pain, crumpling to the ground.

"Ah, Harlow Creston. I must say that I am happy to see you again," the president taunts as the guard makes her sit up. She's limp, propped up like a rag doll in the soldier's arms. His hand cups her chin as she flinches, "Sorry it had to happen this way. Miss Coria fooled you though, didn't she? You really thought she was on your side, even though you knew I was behind it all? I'd expect it from watching that dense young leader, Bryce, but not you. I'd hate to see you growing weak on me."

Even though her mouth is now covered, I can hear the obscenities crystal clear. The president laughs, turning back towards me, "Magic-proof binds. Invented by my very own magical soldiers. They're a miracle. They mute the powers so they can't fight back. This also helps." He produces a shiny needle from his pocket, taking his time to fill it. Harlow screams, fighting and kicking as he stabs it into her neck, then collapses against the guard. They drag her towards the forest.

"Don't worry. Your friend, Harlow, is fine." He looks to me, laughing at my expression, "It's just a sedative. I find it particularly useful for dangerous criminals."

I don't answer. Salty tears trickle from my cheeks and I stubbornly bat them away. I did what I had to do. "I did what you asked. Now are they safe?"

"Well, that's something I must discuss with you, Kenadee." He fakes a grimace, though I can see how his eyes glisten, "I'm a little worried about where your loyalties lie, dear girl. You seem to struggle with this too."

"I did everything you asked!" I point towards the spot where Harlow had been. "I-I brought her to you!"

"I'm no fool. You've been purposely leaving out information for a while now, trying to take their side and keep it hidden. I thought maybe you could use a little bit of… motivation to help you remember who you work for."

He nods at a guard, and the image appears. It looks as if I'm in the room—a dark, grey bunker with a buzzing fluorescent light and… blood. Blood splattered like ink all over the walls.

Dread pools over me as I realize what's happening. The door flings open, and my mother gets dragged into the room. She's limp, and covered in blood. I clap a hand across my mouth in horror.

"No! Please don't!"

Reed appears, a drink in hand as he walks slowly around her. He whispers something, low in her ear, then turns to the soldier closest to him. "Kill her."

I scream, unable to do anything. Tears stream down her face as I watch my mother squirm in their arms. She's my size, barely above five feet tall. It takes one soldier to send her shrieking to the ground. Their voices chant in a low, melodious spell. I recognize from a grimoire instantly. It's a spell for dark magic—for Reed's army to pull off.

My mother begins to thrash violently on the ground, screaming, crying for mercy, but they don't stop. I feel a ragged howl escape my chest as I sink to my knees.

I did this. I killed my mother. I—

Her cries grow fainter, weaker, as her twitching limbs grow limp. Reed steps over her stilled form, nearly kicking her. All the air is gone from my chest. All I can do is stare at her lifeless body in shock.

The room dissolves and the real Reed smirks beside me. His words barely register in my brain, like a distant, taunting echo. "Next time, you'll remember whose side you're on. Goodbye, Miss Coria."

The screen shuts off, and I continue to stare at the spot that my mother had been. I killed her. I killed her. I killed her.

I tilt my head back, suddenly not caring who hears as I scream, a hollow, ragged, aching scream.

25 I LIE UNDERNEATH MY COVERS, feeling angry at the sun for being too bright, and angry at the world for moving on. My clock shines back at me with a ripe green face, taunting me for lying in bed all day. It's 3:54, and I'm here, unable to make myself move, unable to care about a single thing.

My mother's dead. Who knows where Eli is, or whether Reed kept his promise, and Harlow—I betrayed her. I gave her to a man that's tortured her very existence. I'm a monster. How could I have been mad at Bryce when I was the one to betray the girl who offered me a second chance?

Instead, I chose the man that murdered my mother. I hate him with every part of me.

There's a knock on the door, but I don't move, hoping they'll go away.

No such luck, as it clicks open and Tess' voice rings merrily from the hall. "Kenadee? Where are you?"

"Go away!"

The blankets are ripped from their position over my head and Delia appears, arms crossed neatly over her chest. She raises a quizzical brow. "Alright. Explain what you're doing moping around in bed at four in the afternoon."

"Maybe she's sick?" suggests Tess, popping up beside her best friend and watching me with a cocked head.

"I can hear you."

Delia plops down on the bed, tucking a corkscrewed curl behind her ear. "Have you eaten today?" I shake my head no and she sighs. "I'm going to make you some food and you're going to tell us what the hell is going with you. Come on, outta bed!"

For a doctor, Delia is widely unaware that she's about to pull my arm from my socket as she yanks me to my feet and pushes me into a chair in the kitchen. I run a hand over my eyes, exhausted.

"So? What's wrong?" Delia calls, padding over to the far cabinet and rummaging around through the food. "No offense, but you look like a wreck."

There's another knock and Tess bolts towards the door, "Bryce is here!"

He appears behind her before I can react, brows furrowed as he stares down at a map. "Have any of you seen Harlow? She never came in today, she wasn't at home, and she's not appearing on the map." He stops, glancing up and seeing me. "Whoa—what happened? Are you okay?"

All heads turn in my direction as I chew on the inside of my cheek. Reed murdered my mom. I was stupid to trust him, stupid to think he'd spare her. He jumped at the chance to declare his power over me, to make me watch as he had her slaughtered. I turned in Harlow to try and save them, and my mother died anyway.

How could I have been so foolish?

I sniff, balling my fists in the sleeves of my sweater as I shake my head at Bryce. "No... I'm not okay. Can I talk to you?"

He nods, looking worried. "Yeah, yeah, of course. Is this about the attack, because—?"

"No," I say quickly, as Tess and Delia exchange curious glances. "It's something else."

"Yeah, okay." I can tell he's confused, but I don't give him anything else to go off right now. I have to tell him. I have to let it out.

As we walk away, I can hear Delia loud and clear. "Well *that* was strange."

***

BRYCE TAKES THE WICKER CHAIR opposite me as we step out on the porch. The breeze picks up, blowing a stream of leaves across the ground as I shiver, tucking my legs onto the chair.

"It's my fault," I say after a long moment, peeking at him to see if he catches on.

"What do you mean?" He asks slowly, suspicion glimmering in his eyes. I love the warmth in them, the depth of his gaze. Bryce, always so sweet and kind, always trying to see the good in people. Well, probably until now.

THE TRAITOR'S CRUX

I sigh, trying to compose my quivering voice as I spill everything. I tell him about President Reed sending me here to spy and capturing my family. I tell him about the explosions and the phone calls and Alex. Finally, worst of all, I tell him about how I led Harlow over to Reed and his men, like sheep to the slaughter. He watches me incredulously, his lips parted slightly and his forehead wrinkled. His eyes search my face, desperate for an explanation. They're disappointed, afraid. I did this. I'm the monster that destroyed camp. I'm the one that betrayed his trust.

"So… it was all you?" he finally asks, his voice hoarse. He refuses to look at me as he comes to terms with it, searching everywhere but me.

I blink to wash back the tears, "Not everything. Reed didn't tell me about the explosion until later. I didn't do it. I don't know how he did… and Alex? I didn't control her. I just—"

I reach for him, trying to make him understand my side. He pulls away, "Don't touch me! You know, we took you in. Harlow took you in and you just betrayed us all. Don't you think that you could've told us? We can take him! Those people were put in harm's way over nothing!"

I can't hold back the emotions any longer, "I'm so sorry, Bryce. I thought—"

"Whatever, Kenadee." His voice is cold and harsh, ripping into me with brutal force, "Just do me a favor and stay away from all of us. You've done enough damage."

"Bryce—" I cry, but he's already gone, disappearing into the depths of the trees.

***

I SIT THERE NUMBLY, UNSURE of where to go or how to feel. My eyes feel strangely dry, as if I have no more tears left to give. Tess and Delia creep through the door after he leaves, wondering about all the yelling.

I run a hand through my hair, too drained to explain myself. "Bryce will tell you everything, I'm sure."

"Okay..." says Delia with a frown. "Well, he's walking up the sidewalk now with Jay, so..."

My head pops up and for a moment, hope wells through me. Maybe I'm forgiven. Maybe Bryce or Jay will help me.

"What is this?" I whisper.

His eyes are cold as he leans against the railing. Bryce is no longer the boy I fell for, but a stranger. "I considered it, Kenadee, and Harlow was right all along. I didn't trust her... I should have. She knows Reed's games more than anyone and-and I blew her off." Jay avoids my gaze as he comes behind me. Metal cuffs snap firmly across my wrists as Bryce swallows, his Adam's apple bobbing, "So I'm doing what Harlow would do. I won't hand you over to Reed, but I'll be damned if you endanger this camp again."

"Whoa, what?" Tess looks back and forth, mouth open wide.

"Bryce," I struggle against Jay as he grips my arm. "Please, listen to me…"

"No!" he snaps, eyes flashing. My heart races as he comes close to me. Instead, he only lowers his voice to a harsh whisper, emerald eyes like daggers, "You're still better off than Harlow right now. Think of that as you rot in a cell."

26

JAY QUIETLY TAKES ME TO Bryce and Harlow's office, leading me past Julie, and to a closet door at the end of the room. His fingers tap the vault door in a strange pattern, each movement making a clicking sound deep within.

"Take a step back," he warns in a gruff voice, grabbing me just in time as the door flings open, nearly taking me out with its force.

I try to move forward to peek inside the room, but the man lunges for my arm. "Not yet—we have to wait for the stairs."

"Stairs?" I repeat hoarsely.

A loud mechanical clicking drowns out his voice as I spin back around. Lights flicker on, one by one until the entire room is lit up. Sure enough, planks of wood fly all around below, carefully arranging themselves piece by piece into the shape of a grand staircase. Once they reach our feet, he nudges me forward.

No one else is down here, despite the line of cells on each wall. We don't stop until we reach the very last one, which is lit up with blinding fluorescent lights. There's a single cot and a toilet behind what I'm guessing is a clear barrier.

Jay pushes me against a wall once again, ignoring my protests as he sticks a needle into my arm. Once he's done with the blue liquid, he unlocks my bonds and shoves me into the cell.

"What was that?" My head feels groggy. I blink, leaning against the cot for support.

He snaps his fingers as the lock of the black filing cabinet clicks and creaks open. He shuffles through a bunch of files, not looking at me. "A sedative for witches and wizards. Restrains the powers, weakens you so that you can't perform your magic."

I stare at my quivering hands, now rendered useless under the drug's spell. Jay scribbles his signature on a piece of paper and sticks it into what I'm assuming is my file, then snaps again, as the drawer shuts. He comes back towards my cell, watching me with dark brown eyes. "I don't know how you pulled it off, Kenadee Coria, but I'm afraid you're in some deep trouble."

I gulp, "I know."

He rubs a hand over his beard, grimacing. "Look, Bryce is mad now. Everyone is, and rightly so—"

"I—"

He holds up a hand to stop me, "*But* Bryce told me your story. He wasn't sure what to do with the traitor that so desperately wanted to save her brother…" He takes a step closer, kindness in his eyes, "I don't want you to give up yet. Fight with everything you got, kid, 'cause I can take just one look at you and know that you aren't happy with your decisions. You know why Bryce is so good at what he does?"

I shake my head and he smiles, "Not because he has Harlow's brains or fighting skills. No... what makes Bryce a great leader is his compassion. He has this rare, and sometimes naïve, tendency to see the best in people. If you're smart, you'll turn this around and start acting like the Kenadee Coria that he saw. Even an old bat like me could see how smitten he was with you."

And with that, he leaves me to dwell in my thoughts.

***

I LOSE TRACK OF THE days in confinement. A day turns into weeks as I'm left alone with nothing but the white walls staring back at me, mocking me with their solitude.

Jay comes several times a day to bring meals and inject the sedative. As my only company, I've come to look forward to even those small interactions, moments that keep me grounded. He never has news of the raid, though I ask him repeatedly. He says he's not allowed to share that information with me anymore.

"So, tell me, what do I need to do to get a bath around here? I think my smell might be killing off these bugs," I ask one day as the door bangs open. I nearly jump out of surprise when it's not Jay, but Bryce who appears, frowning back at me. "Oh—"

"I'll send a female guard to come help you with that. Wouldn't want to kill off the bugs, would we?"

"I-I didn't know that it was you," I mutter, mortified.

He doesn't smile, but grabs Jay's stool from the corner and props it in front of the cell.

"Look, Bryce—"

He shakes his head, running a frustrated hand through his chestnut hair. "I don't know what to do, Ken, but Jay insisted I come talk to you. How do we make this right?"

"I-I'm not sure," I sigh, leaning against the wall.

Emerald eyes flicker up, "I can't just let you go. I know you were doing it for your family. I understand Reed's been threatening you, but—"

"But what, Bryce?" I throw my hands in the air helplessly, "Tell me, what would you do? Would you do everything you could to save your family, Bryce? Because that's the kind of person I am! Maybe I am selfish, but don't pretend for one moment that I don't feel bad for every single thing I've done since I came here. I can't sleep, I can barely eat. All I can picture is Harlow's face when I turned her over. Look at me, Bryce! Don't you turn away!" My voice cracks with the plea, but he obeys.

There's raw emotion swimming in those brilliant green eyes. I feel my heart break into several pieces as they burn into mine. For a still second, he's mine again and this never happened. But as he breaks the moment, gaze turning downward, I know that things won't ever be the same again.

His pointed gaze doesn't move up again. After a second he says, "We're having a camp meeting about saving Harlow. We'll do what we can to save your family too."

"Let me help," I beg.

His jaw tightens, "Look, we talked as a group and the only reason why I'm letting you out, is because you're coming to the White House with us to break Harlow and the rest of the prisoners free. We need your powers— they're stronger than ours, they're the only chance we have. We did a tracking spell so that we can see your every move. You'll be monitored twenty-four seven. Anything suspicious and you end up back here, do you understand?"

I nod quickly, excitement welling inside me. We're doing it. We're going to break Eli free. "Thank you!"

"Don't thank me. Just prove to me that you're good for something," he whispers, coming up to the barrier and setting his palm against its threshold. He closes his eyes in concentration as the barrier begins to tremble.

I stand silently as it flashes, then comes apart. Bryce opens his eyes, peering back at me. "You're free to go," he says quietly.

"Bryce—"

He doesn't smile as he steps aside to allow me to pass, "Don't think this changes anything."

"Can I at least try?" I want so desperately for him to say yes, for him to grab me, to hold me close. Instead, he stays firmly planted, a crease in his brow and vague interest in his eyes. I continue, "I can tell you what Reed has planned for this camp. I'll tell you everything I know."

27

I SIT IN THE OFFICE chair across from Bryce as he leans on his desk, listening quietly. I tell him everything I know, everything I should have said from the moment I set foot in camp. When I'm finished, he exhales sharply and rocks back in his seat. "Wow... I—I can't believe it. There's really more of you... spies?"

"I *was* a spy," I correct, "And yes. Just one from what I'm aware. I told Harlow before..."

"And you don't have any idea who it could be?"

"No," I admit, "But can't the security team find out something?"

He chews on his lip, lost deep in thought, "It's not that simple. There hasn't been any suspicious activity at all... whoever this is, they've been staying on the down low for a while now. I'll look in Harlow's office and see... if anyone figured out anything, it'd be her."

I wring my hands, butterflies in my stomach, "So, tell me our plan. How are we going to save her?"

"Not our plan. My plan," he says firmly, "You aren't coming, remember?"

"Come on, Bryce! Don't you think I owe it to her to help out? Besides, my brother and my mom are there… I have to do something. I can't just sit idly by!"

"No," he says, walking to the door and holding it open. "Now go clean up before the meeting tonight. No offense, but your comment about killing bugs wasn't that far of a stretch."

"But—"

"*Go.*"

I kick the wall furiously as the door clasps shut behind me, jumping when I realize I'm not the only one in the room. Julie the secretary snickers as I shove past, "Bye little angry jailbird!"

***

WHEN JAY KNOCKS ON THE door to escort me to the meeting, I'm showered, freshly clothed, and still childishly annoyed at Bryce.

The room is swarming with bodies as Jay and I enter the cafeteria, the seats already completely filled with nervous onlookers. Jay and I stand at the edge of the room, tucked against the wall. I see Delia and Tess in the crowd, watching me with grim expressions. I've lost everyone's trust—they all know the terrible things I did.

The door opens and Bryce comes sweeping in, a determined energy to his face. He trots straight past me, eyes stubbornly directed ahead. The conversation falters as everyone's eyes anxiously follow one of their leaders. I hear a few whispers, mentions of Harlow's name. I stare ahead, biting my lip.

At the podium up front, Bryce waits patiently, looking around at all the faces until the noise dies completely. His face looks different tonight, wearing an unusual scowl, his lips pursed with worry. He avoids my gaze completely, looking everywhere but me.

The traitor.

"I want to thank you all for being here tonight. I apologize that it's so late, however, we have a very important safety issue at risk that we all need to discuss. Since we're getting close to dinner time, I'll keep it short."

The room is eerily silent, all eyes glued to the front. Bryce clears his throat and continues, "My friends, a source has told me that there has been more than one person associating with Reed in this camp." Many heads swivel in my direction as Bryce carries on, "All suspicious behavior needs to be reported immediately. Failure to do so means that you're endangering the camp, and you will be punished accordingly."

He pauses, fingers dancing nervously on the edge of the podium, "For those of you that are unaware, there was a recent situation where Harlow was handed over to the President. We've learned from an inside source about Reed's plans. Soon, I fear he'll be coming for us too."

I close my eyes, fighting the sting of his words, the truth behind them. The audience begins to buzz loudly with worry.

THE TRAITOR'S CRUX

"So, what are you going to do?" A man's voice rings through the crowd.

I cross my arms, biting my lip. I have to be calm. I need to prove myself, to show that I can do this. I can redeem myself and this camp. Unfortunately, there's only one way we can surely win. We have to fight fire with fire. We have to defeat Reed. Judging by the worried faces of the crowd, it looks like they all know it too.

Bryce's face reveals the fear we're all feeling. He's just as worried as we are. Without Harlow, he has no one to make decisions with. He's all alone, left with all these people to take care of and look after. He's afraid of failure.

"We have to fight. It's the only way," He admits nervously.

A woman yells out, her voice shrill with fear, "We have children! You expect us to fight? Reed, of all people? He has the entire country on his side. There's no way we can win!"

"I know it's scary. But he will not stop until he gets us, that's been confirmed. All those things he did, the people he used and destroyed? Alex? Harlow? It's a game to him. He's coming for us; he's trying to lure us out. And I think that we need to fight back. We cannot let him do this to us, to our people. Open your eyes. It's our turn to win!" Bryce says, furiously. "I understand that we have families, children, the elderly all in this camp, that's why I'm asking strictly on a volunteer basis. If you believe in this fight. If you want freedom, then please take a stand with us."

Out of the corner of my eye, I see Delia's head turn my way. I catch her gaze for a brief second before she rips her brown eyes away to the floor.

Next to me, Jay waves his hand in the air to capture Bryce's attention. "Sign me up!" He volunteers.

"Thanks, Jay!" This time Bryce acknowledges him, looking right past me, determined to ignore my presence. "Anyone—"

"I'll fight too." He's interrupted by Benson of all people, who, despite volunteering for the cause, doesn't look like he gives a single care in the world.

Slowly, people begin rising out of their seats. I catch eye contact with both Tess and Delia as they stand to volunteer. A few rows behind them, Kenzie rises, sweeping her long brown hair behind her shoulder as she does so. There are about a dozen people, which isn't much, but it's at least something.

Bryce is visibly pleased, a smile in his eyes as he proudly takes in his new army, "Thank you for all of you volunteers. We will be meeting at eight A.M. sharp tomorrow morning to discuss strategy. Don't be late."

His eyes fall on me with the last, unspoken warning. I hear it loud and clear. *Don't you dare try anything.*

28

I TAKE EXTRA CARE TO wash my hair the next morning, massaging my scalp carefully as I spread the foamy bubbles across it. I close my eyes and let the water run down my face as I rest my head against the tile. Bryce came to my door last night after the raid's strategy meeting I wasn't allowed to attend, and told me that we were leaving this morning at seven.

All I can think is that it's happening, today. We are leading this rebellion, getting our prisoners and our homes back.

I'm going to get my brother back.

No matter how many times I say it to myself, I can't believe it's going to be true. I wonder what Eli looks like now. He was always a handsome child growing up—the kid that chased the girls and had many girlfriends by the time he was in kindergarten. It was something in his dimples, or that sly wrinkle of his nose. People adored him. I wonder how much he's changed, how much Reed has gotten to him. I don't know if I'm more anxious or excited.

As soon as I'm out of the shower, I run a comb gently through my tangles and gather my hair back into a small bun at the nape of my neck. I brush my teeth and find my oldest pair of pants, figuring it'd be the best if they got ruined. I throw on a long-sleeved t-shirt and a black hoodie. Winter threatens us each day. Lately, we've even gotten some snow. It won't be long before it comes knocking in a full raging winter storm.

"Morning, Jay," I say automatically as I find him leaning against the porch, "Did you ever go to sleep last night?"

He laughs, "For a few hours. You don't see him, but another guard takes my place overnight. I care for you and all, but I need some sleep too!"

We joke as we make our way to the outer edge of the camp borders, where the group waits. Today, it looks like everyone wanted to be ready. We're all too nervous not to be. Bryce claps his hands together as we arrive, waving everyone into a tight team circle. There are many faces I already know: Tess, Delia, Benson, Jay and Kenzie. There's also some new ones. People I've seen around camp. One girl is named Emery, a barista at the coffee shop, with a curly mane of hair, large amber-colored eyes, and a serious straight line for a mouth. She's with her little sister, Olive, who seems undoubtedly the opposite of her sister—energetic and loud, and looks practically identical despite having shorter hair and eyes that match her name.

Across from Olive is Kai, one of Bryce's friends. A young man probably in his mid-to-late twenties, with slanted cheekbones and jet-black hair reaching slightly past his ears. He looks around the room darkly, as if assessing whether or not he really wants to be here.

"Alright, looks like we're all here. Everyone ready for Operation: Infiltrate the White House?"

He's greeted with a dozen different cheers and battle cries, breath steaming in the crisp morning air.

"The first part requires everyone's participation. Everyone, *Kenadee*." He spits my name like it's a curse word.

"Got it," I say, nodding. I can do this. I have to for my team, to get the others back and win. He looks at me firmly, his green eyes meeting mine for the first time in days. I know he's upset and hurt still, but I'm glad we're making progress at least. Eye contact is a start.

"Alright, then, let's go. Transportation devices out!"

"On three! *One… two… three…* Go!"

I clench my eyes shut and imagine the lawn from what I saw on the map. Elaborately decorated gardens, trimmed shrubs, and endless guards. Before I know it, I feel like I'm being swept off my feet and into the air.

I open my mouth to scream, but nothing comes out. I'm lost in a sea of air as we fly, closer and closer to our deaths.

We're falling, why isn't anyone doing anything?

I seal my eyes shut once more, no longer feeling brave enough to watch. If I'm going to die, I'm not going to watch it happen.

I expect it to hurt, but I feel absolutely nothing as I open my eyes into the blinding sun. The trees reach high above me, shedding their russet colored leaves. One even falls onto my nose, fluttering gently in the wind.

I groan, pulling myself up to a sitting position.

I'm on a sidewalk, the sights and sounds of the city all around. Somewhere in the distance, sirens wail, and people mill all around us, not minding any attention to our strewn forms.

"Bryce... they can't see us, can they?" I ask, peering at my hands to make sure that they're still visible.

He pushes himself to his feet, "No. I did a cloaking spell. I figured people would probably call the authorities right away if they saw us appearing out of nowhere. They're afraid of magic, we don't need to call any more attention to ourselves."

"Good thinking, boss," says Jay, throwing his head in the direction of the tall iron fence that separates us and the White House, "Now, what are we going to do about those guards that are comin' towards us?"

"I thought you said this was a cloaking spell!" I cry as several figures move in on the gates.

He shrugs, eyes set straight ahead, "I meant for non-magic. Reed's wizards, on the other hand... they can see us. Kenadee, you need to get the barrier down, now."

I don't hesitate. My hands find the marble-smooth edge that keeps us from Reed and his world as I concentrate. Feeling the magic radiating in my fingertips, I begin to chant.

One by one, each member of the group takes their position, ready to fight. More guards begin to appear, their radios buzzing loudly with the news. The wall doesn't budge.

I grit my teeth, feeling them edging closer and closer. All those weeks imprisoned took their toll—my magic falters underneath my quaking hands.

"Why isn't it working?!" Tess shouts. Her tiny voice is drowned out by a cascade of magic, aimed directly towards us.

"Don't let go!" Bryce orders, "Keep low to the ground. Be ready to fight when the barrier breaks!"

A low crackling sound is music to my ears. A hairline fracture appears in the barrier walls underneath my fingers. "It's working!"

Someone down the line screams as the magic sizzles on their flesh, their body hitting the concrete with a loud thud. Somewhere inside the White House, an alarm pierces the air.

The fracture spreads, splitting wider and wider. I nearly laugh out loud with relief as it spreads just wide enough...

I throw my powers forward with every ounce of strength I can find. The others are flung off their feet with the force as my spell hits the crack. With a sound like breaking glass, the barrier shatters.

We're all up on our feet in an instant. While Jay, Benson, and Bryce position themselves in front of the guard, Delia crawls beside Kai's crumpled form. There are red hot burns on his skin. One hand settles on his shoulder, holding him down, while the other hand spreads a salve that she'd produced from her bag. He screams and thrashes in pain as I tear my gaze away.

Kenzie, Olive, and Emery are beside the boys in an instant, clasping hands as they begin to chant. Something slams into the back of my head as I go tumbling to the ground, momentarily plagued by stars. A female guard stands behind me and flicks her hand. I feel myself lifted off my feet, tumbling through the air. I gasp, climbing to my knees in recovery as she comes closer.

I snap my fingers, but my magic won't come. I swear under my breath as she takes a menacing step forward; I burnt out my powers with the barrier spell. If it weren't for Bryce and the sedatives I'd been given in prison, I'd be fine.

Somewhere, my friends continue to chat. Overhead, the slight breeze turns to a hurricane; their voices grow louder as the female guard glances up in horror. I take advantage of her distraction, Markus' and Harlow's trainings kicking me into gear. I roll away from the guard and jump to my feet, slamming into her like a football player.

"Kenadee! Watch out!"

I look up just in time as the whirlwind comes my way. Someone's hands grasp my arm as they yank me out of the way.

The guards are picked up by the wind, flung into the air like helpless rag dolls and swept into the distance. We watch it twirl right into the skyline before disappearing for good.

Bryce glances down at me as if he just realized that he's still clinging to me tightly. He lets go quickly and stumbles upward. "Who needs mind spells when you have the wind? Good thinking you three! Now come on! There's no time to waste!"

"Look!" We all follow Emery's gaze to the lawn, where the sirens still shriek. A large group of guards races towards us.

"You guys go, we got 'em!" Jay says in a low voice.

"Are you sure?"

Jay just gives me a look, a small smile on his lips. "They'll be no problem. Just go!"

We say no more. Jay and Benson greet the guards with a sea of colliding powers as the rest of us duck out view. We rush past the fountain and across the neatly trimmed lawn before ducking behind an elm tree. The front entrance sits diagonally from where we stand, nestled behind four gigantic pillars.

We race up the steps, reaching the front doors, where several more guards stand ready. In a single swipe, Bryce summons the bricks from their feet. They're swept off their feet, and Bryce is instantly sending the bricks collapsing on their heads. We don't hesitate before slipping inside and gaping at the mansion around us.

The entrance hall of the White House is magnificent. The crystal chandelier reflects against the freshly polished marbled floors and the grand staircase is decorated in plush red carpet.

"Alright. Group one, you're going to the main prison. Remember, get them all back to camp as quickly as you can. We'll all meet back there when we're done. Group two—" he motions to me, Emery, and Olive, who stand quietly behind Tess, "You're coming with me. We're going on a scenic tour of the mansion. Everyone good?"

A few yeses are thrown his way and he nods briefly, "Alright team, let's do this."

We part ways, as the others rush off. Bryce waves the two sisters and me in impatiently, glancing past me to make sure there's no one around, "Grab hands, we have to transport there."

"What? Why?" Olive frowns.

Emery tucks a loose curl behind her ear and reaches for my hand, "Reed had his magic soldiers hide it. All of his prisons are off the map. You have to transport in and out—his soldiers have to get him there if he wants to visit them. Think of them like secret rooms."

We all close our eyes and imagine the prison. My mind wanders to Harlow and my family. I'm so close I can feel it…

We're whisked away by magic's reign and welcomed by hard marble floor. I groan as I pull myself up, considering how many times magic has beat me up today.

"Get back!" Bryce hisses suddenly. Using his arm, he shoves us against the wall in a hurry. Olive mutters a spell under her breath and our bodies disappear into the cream-colored paint.

From around the corner, I hear booming voices. Two men—coming straight in our direction.

Reed's magic guards. They've known that we were coming all along. They've been waiting.

I don't breathe as they come past, their shoulders nearly brushing my forehead. "Which one is that?" the guard furthest from me asks.

The other guard laughs, his blonde head bowed over some paper in his hands. "Creston. Remember? She was the hardest one to break, but we did it."

My stomach flips. *Harlow. They're talking about Harlow.*

I look to my partners, but can't see them. They're still blending in with the wall. I can feel the tenseness as they stand, not daring to breathe.

"And what does he want us to do with her?" asks the first guard.

I try to crane my neck so I can hear as slowly their voices fade around the bend of the hall. I can't make it out.

Our bodies reappear, and we all gasp for air. "Follow them," mouths Bryce, nodding towards the hall that they disappeared down.

We creep along the walls, our backs against the cream-colored paint as we watch, careful not to get too close.

It gets harder and harder as they take every strange turn possible. We quicken our pace with each step, determined not to lose them. We watch from the corner as the pair of guards make their way up another carpeted stairway decorated with red and gold, and a pearly white bannister.

We have to act now.

THE TRAITOR'S CRUX

Ignoring Bryce's protests, I dart for the staircase, looking both ways for Reed's guards. They've just... disappeared.

Something wraps itself around my throat, slimy, cool. Like a leash, it yanks me by the neck, tossing me to the floor. I gasp, trying to turn around.

"What do we have here?" the guard laughs, boots padding against the carpet. "A rogue little witch, hmm?"

"Let go!" I croak.

"What was that? Tighter?" he clutches his hand into a fist, and the air escapes my lung. I gasp on the floor like a fish out of water as a loud crash echoes through the hall. The guard holding me back falters with surprise, letting go for just a second as I take control.

I push myself to my feet, then shove him back with all the power I can wield. I throw him over the bannister, watching as he lands with bone-crunching force.

I turn to find Bryce right behind me. The guard he battles leaps into action, hands swallowed by flames. I gasp as a flying fireball zooms over my head and nearly takes out Emery. Luckily, Olive stands ready. She counters the spell, swirling it in mid-air and sending it backwards like a boomerang.

The guard screams as the flames lick upwards, dancing from the sleeve of his shirt to his chest.

We head up the stairwell, where the hall takes a left turn and ends abruptly, nothing but a large iron door. Bryce lets out a relieved sigh, "This must be it!"

"How do we get inside?" Olive raises a brow, "There's not even a door handle."

Emery raises her shoulders and slides in front of her sister. She examines the door for a moment, head cocked. "Wait... I know!" she trails off, closing her eyes until her fingers glow a lime green hue.

"Sis, do you know that you're glowing? 'Cause I think we might have a problem if not..."

"Shh!" says Emery, not looking to us, "Now you're all going to want to take a step back."

Olive shrieks as the door pops, a dent appearing in its surface. There's another, then another—with a final burst of energy, Emery sends the door crashing inward, flying off its hinges. We all stare at a brilliant white room.

"Alright," Olive nudges her sister happily, "I take back every mean thing I've ever said about you! Now come on guys!"

My heart pounds in my chest. I could be feet away from my brother. He could be in this very room.

I move first, my footsteps loud against the concrete floor. The lights buzz and flicker overhead, unnaturally white. It's so silent and still. My breathing seems too loud as I go further in, coming across cells on each side, smashed together tightly. Each cell is small and cramped, with narrow walls and no furniture. Most are empty. I hold my breath as we walk, four pairs of feet in this too-quiet room.

My heart pounds with the sound of my brother's name. *Eli, Eli, Eli.* So close. He has to be.

"You okay?" Bryce whispers from behind me. His expression is still stern, but his green eyes watch me sadly.

THE TRAITOR'S CRUX

I nod, taking in a big gulp. "I'm not sure. Let's just find them and get out."

"Guys, here," Emery calls, worry dripping from her voice. She stands at a lone cell with a little boy inside. The doors don't budge as she pushes, trying to ease him out. The young boy inside cowers in fear, cuts and bruises all over his face.

Bryce whispers a spell as the glass breaks and the boy cries.

"You're okay. You're safe," Emery coos softly. "We're here to get you out."

I continue to walk, feeling as if my heart is going to explode from my chest. This prison seems never-ending, as if it could go on forever with its vast white walls. Finally, we near another cell with a crumpled form inside.

"Harlow!" shouts Bryce, running to the glass. I stop to do a double take. The cell is bloody and dim, with a flickering light bulb and no furniture, just like the others. Harlow looks tiny and fragile, her arms shackled high above her fallen form, her feet bare and her ankles caked in dried blood. She doesn't move as Bryce breaks the walls and kneels beside her.

"Har—Har, wake up!" Bryce shakes her softly, panic filling his voice.

Slowly, gently, her eyelashes flutter and her unfocused blue eyes meet Bryce's. He gasps, tears on his cheeks. This was too close of a call.

"Har, we're breaking you out. Can you walk?"

I can barely make out a nod, as Bryce wraps her arm around his shoulder to help her up. As soon as she tries to stand, her legs crumple beneath her and Harlow falls weakly to the ground. Bryce catches her swiftly, scooping her into his arms. "It's okay, don't push it."

"Hey, we checked—they're all the prisoners in here." Olive comes running up, panting to catch her breath.

"What? No! My brother should be here. And my mom—" I say, shaking my head defiantly.

Olive only shrugs, "You can check, but it was only these two that we found. We checked every cell."

"We'll check again. It's okay. We'll find them." Bryce's eyes meet mine, steady, calm.

But before we can move, the white halls are lit with a bright red light and the shrieking wails of a siren. *The alarms.*

"Shit! Again?" swears Olive, "How did that happen?"

"I don't know, but we—"

"You just weren't fast enough." A familiar female voice echoes from behind me. Chills raise on my neck. "Hello, Kenadee," says my mother.

29

"MOM?"

I feel my mouth fall open as I stare at the woman looking back at me. "You—Reed killed you."

"Magic is a wonderful thing, is it not?" she shrugs, heels clomping against the floor as she steps closer. "You have such a trusting soul, you didn't even question the performance."

My cheeks turn hot as she brushes the loose hair from my face and laughs. I catch her scent and it's different... she smells of expensive perfume and champagne. I look at her clothes, a fitted suit and shiny heels, and feel disgusted. "You never suffered a day here. Is Eli—?" I'm about to say a traitor too, but I stop myself.

"I haven't suffered because I took the right side. You never really thought about where your magic came from? You never thought that I was just like you? I spent so long afraid of myself, afraid of my children because I knew that you shared my power. President Reed has helped me overcome that fear. He's helped me see what I could become. Eli's like you. He doesn't see that we're trying to help the world—"

THE TRAITOR'S CRUX

"Help the world?" I scoff. "Reed has done nothing but take innocent lives!"

My mom makes a small sound in the back of her throat, and turns to the guards behind her. "Well... think what you may, but I'm going to need you to all come with us. Don't try to resist. These cuffs have been crafted by the President's magic team so that even you can't break through them."

A guard behind me yanks my shoulder backwards. I can hear it pop as he clasps my wrists together in cold metal cuffs. He spins me around as the other guards do the same to the rest of the team. It takes several to yank Harlow from Bryce's arms and subdue him enough to chain him.

"Leave them alone!" I hear myself shout as the guards try and force Harlow to her feet. Her legs collapse, and they drag her instead.

My mother clasps her hands together in excitement, "Good work, men. Take them to the President's office. He came all the way home for this little... reunion."

We're taken to the Oval Office, where the guards hold us back and my mother raps on the partially open door. I can hear his voice, low and quiet, but creepy as ever, as he talks to someone unseen. I can't make out his words, but his voice reminds me of a snake, smooth and dangerous. He seems to be threatening whoever has the unfortunate luck of standing in that room. As my mother knocks, his voice stops. He pauses for only a brief second before everything changes entirely. His tone becomes falsely pleasant as he calls us in.

Our captors bow their heads in respect as the door creaks open. I bite my lip, refusing to look the monster in the face. The President stands before them, arms crossed as he leans against the desk.

"Mr. President, sir. We have them," says my mother in an official tone.

"I can see that, thank you. Kenadee, it's nice to see you again. Unfortunate that it has to be under these conditions." We're shoved to our knees on the carpet right in front of his shiny black shoes, which don't budge as he takes in our ragged forms. "Do you really think that was a clever idea? You really thought you could win against me? Now look at you. Pathetic."

"Screw you," I spit, earning a swift kick right in the back from my guard. Throwing his head back, the President laughs cruelly.

"You know, Kenadee, you've disappointed me greatly. That's the thing with you magic people. Your loyalty is shaky at best. Always living to serve yourself, aren't you?" Reed's dark eyes drift from my face, to Bryce's, lingering there for a moment as they glare at each other. Something hangs in the air like a heavy cloud, a secret, something unspoken. But before I can ask, Reed's scrutiny is back on me. "I honestly thought your mother's faked death would be enough to steer you back in the right direction. Clearly, you haven't learned. So, what must I do to get the message to you? How many times must I explain before—well, you know. Bring him over." One of Reed's men nods dutifully and pulls open the large white door, summoning to someone just outside. Seconds later, several more guards enter, shoving forward a young man. It's been years, but I recognize him immediately.

"Eli!" I shout, shoving my way forward. Or, at least, trying to. The guard grabs me, yanking me backwards so that I fall at his feet. *My brother. Here. He's alive.*

He's gagged and I can see the shock in his hazel eyes. His muffled cries ring through the room as the President continues to chuckle. "Poor Mr. Coria. What'll happen to you? I have to say, I am rather sorry to see you go. But I promised your sister she'd witness your death if she defied me."

"No!" I shriek, stumbling forward again. I thrash and fight as my guard tries to restrain me, "Don't you touch him!"

Eli's guards pull him to his feet as he kicks and elbows, trying to free himself despite the heavy restraints binding him. I can feel myself screaming and the tears rolling down my cheeks as I'm hauled backwards. At this point, I no longer care about anything but Eli.

Reed casually pulls a handgun from his pocket, taking his time to load it. One bullet.

He makes his way to my brother, aiming straight for the heart. My eyes are blurred with tears as I scream and thrash. He can't do this—he can't!

"With all due respect, *sir*, why don't you drop your weapons?" A slow, calm drawl makes my heart skip a beat.

Jay stands at the door, his hands around my mother's thin neck. The President draws back, surprised as the whole team floods in through the doors. *Our team, our heroes. They came back.*

Reed's guards take position immediately.

"Now I wouldn't do that if I were you." Jay says, clicking his tongue. "I'd hate to break her pretty little neck when she's been such a dutiful servant."

But Reed only laughs, giving an indifferent shrug, "Kill her. I'll find another."

It's the only cue his men need. They leap into action, power spiraling through the room. I press myself against the ground as the spells fly overhead. I need to find a way to get out of these cuffs. A body falls, a limp hand landing outstretched on my arm. It's the soldier that had been holding on to me, but now he stares at the ceiling with blank eyes. I shudder and roll away, nearly landing on top of Bryce. "How do we get out of these?"

"I-I don't know," His eyes scan the chaotic room frantically. "It needs a spell…"

There's a crash and more guards spill through the doors. I look up just in time to see Reed flee the room, three guards in tow.

Crap.

"Don't worry," says Emery, "I know a spell!" She crouches down beside me and sets her hands to the cuffs. "Sorry, this might sting."

A sharp hiss escapes me as sure enough, the metal begins to grow hotter. It tingles against my skin and pop!

The handcuffs clatter to the floor.

"Thanks Emery!" I rub my aching wrists, the burns from the spell already making my skin a tender pink.

Everywhere, people fight. I turn just in time to see Tess' head crack into a wall. The guard steps over her lifeless body with a smirk.

"Leave her alone!" I cry, and the woman's eyes fly to my face. I don't give her any time. "*Praemium!*" The woman freezes in mid-air, staring at me as she realizes what's happening. A second passes, and with a large crash, the woman explodes.

I kneel beside Tess to make sure she's still breathing. There's blood dripping down her forehead, but her chest rises with each steady, deep breath. I sigh with relief, then push myself up. My team battles hard, but I can see the fatigue written into almost all of their faces. They know there's no way we'll win this. Not against magic this dark.

An idea pops up in my mind.

I rush to my brother, using my power to knock a guard out of the wall. "Eli! I need you—come here!" I don't turn to see if he's following as I kneel beside Harlow. She's slumped against the wall, barely conscious, but her head turns just slightly toward me. I reach for my brother, helping him down as I explain. "I need you both to combine your magic with mine. You're weak, but with three of us it might work. Give me your hands."

Eli's brows furrow, but he obeys silently. I close my eyes as Harlow's weak fingers clutch mine. I draw in a deep breath, and focus on our powers. Every nerve in my body begins to tingle as it rises, gaining in strength, letting me build it up.

Somewhere there's a shout. I release their hands, glancing up just as a soldier marches towards us. She raises a hand but I'm faster. I'm more powerful. I send the President's desk flying at her, clutter flying from its top and knocking her back into the wall. I'm on my feet in the blink of an eye, feeling the strongest I've ever felt. The magic practically seeps from my skin as I knock Reed's soldiers out like a line of dominos.

"Kenadee!" comes a warning voice. My mother is the only soldier not affected, looking calm as she steps toward me. I don't wait. I set flame to the arsonist's office, motioning my friends closer. Jay wraps Harlow's arm around his shoulder as he helps her up, and Benson takes the other side. A bloody Tess looks like she's about to pass out, and Kenzie helps sport her. Bryce is already reaching for the transportation device when my mom's magic rips through the air.

"Get down!" I shriek, pushing Eli just in time to avoid the spell.

Olive is too late. Emery screams as blood spews from her sister's mouth, her ears, and her nose. Delia grabs Emery, yanking her back as Olive falls backward.

Dead.

Bryce murmurs something that I can't hear, and we disappear into the daylight.

30

MY REUNION WITH ELI IS short-lived, as Delia carts him off to the hospital a few minutes later. Too tired to argue, I go home and shower, falling asleep as soon as my head hits the pillow.

Delia is the first person I see the next morning as I weave through the dark hospital halls, excitement in my chest at the thought of seeing my brother.

My brother is here! He's actually here!

"Kenadee!" I frown as Delia emerges from behind the nurse's station and plants herself in front of me. "I've been wondering when you were going to come around."

"You have?" I ask, confused. None of my friends have exactly been friendly with me since I've come back from the prison.

"Of course! Hey, you wanna take a walk? I promised your brother I'd pick him up breakfast. But since you're here, you can come with me!"

"Uh... well, I was going to see Eli..."

"You can see him when you get back. Come on!" She grabs my arm, leading me out the large glass doors and towards the hospital cafeteria. "I ordered ahead of time.

The cooks said they'd have it ready for us. I ordered for your brother and Harlow, *if* she feels like eating."

Harlow's name makes my mind flood with guilt. The memory of her crumpled in the cell, covered in blood. It happened because of me.

"You okay?" Delia's voice brings me back to reality. Her deep brown eyes watch me with worry. "We haven't talked in a while and well… I figured you could probably use a friend."

I shake my head slowly, "It's my fault Delia. I was so focused on protecting my family that I became just as bad. I actually came here with the intentions of taking everyone down. I'm a—"

"You know what I think?" Delia interrupts, a thoughtful expression on her face. "I think you need to give everyone a little time. It was a horrible thing that you did, and I understand, I do, but it doesn't change the fact that you betrayed us. Trust isn't so easily earned after something like that."

I shake my head. "I did such horrible things. Harlow—" Tears well in my eyes as I try to find understanding within myself.

"Look, Harlow's pretty beat up, but she always pulls through. She's tough. And she'll probably be pissed, but doesn't she have a right to be? You have to make things right with her. I think she deserves that at least, don't you?"

I gulp, "Yeah, she does. But I don't know how I can even explain it to her."

"Oh, please. She appears mean and tough, but the girl's really a big softy. Just go talk with her. Fix things. Figure it out."

I hold the cafeteria door open for Delia, about to respond when she stops mid-stride in the doorway. The cafeteria is strangely crowded with bodies, all gathered around a floating television in the middle of the room, murmuring intensely. Sharing a curious look, Delia and I hurry forward to watch the screen.

A journalist in an ugly yellow dress talks sternly into the microphone, standing in front of the White House fence.

Oh no.

"Yes, Henry, days ago terrorists invaded the White House and freed hundreds of highly dangerous witches and wizards. It's believed that the terrorists possessed magic themselves and used it against the guards. President Reed spoke about it earlier today in a press conference, calling this an act of war." She pauses dramatically as the camera switches to the press conference, where Reed stands at a large podium, flashing beams of white light from cameras flickering in the background.

"My fellow Americans, I'm afraid that our security has been compromised. These witches and wizards still plaguing our country have been an issue for too long. War, poverty and destruction! Each of these is the result of magic's dark influence upon our beloved nation. So, I am making it my promise to you, to the citizens of the United States of America, that I will not rest until each witch and wizard is brought to me, dead or alive. We will make them pay for what they've done!"

Bile rises in my throat as the camera now shows the streets of Washington D.C. People marching, rioting. Brilliant red-orange flames licking the sides of walls and vehicles. Angry shouts and cries of death.

The people are furious, and they're not going to rest.

In my head, I can hear Alex's voice, distant and shaky as the gun spun uncontrollably. *You're dead, you're dead, and so are you.*

Bullet shots, loud and clear, one by one, shell by shell. *Dead, and dead, and…*

31

I PAUSE AT MY BROTHER'S door, suddenly feeling nervous and shy. This isn't the Eli I knew. He's gone, replaced by this young man that I don't know. How do I talk to my brother that's been gone for nine years? How can I pretend to relate to what he's going through?

"Hey," Delia says warmly, reaching for my hand and squeezing it. "He's here. That's all that matters."

"I don't know what to say…" I look at her helplessly.

"Right now," Delia replies, "It's not even about words. Think of what he's gone through. Right now, what Eli needs most is for someone to be there."

I let her open the door, following bashfully in her footsteps. Eli glances up from his bed, clothed in a white hospital gown and surrounded by blankets. He looks so different. Nine years of imprisonment has made his cheeks hollow and his skin pocketed by scars. He's still handsome, with hazel eyes that are now dark and tormented and visible dimples in the corners of his mouth. When his eyes land on me, they take a second to register who I am.

I don't know where to begin. I slink past his bed and perch myself in the chair next to him. "How are you feeling?"

"Alright," he murmurs wearily, then adds. "It's just a lot to take in, is all."

"Don't worry," says Delia kindly, placing the Styrofoam box stuffed with French toast, scrambled eggs, and two long strips of bacon on the table in front of him. "You'll get there. You've been through a lot... no one heals overnight."

He thanks her for the food, then opens it tentatively. She stops at the door with one hand on her hip, "Take it slow, or you'll make yourself sick. Your appetite needs to build itself back up. I'm gonna go give this to Har and give Bryce a call. You need anything?" asks Delia, her eyes betraying her worry.

"No, we're good. We'll wait here." I give her a forced smile, my heart pounding in my chest. I think back to the news. What does this all mean? Is Reed coming for our camp? So far, it seems like he has the whole country on his side.

Eli waits for the door to shut behind Delia before he turns back towards me, "What was that all about?" He holds up his plastic fork and stabs at a piece of egg.

I sigh, smoothing out the blanket at the edge of his feet. "The President isn't happy about what we did yesterday."

He quirks a curious brow. "You thought he'd take it nicely?"

"Well… no," I admit, rubbing my dry palms together, "I'm just worried about what he'll do."

That's an understatement. I'm terrified about what he will do. There are still prisons all over and judging from the amount of people that volunteered to help with this raid, we won't be powerful enough to free anyone else. If Reed continues to build and strengthen his army, we're the first ones he'll come for.

Eli shovels his fork through his food, playing with it more than actually eating it.

"You've taken him on before," he replies finally, "That thing you did when all those soldiers were there... you just took them out."

I think of the combining spell that he talks about and shrug it off, "All I did was combine our three powers." I tell him about dark magic, and how I know he has it because he did the death timer on Harlow. "It was really the three of us that did it. I couldn't have done it myself."

"Regardless," he says softly, "it was because of you that we got out. Give yourself more credit."

I'm about to answer but then someone knocks gently on the door. It creaks open softly, revealing Bryce—his face riddled with worry. "Can I come in?"

"Sure." I let out a quiet breath, watching Bryce walk nervously into the room. His throat bobs as his eyes find me.

"Uh- sorry. Can I steal you for a moment?"

In the fluorescent hall light, I can see the deep bags under Bryce's eyes and the unshaved stubble on his chin.

THE TRAITOR'S CRUX

He looks at me for what feels like the first time in ages, something other than hate in his eyes. "Look, I'm sorry for the things I said. I was frustrated and angry, but I know why you did it. Reed has a way of playing people."

"Bryce, stop. You had every right to be furious at me—I'm mad at myself for even believing him." I hesitate, meeting those clear green eyes, "But, I do have to ask... What does Reed have on you?"

His eyebrow shoots into the air, "What are you talking about?"

"Don't play dumb, Bryce. I saw the look. What happened between you two?"

He bites his lip, clearly contemplating what to say. "He killed my parents when I was young. It was before anyone knew I was magic—even my own parents. He came for my mother. She was magic too. No one knew I had powers until the soldiers tried to grab me—I used them to get free." He shakes his head, voice breaking.

Tears sting at the back of my eyes. "Bryce..."

He cuts me off, "My dad... he told me to run and I listened. *I listened, Kenadee.* What kind of kid does that? Who runs when their mom is being attacked? I didn't even try to help them!"

"Anyone—" I try, but he isn't listening.

He shakes his head sadly, "No one. I hate myself for it, Ken. You wanna know how I found out they were dead?" He doesn't wait for an answer. "I was here, at camp. Safe and free, eating breakfast when the news came up. My mother was an example. They tied her and my dad to chairs and set the house on fire. Filmed the whole thing and then said I was next..."

I reach for him, pulling him to me as tears well in my eyes. The only thing I'm able to muster is a simple, "I'm so sorry."

I can feel him nodding into my shoulder, "I know." He pulls away, almost desperately, shaking his head. "I-I can't do this, Ken. Not right now. What you did—"

And just like that, I swear I feel my heart shatter into a million pieces. I take a jagged breath and nod at my feet. "I know."

Suddenly the distance between us seems like an entire sea. We stand in silence, unsure of ourselves, of each other, of what happens next. A bone moves in his jaw as he swallows, looking down the hall where Tess' voice echoes and pushing himself off the wall. "Oh, um, I originally came to tell you that we're having a meeting about the recent news. We're all in Harlow's room if you'd like to come."

"Uh—sure." I finally manage to whisper. I was trying to put off any interactions with Harlow until I could figure out what to say to the girl.

Several heads turn as we enter the room, suspicion in their eyes as they regard me. Delia sits cross-legged on the floor with Tess's head in her lap as she braids her hair. She's the only one that waves me over, still looking slightly dazed from her head injury, even though it's been mostly healed by Delia's touch. I hug an awkward arm to my chest and plop down beside her.

The room is dark and grey, similar to Eli's. Harlow's bed is in the middle of the room, decorated with drab white bedding and beeping monitors. She's sitting up, but looks pale and small, black and blue bruises spotting her arms and a stitched-up gash on her forehead. She stares out the window with a troubled expression, her blue-eyed gaze distant and sad. She barely blinks as Bryce starts the meeting, throwing her an anxious look in the process.

"Alright guys, I'm proud to say that our White House attack went well, but today, I'm afraid we have some heavier matters to discuss."

"Oh, my God, please tell me it's about those disgusting excuses for burritos in the cafeteria," Delia suggests, trying to lighten the mood.

A few snickers sound around the room, and even Bryce tries to hide his smile. "Uh, no. Sorry. Although, I do have to say I agree about those burrito things. But no, this is about President Reed. I'm sure you're all aware of his message today."

The entire group tenses a bit at the name, and no one seems to breathe as we watch Bryce, waiting for what he'll say next.

"We all knew he'd be coming back for us. But now, he's turned the public against us as well. I don't want to create a panic around the camp, but I think it's time we start planning for an invasion. Reed is powerful and he's building a civilian and wizard army that both want us dead. We need to consider the risks and move the members of this camp to a safer location where families and children will not be harmed. As for us, I think we need to do something about Reed once and for all."

Jay raises a hand, stroking the stubble on his chin with his fingers. "Where do you plan on moving everyone? I mean, while it sounds like a great plan in theory... won't Reed find us?"

"Yeah, I have to admit that I'm worried about it. There are, however, many camps that have offered to take our people. Their only conditions are that they stay clear of warfare and remain hidden. They're afraid they're security will be at risk."

"I think if we can get everyone at camp to unite against him, we could beat them," Delia offers, hope dripping from her voice.

"Perhaps, but let's be honest: no one really wanted to fight before. The entire camp knows what Reed can do and they're terrified. We were the only ones that even volunteered to do something. What makes you think we can convince people to fight this time around?" Bryce argues.

"Yeah," says Kenzie, "Especially because they all have dark magic!"

I clear my throat and all eyes except Harlow's turn to me, "Well, this time we have a lot more at stake. We have prisoners, for example, that were held captive by him. I doubt they'd mind a bit of revenge."

"Maybe, but my guess is that it's also terrifying for them. They've spent so long cooped up in cells, they probably aren't looking for any more risks. If they're caught, worse things than that will happen to them," Kai says.

"But if we don't fight, we die. That's all there is to it," Benson says, breaking his usual silent streak. His dark eyes meet mine, and I give him a small smile for supporting me. He looks away quickly, folding his arms across his chest.

"Aww, look at you Bens. What has you kissing her butt all of a sudden?" Kenzie pipes up, her voice saturated with sarcasm. Benson blushes, looking down at hands.

"Kenz—" warns Bryce, but she doesn't listen.

"Funny, how Bryce said that the new girl would be locked up and watched, yet, she was still there and fought. I always thought once a traitor, always a traitor."

"Yes, but you guys should know th—" I begin but she only laughs darkly.

"Stop pretending that you're on our side. You don't care about anyone but yourself. What's the plan this time? Have everyone fight for you, then corral us up like a bunch of cattle while you get a gold star from Reed? Is that it? Turn us all in like you did to Harlow?" Kenzie grins evilly, knowing full well how hard she just hit.

At the mention of her name, Harlow turns back to the conversation, looking confused. Kenzie continues, "Huh, Harlow, I'm right, aren't I? She turned you over to Reed. It's her fault that all this happened!"

For a brief second, Harlow's eyes flick to mine before she looks back towards the window. "Drop it, Kenzie," her voice is hoarse and scratchy as she murmurs.

"Wha—Are you—" Kenzie stammers, taken aback.

"You heard me," Harlow says curtly as she turns back to Kenzie, "It's not your place."

Stiff silence breaks over the room as Kenzie gapes at Harlow and Tess and Delia snicker loudly.

Bryce is the first one to break the quiet buzz of the room, "Like it or not, we're a team and we should only have one enemy. Reed is the problem here. I'll call a camp-wide meeting and see if we can get more volunteers for the cause. Right now, it's your job to be prepared mentally and physically. Train, practice. Do what you have to do so that we can win. We won't let Reed destroy us. He's a problem we've had for much too long. Who's in?"

The room erupts in cheers and hollers, excitement for the cause. We can win this thing. My mom, President Reed—they'll pay for their crimes. They'll pay for the murders and the tortures, all the deaths they've caused. If it's games Reed wants, it's games he'll get.

32

THE DAY OF THE BIG meeting, the cafeteria is more cramped than ever with bodies. People shove their way past one another, finding spots on the floor, against the wall, even in the hallways, where they anxiously crane their necks to see in.

Children weave in and out of the rows, some new to their freedom as they play games with the original camp kids, squealing and giggling as they find each other's hiding spots. The older members seem antsy, bouncing their legs and barely making small talk as their eyes dart nervously around the room. I think many of them aren't sure what to do, or what to expect. All they know is that Reed declared war yesterday, and if we aren't careful, we're going to be dead.

Delia sees me coming and scooches over, patting the open seat to her left. "I was wondering about you! You okay?"

I wave a dismissive hand, crossing one leg over the other as I lean back in my chair, "I'm fine. It's nothing…"

"You know who else is fine?" Tess giggles, fingers smoothing down the stray hairs that poke out from her braids and gesturing towards Eli, who just got out of the hospital this morning. He stands with Bryce at the edge of the room, talking, "Your big brother. Why didn't you tell us he was so good looking?"

We all turn to watch them. Eli still moves cautiously, always on the edge like he's trying not to call attention to himself. He smiles faintly when he talks with Bryce, but I know it's all a show. Reed, and my mother, did horrible things to all the prisoners and my brother was no exception. No matter how well he hides it, the damage is evident.

"He's sad," I say, softly, not turning towards the others. I can feel their gazes turn to me, then to Eli.

"Yeah, they all are. Reed's a horrible man and they were prisoners for a long time. It's got to be pretty hard to get over. I don't think Ha—" Tess cuts off, clamping her mouth shut and looking away conspicuously.

"What?" I ask, looking from person to person. They look at me sheepishly.

"Nothing. Nothing at all." Tess says a little too quickly.

"No, what?"

Tess shakes her head, her copper-colored braids flailing behind her, "It's just that Harlow's not the same. Reed did something to her this time – even worse than the others. She was arrested by him several times, but I've never seen her like this before. It's like she's barely here."

Delia reaches for my hand as my stomach twists itself into a knot. All I can think is that Harlow's ruined because of me. Reed harmed her and I allowed it to happen. Delia swivels her head so that I'm forced to look into her eyes, "Kenadee, I know what you're thinking. This is Reed's fault. He was the one who did it. You didn't torture her, you didn't—"

My voice is harsher than I mean it to be, "She was only there because of me. I turned her in. She wouldn't have endured any of it if I hadn't. We followed some guards when we did the White House raid that were talking about her... they said she was the hardest, but they finally broke her. Like they deserved some kind of award. And I can't help but constantly think it's my..."

I trail off as the two girls press fingers to their lips.

Harlow stands right behind me, pausing as she clearly heard everything.

"Harlow, I'm—"

She cuts me off, looking stubbornly ahead at Tess and Delia, "Have you seen Bryce?" Her voice is still raw, her eyes brimming with some unreadable emotion.

"Yeah, he's over there with Eli." Tess looks back and forth like a deer caught in the headlights, eyeballing the door in case of a fight.

"Thanks," Harlow says quickly, then walks away before I can say another word. We watch her go, limping painfully. Her blonde ponytail bobbles through the crowd as I see her find Bryce, leaning in to speak.

The three of us sit in silence as slowly, the crowd quiets down and Bryce and Harlow find a spot at the microphones. Nadine and Jay stand beside them, as well as a few other government staff. Eli appears beside me as I scoot over to give him a seat. Bryce smiles warmly, his eyes scanning the vast number of people. "Hello, everyone, and thanks for coming today. Harlow and I weren't sure how to break this to you, but I'm going to put it bluntly." He takes a moment to look around, a small, sad smile on his lips, "We've known that Reed has been eyeing this camp for a while. If you haven't heard the news, after our break in, Reed's hinting about an attack."

The room doesn't take long to explode. "What are you going to do about it?" A middle-aged man stands fiercely, pointing a finger at the two leaders at the front of the room. "We can't live this way!"

"Trust me, we're doing everything we can—"

"Reed ain't gonna stop!" the man spits, cutting Bryce off, clearly worked up at the subject.

"You're right, he's not going to stop. That's why we need to step up and fight back. We need volunteers to join our resistance. Anyone. Young, old—we have to fight back because he will not stop until he has every single one of us. We all have a duty and a camp to protect. However, for those of you who don't wish to stay and fight, the leaders of various camps and I have been working on a method of evacuation. We've created an underground network, the safest place from Reed and his soldiers. We're going to start evacuating immediately, families first and small groups so that it doesn't attract attention. They will hide and protect you."

The man looks taken aback and glances around nervously. People begin to murmur. My brother, surprisingly, raises a hand in the air. "You know I'll help. I mean, what can he do to me that he hasn't already?" A few chuckles come from around the room as, one by one, people begin taking the bait. I stand with them, raising my hand in the air to acknowledge the fight.

"Good, good!" Bryce says happily, "Keep it coming, guys! We need more than the White House plan had. We can't fight back with only a few witches and wizards. We need an army! We have to defeat him!"

I'm amazed at the sea of people, standing tall like soldiers. There's at least a few hundred bodies, mainly young, but a few older as well. Others in the camp huddle closely, clutching one another in fear. I don't blame them. I know what the President is willing to do to get his way, even if it means yanking children from their families and torturing them.

More and more people take the stand, smiling back at the two leaders proudly. They're willing to fight, eager to protect our world. Hope flutters in my chest and I can't help but smile to myself. Together, we will stop him.

I want to see his face when he dies, when he sees what it feels like to die a slow, painful death, just like those that were murdered at his hands.

We're the ones Reed will be afraid of, the ones that will destroy him and his legacy, once and for all. An electric energy overcomes the room, as slowly, a chant begins to rise, louder and louder, echoing off the walls. We can do this. We are one.

33

EVACUATIONS BEGIN ALMOST immediately the next day. All but the handful of witches and wizards in the resistance will be moving on to different camps across the country. Reed has been to this one before and I'm sure it won't take long for his soldiers to find a way to break our border. The sooner we can get people out, the better.

From my room, I can hear doors opening and closing as people stream through the halls. I can hear their voices echoing as they hurry—eager to get away from immediate danger, ready to move on to their new life.

When I get to the mess hall for breakfast, I find the room nearly empty. Most people ate earlier so they could start packing. With a book tucked under my arm, I find a plush booth nestled in the corner. It faces out, so that I can see the rest of the world as it passes by. I order myself a coffee and oatmeal, distracting myself in the crinkly spine and old pages of my latest read.

My breakfast pops up and I set my book aside, marking the page for later as something else catches my eye. The giant television that drifts from room to room in the camp now has popped up here in the cafeteria. I lean in, trying to hear the nervous-looking journalist.

"Breaking news. There has been an attack today in Chicago during a parade in honor of the President. It is believed to be the acts of a terrorist group of magical citizens." The camera flickers, now showing footage of the streets as explosions seem to hit each float, knocking people straight into the air as flames devour everything in sight.

A man stands before the scene, looking solemnly into the camera, "Thanks, Judy. I'm here, in the streets of Chicago, which are wild with fear and destruction after an earlier terrorist attack. The President spoke about the issue today, calling it an unspeakable act against the human race. The people are calling for action, and surprisingly, so is this magic world. As it turns out, magical soldiers are lining up to help the cause against these rogue groups…"

Fires, broken buildings and mobs of angry people are shown on the screen, spraying graffiti messages aimed at us. It now zooms back to the first journalist, wearing a frown as she begins to talk. "Thank you, Jim. Although we do not have one for each individual escaped prisoner, we have mugshots for those considered the most dangerous witches and wizards. Please, if you come across them, do not try to engage with them. Call your local police immediately and they will take care of the situation."

Mug shots pop up, making my stomach reel uneasily. Harlow, Eli, and even a few little kids that were found inside the prisons.

I'm suddenly not hungry. I grab my book and scoot out from the booth as the journalist calls their names, describing them one by one. In the lobby, I break into a sprint, not even bothering to stop as I accidentally slam shoulders with a young girl. I can hear her angry shouts, but keep going, determined to find Bryce.

I don't stop when I reach Julie's counter, but slide around it and dart around the corner. *He's not here.*

"Where's Bryce?" I can't control the fear in my voice, which obviously worries Julie. Her eyes are round with fear as she takes me in like an insane person.

"Then is someone here?" I demand again, slowing my words for emphasis.

"Harlow is," Says Julie simply, examining her nail beds.

I don't respond. I run to Harlow's door and knock loudly. "Hello?"

She looks up briefly as I enter, then immediately glances back at her work. "Go away."

"Harlow, please!" I beg, "Listen to me!"

"Listen to you?" she scoffs, pen pausing in mid-air, "You're lucky I'm in too much pain to *kill* you."

"I know, and you have to believe how sorry I am—"

"Well, in that case..." she sucks on her teeth, "I don't care. Tell me what you have to say and leave me alone."

"Fine," I lean back in my chair with a sigh, "I saw the news in the cafeteria today. There was an attack in

THE TRAITOR'S CRUX

Chicago and they're blaming us. It said there are more dark-magic soldiers enlisting, Harlow. What does that tell us? His army is growing stronger!"

She takes it in silently, thinking for a moment before she speaks again. "Okay, is that all?"

"What?" I stammer, surprised at her calm exterior.

"I asked you if that's all," she says a little more sternly this time, the old Harlow poking through.

"Harlow, I don't think you understand. They have your mugshots, descriptions everywhere. We have to do something."

"No…" she scoffs, "*We* aren't doing anything, *I* am. You can go talk about how bad you feel with Tess and Delia if you want. I'm sure they'll listen."

"Look," I slam my hands down on her desk, trying to catch her attention as she jots something down on a notepad, "You know how sorry I am. I did something horrible and can never make it up to you. But I want to at least try to make things better."

"Oh yeah?" Fire suddenly rages in her blue eyes, "That's really great of you. Really great. Why don't you go tell that to someone else? I'm done with you. You had your chance. I offered it to you myself and you lied to my face. You don't know *anything* about what Reed is capable of. You tell everyone you did it for your family? That's really sweet, Reed's all about family. He has my brother—remember him, from visiting my memories? Yeah. Well he works for Reed now. My sweet baby brother is one of his best, hate-filled soldiers."

Tears fill her eyes, desperate and angry, "He got a turn with the fun new torture device, just for us magical people. Oh, yeah, it's wonderful. I've never felt such intense pain; four whole beatings a day. It's okay. They were careful not to do it too long—didn't want me dead before my timer goes off. Must be an extra special death, huh? So why don't *you* step aside and trust me when I say I am doing *everything* I can to keep him from us, because I can't stop thinking about the things he can do. Just go back to your new friends and your brother and Bryce and cry to them about how bad you feel. Maybe they'll care."

"I'm so sorry," I finally whisper, feeling hot tears trickle down my cheeks.

Realization dawns in her blue eyes as she bats a stray tear and clears her throat, instantly switching facades. She clenches her shaking hands into fists and in a breaking voice, says, "You can go."

34

THE TRAINING STARTS EARLY IN the morning when the camp is quiet and asleep. Winter is approaching fast. I throw on a hoodie and thermal pants to avoid the early morning chill, grab an apple, and head out the door.

Everyone's already in the training room, stretching and warming up as they talk excitedly. I choose a corner by myself to shake lose my tired limbs as I prepare for whatever this training session might include. I ignore Kenzie as she swats her ponytail from her shoulders and glares my way.

"How's everything this morning?" All heads turn in shock as Bryce enters the room instead of Harlow, who usually handles magic training. He's surprisingly chipper as he throws his things aside and waves us in. "We'll start with some fitness warm-ups. Three sets of ten push-ups. Go!"

The group groans collectively as we drop to our knees and do the exercise. It's been a while since I last trained with Harlow, and my limbs ache in protest. We follow the push-ups with sit-ups, planks, jumping jacks, and burpees.

Bryce is the first one finished. He jumps back to his feet, clearly the only one energized by this whole thing. He watches until we're all finished, cheering us on like an over-excited jock. "Good work! Water break, then we're going to focus on defense spells. You have three minutes before your due back here."

I crumple to my knees, panting. Delia laughs, watching me from her spot against the wall, "Really, girlfriend? I thought Harlow whipped you into shape before."

"She did, but I stopped training when—well, you know," I say sheepishly, taking a big gulp of water.

Delia grimaces, "I know… I hope that she'll be okay. I mean, for her to miss a training like this is unusual. It's like she's just… shut down."

I'm grateful for Tess as she comes bouncing towards us, a whirlwind of energy. She talks so quickly, I struggle to keep up, "Oh my gosh, this is so hard, I forgot how much I hated exercise. Why can't I eat and not get fat? Then I'd never have to exercise. Why…"

My mind, accustomed to tuning out the many rambles of Tess, drifts off. We've all been worried about Reed's next move. He seems to always be one step ahead. His next move will be sly. It'll be cruel and calculating, just like the President himself. Like my mother. Like all of Reed's mindless drones. He has the entire country at his disposal. My skin crawls to think of what they'd do to us if they got ahold of us.

Bryce joins me at the wall, batting the sweat from his forehead with the back of his arm. I watch him for a moment as I screw the lid back onto my water bottle. "So, we haven't talked. How are the evacuations coming?"

He gives me a contrite glance, lowering his voice to a whisper, "We're pretty worried. The underground tunnels will only work a while before Reed's soldiers track us down... we're lucky that we have more numbers, but we still need to find a way to keep them out for good."

"They have dark magic, Bryce. If it's anything like mine, then..."

He frowns, "That's what we're scared of. They've been roaming the forest already. We've had to send our guards to go attack..."

"What?" I gasp, "You didn't mention they were here already... That means—"

"I know," he whispers, emerald eyes flicking to my face, "Plus we can't find anything about that damn spy that you mentioned. Whoever they are, they've been lying low for quite some time. We think they're just a quiet observer, telling Reed everything."

"Can't you look at footage from the attacks? Something to trace their magic?"

He shakes his head, "We looked several times. It's the weird thing... it's been tampered with. Harlow's been investigating each guard, but so far, nothing..."

"So," I ask, as calmly as I can, "what do we do?"

He kicks himself off the wall and throws his water onto his bag, "We train and we keep moving forward. It's all we can do. Speaking of which—"

"Of course. Go."

He groups everyone together and we get back into the session, this time, pairing up in groups of four for defense spells. Bryce walks through the aisle with the help of Jay, setting down bowls of water in front of each partnership. "Most of us here, save one," he nods in my direction, "have limited powers. This means we can use and manipulate objects directly in front of us."

"Yawn!" says Kenzie, "We learned this forever ago. What's your point?"

"Thanks for the unnecessary sass, Kenz. If you'd let me talk, I'd get there," says Bryce pleasantly as I snicker to myself, "*Anyway*, we can use anything, as long as it's available. A trickle of water, for instance, can go a long way."

He takes a step back to demonstrate, squaring his shoulders and sprawling his hands. Slowly, they raise to the air, the glistening whorls of water trailing his every move. He brings out his hands to either side and the delicate arc of water grows wider, expanding until it crashes to the floor like a waterfall. We all jump back as the water laps at our ankles before dissolving into the mats.

"See?" says Bryce, arching a brow, "Simple as that. I want to see you all try it with your partners."

***

I'M BACK IN MY ROOM, barely slipping a clean shirt over my head when the room begins to blare with a ringing noise. I don't have to look to know who it is. Reed wants to talk. I hurry fast, yanking the shirt down and meeting the secretary. She doesn't look at me, as always, smacking her gum with the same boredom I see in her every time.

"Miss—"

"I know, I know, just bring him in," I say dryly, cutting her off without hearing the rest.

The girl rolls her eyes at me, apparently offended, but rings me in nonetheless. President Reed's face appears moments later, the usual glass of alcohol in his hand and a cocky smirk transforming his lips. "Ah, there she is. How is my lovely girl?" he says slowly, the alcohol doing its duty.

I ignore his question and glare back, "Why are you calling me?"
He raises his hand, large, with gnarled fingers and aged spots on his skin, "Please, Kenadee, don't go any further. You knew the consequences of your actions. I'm sure you've come to terms with it."

Rage swarms through me, making me clench my fists. *How dare he?*

"You—"

He cuts me off with a raised hand before I can even let the insults come streaming from my lips.

"Kenadee, we've been watching you very closely, and we weren't happy with the results we got. We especially didn't appreciate your part in breaking into the White House. Didn't I give you enough warning of what would happen?"

"You're a monster. You thought you'd get away with this?"

"Oh, now that's unfair, isn't it? I promise that all of you will pay and it will be entirely your fault. You think that you can just steal my prisoners from me? You think we won't find you?" He chuckles quietly, as if it's a funny inside joke, "I will find a way into that camp of yours and I'll make you pay. I'll kill each and every one of you if that's what it takes. Miss Coria, I always get my way. Don't fight it."

I say nothing else to the man. *I can't...*

Throwing his head back, he laughs at his victory. "It's always a pleasure, Kenadee. Unfortunately, the next time that we see one another will be under grimmer circumstances. Have a good night, dear girl."

The screen folds itself away as I clench my fists, trying to fight the mixture of anger and fear coursing through my body. Why can't he just let us be? Reed has dragged my entire family into this mess. I don't bother to stifle my sobs. The device weighs heavy in my palm as I send it throttling through the air, slamming straight into the wall with a sickening crack. My heart pounds like a drum in my chest as the next move becomes clear. I *will* make them pay for what they've done.

Mark my words.

***

BRYCE ARRIVES AT MY DOOR shortly after the meeting with Reed, his green eyes growing wild with confusion at the sight of me. "What's the matter?"

"R-Reed..." I manage to spit out.

He says nothing more, but uses a gentle hand across my shoulder to lead me to the couch.

It's all I can do to apologize, again and again, as he quietly comforts me.

"Ken, I know that you're scared, but will you tell me what happened?" Bryce's voice is calm and soft, bringing me slowly back into this world, momentarily forget my fears.

I take a few shaky breaths, wiping at my eyes as I begin my explanation. "Reed, he...he called me. He has this device that does a video chat thing—he used it a few times before when, well, you know..."

Bryce's dark brows furrow. "Wait... you talked to him? Just today?"

I bite my lip, saying nothing as I nod. I can feel his anger from here as he throws his arms into the air. "That's just great, Ken! I thought you were done helping him!"

"I am done, Bryce!" I hiss, "He called *me*! Not the other way around. I forgot it was even in my room!"

Bryce opens his mouth, then clamps his jaw back shut. There's a look of ferocity in his eyes that I've never seen before.

I break the intense silence. "I swear to you that I'm not helping Reed. He's destroyed everything, Bryce. All I want is to make him feel some of that pain."

He stares at me for a second before slowly nodding. "I believe you. Right now, he's tearing us apart without even trying. If we're all going to work together, we have to be able to trust each other. Tell me what he said."

I hug my knees to my chest, a vain attempt for comfort. "Bryce... I think we're out of time. He made it sound like..."

Realization dawns over his features. "Damn it!" Bryce rises to his feet, running his hands through his cropped brown hair.

I don't look at him. I stare at my feet, instead, a crazy idea filling my brain. My heart seems to race a bit faster as I climb to my feet. "Bryce... I know what we can do."

35

I ALWAYS HAD IT IN my head that I was somewhat immortal. My mother always told me to be careful and watch my actions. "Don't get hurt!" she'd warn. I'd always ignore her, too lost in my own naivety, until I came home crying from a bike wreck or a skinned knee from doing something stupid. My mom blamed it on the childhood years, saying that kids always think that they'll live forever. But they don't.

Bryce stares at me in horror as the idea spills from my lips. It takes him only a matter of seconds to shut it down completely. "Absolutely not! You cannot go back there! Are you insane?"

"Just hear me out!" I plea.

"No, it's final! No one goes back there. It's way too dangerous!"

I scoff, "You don't get to tell me what to do, Bryce. Besides, this is just an idea. Maybe it'll give everyone enough time to flee!"

He takes a deep breath, clearly trying to calm down. "Look, Ken, can you please just—just don't! You don't have to play hero. I can guarantee that Reed and his men are out there, right now, coming for us. We're lucky that they can't get in, but we all know that's only a matter of time. It's our job to get our people out of here. These walls are the only place where magic can be used freely without getting tracked. Let's focus on evacuating the people that are depending on us for safety. Going out there to find Reed will only make matters worse. Please, listen to me when I say that this is the only way."

I chew on the inside of my cheek, hiding all the words I really want to say. I know that finding Reed right now is a crazy idea—but if it diverted their attention for even a second, it could save our people. We don't know who sits outside the camp walls waiting for us. The second that Reed finds a way in is the second we're handed our death sentences.

Bryce and I sit in silence for a minute, unsure of what's next. I turn my attention to the window, pretending to watch a scene down below. My backyard overlooks the mountains in the distance. I usually love the view, but today, it feels confining. What enemies lurk beyond our borders? I watch the small children below as they weave in and out of the snow banks, popping out at their mothers and fathers who carry large loads of bags.

"What do you say?" Bryce finally asks, breaking the silence as he joins me at the window pane.

"You're right. It's probably a reckless plan," I admit. And yet…

As Bryce takes a spot at the window beside me, I wonder how reckless I'm willing to be.

I TAKE A WALK, UNABLE to handle the thought of sitting inside.

People everywhere are in full-swing evacuation mode. A large portal is open in the middle of downtown as people make their escapes to their new home—wherever it may be. The security team stands close by, hands clasped behind their backs. They've already taken extra precaution, casting the same barrier spell that keeps everyone else out of the portal. Still, they lurk close by, as if Reed himself were about to appear.

I go for a coffee, sliding a tip in the jar as the barista gives me a dirty look. Unfortunately, everyone knows what I've done, which means friendly faces aren't something I've been experiencing. I thank the barista anyway and step out into the cool winter air.

I take careful sips, my boots crunching loudly over the crisp snow as I watch people bustle about with their boxes. I weave off the path and head up Harlow's and my former running trail. It smells of minty spruce trees and smoked wood wafting through the chimneys. Tiny tracks in the snow reveal that a fox had been hunting a mouse.

I reach inside my pocket and pry my gloves on my hands, not watching where I'm going until it's too late. My boot lodges on the gnarled edge of a log as I go flailing to the ground.

"*Really Kenadee? Really,*" I whisper to myself, furiously, looking at the remains of my coffee, now splattered

THE TRAITOR'S CRUX

down my shirt and all over the snow. I'm to my feet in a huff, reaching for my empty coffee cup when something catches my eye just beyond a particularly fat pine tree.

Something red.

I take a daring step closer to examine the scene.

It's a message, carved into the trunk of an old aspen tree with jagged, capital letters.

You're dead, you're dead, and so are you.

I scream.

36

THEY FIND THE BODIES A few hours later, hanging lifeless in the trees above. They'd been hung, and I know exactly who's responsible.

Bryce and Harlow stand with Jay, Nadine, and Benson, discussing the scene in hushed tones. I interrupt the conversation with a low voice, "We need to talk. *Now.*"

"Excuse us," Bryce says urgently as they follow my lead out towards the trees.

When I'm sure that no one else is listening, I talk. "Whoever this spy is, they aren't laying low anymore. How are they doing this?"

Bryce frowns, "There were guards all over. They shouldn't have been able to do without being seen."

"That's because they have powers like ours." Harlow's keen eyes land on mine, "See those drag marks in the snow? The victims were literally attacked by those ropes in the tree. If you ask me, the killer has a real sick sense of humor."

Bryce's eyebrows raise, "Well, great... you've trained practically everyone in this camp. We have records. Why don't we just find the ones with dark powers?"

"It's not that simple. Whoever this is, they've been smart enough to hide it since day one."

"So, what? We sit around and wait?" Bryce motions in the direction of the hanging bodies, "Watch more people die?"

"I didn't say that," Harlow says with a sigh, "This asshole is helping Reed play with his food. The fact that he's so cocky is what terrifies me—I think Reed knows something that we don't."

"You think he's stronger then he let on?" I ask, realization dawning over me.

Bryce looks like he's about to be sick as his mouth opens and clamps back shut. "But... it doesn't make sense. Why doesn't he come and attack?"

"*Because*," Harlow limps towards the nearest tree and leans against it, "Plot twist: miracles exist and Kenadee finally grew a brain."

"*Ha-ha*." I roll my eyes as Harlow snickers to herself. To Bryce, I say, "Remember how I was needed to break down the barrier?"

He nods, "It's the one thing keeping Reed from us."

"Exactly. You guys did such a good job with the security that he couldn't attack until it was down. He knew he couldn't start the war until he had it figured out. These attacks... they never happened before I came?"

They both shake their heads. Dread washes over me as I finally understand. "He's declaring war because I'm going to break the barrier."

Bryce blinks, staring at me with a hard expression. "Say that again?"

"Of course..." Harlow says in a low voice, "That makes so much sense. This spy of his couldn't do it, so he's going to use you instead."

"Stop!" Bryce forces himself between us, "What are you talking about?"

"The night of the fireworks, remember? I was new to magic, I was weak. He got inside and used me to do that spell."

"No..." he says, eyes widening with horror. "We won't let it happen!"

I gulp, my stomach twisting on its self. How do I stop something I don't even know is happening? If Reed has access to the camp, he'll slaughter everyone. "I-I have to do something," I whisper.

"It's actually quite simple. We'll lobotomize her," Harlow suggests.

"You'll *what?*" I recoil, noting the wicked gleam in Harlow's eyes.

Bryce glares at Harlow, "It's not really called a lobotomy spell—that's just Har's way of trying to be funny. The spell basically defends your mind, keeps it protected from any outside magic. The only thing is, it doesn't last for long."

"Don't worry, I won't scramble your brain," the blonde mocks, "But you will have to stay under constant supervision so that we know you're not off doing Reed's dirty work."

If I didn't feel unsettled before, I sure do now. I regret the words the moment they come from my lips, "Do what you have to do."

"Great, then it's settled. Come by my room tonight and I'll do the spell," she says, "But now for the fun stuff. We need to talk war."

"We can't risk it." Bryce folds his arms, voice firm, "He has a growing army of dark powers, a regular army with guns and bombs, and—"

"*But*, without me to take down the barrier, we're at the advantage," I remind him, "As long as you do that spell, then they can't get in. Your security team alters the spell to block out his army, right?" Bryce nods. "Then it's perfect! That means their weapons can't get in either."

"You forget, Reed's aware of this too. He has people like you running around under the radar." Harlow rubs her tattooed hand absentmindedly. Her fingers are slightly crooked, like a broken hand that never healed properly. She sees me watching and drops her hands to her side, turning to Bryce, "Call a team meeting for everyone that was involved in the White House raid. I'll work with the security team on creating a stronger barrier. Kenadee, come with me. It'll require all the power we can get."

"And then what? Our people are still in danger."

She kicks off the tree she was leaning against and circles slowly around Bryce, "They'll help, like it or not.

This is their home too. They're going to help us play his game right back."

"Play his game?" Bryce's face contorts, "All he does is kill to get his way. Are you suggesting—?"

"I'm hurt that you'd even say that. Believe it or not, I'm not a psychopath, Bryce," She scoffs, clapping a hand over her chest to feign offense, "All I'm suggesting is that we take back our people."

"The magic army?" I ask. A gust of biting wind makes the leaves tremor above as I zip my coat to my chin.

Harlow nods, eyes glimmering. "Exactly—knock them around a bit until they see what they're missing."

"You're enjoying this too much, you know."

She holds up her hands, walking backwards, "I'm dying, Bryce. Let me get back at Reed and have my fun while I still can."

Bryce looks to the sky in exasperation as Harlow heads back towards camp without another word, navy ski hat freckled with snow, "Lord help us. You know, I actually fear for Reed when Har gets her hands on him."

37

THE LIBRARIAN GIVES ME A wide-eyed look as I pile in through the door and stomp the snow from my boots onto the mat. I crane my neck to see her over the grimoires—my latest haul was my smallest yet, only nine. Ever since the leaders made it clear they don't we me to attend security meetings, I've had a lot of time on my hands.

I stick the pile on a small table and the books fly up the stairs toward their resting place. Dusting my hands on my jeans, I follow their lead to the grimoire section, the musty smell of their old spines filling my nostrils. My hand lands on one, a particularly shabby journal with yellowed pages that stick together as I try part them. I narrow my eyes, catching a title on page in bold letters that catches my interest. I flip until I find it, sticking my finger underneath the words.

CONTROL IN DARK MAGIC.

I plop to the floor excitedly. I know this grimoire—it was the same writer of the last dark magic grimoire I found. I thought it was here on accident, but now...

I scan the nearly illegible scrawl hurriedly until I find what I've been looking for.

Mind spells: most common method of obtaining control over ones' victim. They're simple, but only last as long as the user is in the victim's head.

Death Timer: tattoo placed upon victim's skin. Causes both mental and physical effect on its wearer. Most people are unaware that the D.T. is considered the most powerful control spell because it weakens the victim's bodies, making them easier prey for those seeking long-term, full-victim mind and body control.

I read the last few lines again and again. Reed must not have known, or he would have had Harlow serving in his ranks. I draw my knees to my chest and prop up the book as I continue to read.

Venenum: vocal spell, nicknamed "Poison spell". Less common. Requires enchanted objected to get control over victim. They must use it often in order for the user to ensure that it works fully. Long-term as long as object stays enchanted, and victim continues to use it. Caster of spell can slip in and out of mind without victim knowing. Full mind and body control. Victim suffers memory loss.

I slam the book shut, tucking it under my armpit. It all makes sense: the communicator. It had to have been. I used it daily—before they returned it to my doorstep, they must have charmed it.

I land in my living room and reach into the junk drawer of the coffee table. I pick it up with my magic so that I'm not touching the device, and whisper the word. "Praemium."

JESSICA PRATHER

The communicator explodes into a million pieces, spiraling to the carpet and flickering out like broken stars.

38

I STEP FROM THE SHOWER, emerged in a cyclone of steam. Shaking my hair dry with a towel, I freeze. Somewhere in the house, a door slams shut.

I throw on my clothes as fast as I can, feeling a strange panic overcome me.

"Eli?" I call, heart skipping faster with each step down the quiet hall. "Eli, is that you?"

Silence.

After checking every corner in the house, I slip into the living room, my eyes instantly landing on the spot where my grimoire had been. Instead, a note sits in its place.

Just because you destroyed the communicator doesn't mean you're free. Turn around.

The hairs on the back of my neck rise as I turn slowly, not expecting what I might find. Directly in front of me, in the spot where it'd been destroyed, the communicator begins to buzz.

I leap backward, falling over my couch as Reed and my mother appear on the screen.

"Kenadee," Reed rocks back in his chair, "I hope they didn't startle you too bad."

"Where's the grimoire?" I hiss.

Reed smiles faintly. "Oh, don't you worry about that ole thing. It is being put to good use."

"What do you want from me?" I ask in a low voice. "I don't work for you anymore."

"*Au contraire*. We know all too well what motivates you, dear girl. We have been studying you *very* closely. I'd hate for someone to die because you refused to help."

No. This can't be happening again.

Reed turns to my mother, and she pulls up one of those spells. I gasp as I realize what they're watching. My friends stand outside, helping with the boxes and the chaos of the evacuations.

"Right now, I have eyes on each and every one of them. There are so many that we could harm, just like that." He snaps for effect. "Take your brother for example." He pops up under the spell's watchful eye, pointing at something in the distance as he talks with Benson. "Poor, poor Eli. Nine years of torture… he really could use a break from all the pain, don't you think? Or there's sweet little Tess, so full of optimism. Delia, the kind-hearted healer. She's one of your only friends, isn't she?"

"Leave them alone." I growl.

He only continues, "I'm not even to good ones yet. There's always Harlow." He zooms in on the blonde as she tosses a box into the portal. "You know how much I love to see her in pain. Or Bryce. The boy you lost. What if you lost him for good?"

"No," I shake my head, "Please, don't! I'll-I'll do it, just leave them alone!"

My mother closes the spell as Reed taps the tips of his fingers together wickedly. "You're going to break the barrier, and turn yourself in to me. I want you in my army, Kenadee, and I won't take no for an answer."

"Okay." I swallow. "Fine… but leave them alone."

He doesn't acknowledge this, only raises a brow. "You have until morning light. I suggest you make the best of it."

39

I SLIP THROUGH THE DARKENED halls like a ghost, my heart breaks with every step I take.

I hate to leave, to abandon them in this time of danger, but I know what I have to do.

I wear nothing but the clothes on my back: layered shirts, a jacket, my boots, and mittens for warmth. All I need is magic.

I pause outside my brother's door, swallowing back the tears.

I always vowed never to let my brother leave my side, and now, I'm the one leaving him.I hope he'll forgive me one day.

I kneel down and tuck the note underneath his door, batting angrily at a tear that cascades down my cheek. I take a shuddering breath to steady myself, and move on to Bryce's room.

The boy that was mine. He wasn't just a leader, but someone who tried to see the good in everybody. He was the guy with the calloused fingers from constantly strumming his guitar, who had bright emerald eyes and the kindest smile I've ever seen.

THE TRAITOR'S CRUX

The boy that I think I love.

So, like the coward I am, I shove the goodbye note through the crack underneath his door and walk away.

I wind through the hall and make a final stop at Harlow's door, clutching the paper tightly in my hand. This was the hardest goodbye note, the message I'd been putting off too long.

HARLOW,

THERE'S NOT MUCH FOR ME TO SAY. I HOPE THAT YOU KNOW HOW SORRY I AM FOR THE THINGS THAT I'VE DONE. YOU ESPECIALLY DIDN'T DESERVE THE THINGS THAT HAPPENED TO YOU. I DON'T KNOW THAT I'LL EVER MAKE IT UP TO YOU, BUT I'LL SURE AS HELL TRY.

THE TRUTH IS, I'VE KNOWN FOR A WHILE THAT THIS MIGHT BE THE ONLY OPTION. I JUST NEVER REALLY WANTED TO FACE IT. AS SOON AS YOU GET THIS, CLEAR THE PEOPLE OUT OF CAMP. GO SOMEPLACE SAFE, SO WHEN REED HAS ME BREAK DOWN THIS BARRIER, THERE'S NO ONE LEFT TO KILL.

I'M SO SORRY, HARLOW. I HOPE YOU'LL UNDERSTAND.

SINCERELY,

KENADEE

(P.S., DO ME A FAVOR AND WATCH AFTER Eli, WILL YOU?)

I push it through then climb to my feet. My palms are sweaty and my head pounds anxiously. This is really it. I'm leaving...

I force myself to look away, sniffling as I refocus my thoughts on the task ahead. It's the perfect time of morning to slip away—where everything is the strange dark gray from night, but the sun is beginning to peek from behind its shelter in the silhouettes of the mountains. It'll give me ample daylight once I'm out of the camp, and I won't have to worry about sneaking around in the dark in the woods. That brings on a whole new world of dangers that I don't really care to face.

Kai is on guard duty this morning. I can see his frame from my perch on the balcony as I stare from the large windows facing outwards. He's slumped against a tree, carving something with what looks like a knife to keep himself busy.

I go downstairs quickly and walk right through the front doors of the camp. Kai looks up in surprise as he hears my boots crunching in the snow. "What—what are you d—"

"I'm so sorry!"

He leaps to his feet, as agile as a cat, but he's too late—I put him to sleep with the swipe of my hand. I look around for any sign of danger as he crumples to the ground, making sure that no other guards noticed. When I'm sure that no one else is around, I duck into the shadows.

I run until I find the lightning-warped tree and the edge of the camp that I've grown so familiar with. My hands thump against the hard surface as I take a few breaths to calm my racing heart.

This is it. All I have to do is get through these barrier walls.

Power rises warm within me as I recite the spell. It breaks easily under my guidance, eager to obey. I clamp my fists tighter until the barrier shatters in mid-air.

I let out the air I'd been holding with relief. Sirens begin to shriek at camp, a security alert that I take as my cue to go.

Someone behind me clears their throat. "Where exactly do you think you're going, new girl?"

"Harlow!" I gasp, turning and clapping a hand to my chest, "You scared me! How'd you know I'd be here?"

"What can I say? I have nightmares. But really, I'm more concerned about this." She pulls the note from her pocket and dangles it in front of me.

I sigh, "I have to, Harlow. He's never going to stop unless I do."

"What's he got over you?"

I shake my head, "I can't say. All I know is that you need to find that other spy, as soon as possible. Harlow, it can't wait! Reed—"

"Reed is a bully. He knows that he can scare you into submission—don't let him, Kenadee."

I look to the place where the barrier once was, then back to the camp, mind racing. I can't just defy him. He'll kill them…

Harlow takes a step closer, forcing me to meet her gaze. "I hated you for what you did, you know. But… I know why you did it. And if you ever repeat this, I'll deny it, but I guess you've grown on me and I don't want Reed to hurt you."

I give her a mischievous grin, "You know there's a word for that, right?"

She rolls her eyes, but doesn't try to hide her lopsided grin, "Say it and I'll punch you."

I'm honored, really. The great Harlow Creston considers *me* a friend. *And* she only looked mildly sick while saying it. "What's wrong?"

Harlow's brows furrow as she stares in the direction of the camp where the alarm still blares. "The alarms have been going off for several minutes now and no one's reset them."

"That's because they're taking a few visitors right now," says a familiar voice. My mother emerges from the shadows. "And the President doesn't like rude hosts."

40

"OH, *COME ON*," HARLOW GROANS at the sight of my mother, "It's not even five A.M. and this is already a terrible day. Can't I have my coffee first?"

"Would you shut up?" I hiss at Harlow.

"No, it's alright," my mother says, taking a step closer. "I'm quite used to Ms. Creston and her bad attitude. Maybe she just needs a small lesson in respect."

"No!" I scream as flames emit from her hands, racing toward Harlow with a fiery rage.

My shouts are short-lived, however, as Harlow raises a bored hand and the flames ricochet, spiraling towards my mother's head. My mom redirects them just in time.

Harlow frowns, head cocked, "Damn. I missed."

I make the next move, using both hands to summon my magic, pinning her against the tree. She looks up in surprise, then her face twists into something else. Something full of rage and horror.

"Why are you here, mom? You and Reed just called me from D.C.!"

"Wait, what?" Harlow scoffs beside me, "Is that why you were leaving? To go play house with the president?"

My mother ignores her, eyes only for me. "We saw Ms. Creston come and we knew you wouldn't go through with it. We decided to take the situation into our own hands."

"So... where is everyone?" I breathe, air fogging in the navy night, looking around. No soldiers.

My mother grins wickedly. "They're in the camp, of course. You took down the entire city border, after all. Even our other little rat couldn't do that."

"Who is the rat?" I spit, twisting my hand as she gasps in pain.

"You know," she wheezes as I grip tighter, "Magic is so fun. I never knew what I was missing all these years by not practicing. Now, I can do things like this."

She throws both arms to her knees and Harlow and I are thrown backwards into the snow. My mother's feet crunch towards us. "Dark magic...It feels so wonderful, doesn't it, to just let go?"

Harlow strikes, but my mother is too fast. It's her turn to pin the blonde against the tree. "I don't see why everyone is so afraid of you. You're so... broken, aren't you?"

"Let her go!" I hit my mom in the stomach with my magic and she doubles over, but doesn't loosen her grip. Nostrils flaring, she sweeps me off my feet too, shoving me into the tree.

"Kenadee, we have to thank you again for that wonderful grimoire. The information was just fabulous. I learned something new that I could try out tonight."

Realization dawns on me as my mother turns to Harlow.

"As it turns out, Death Timers make for the best kind of servants. It's the only way I could control someone with power like yours. You're going to be my weapon."

Before I scream, my mother drops Harlow, hand flying to the shoulder that sports the tattoo. There's a glowing from her hands, a sickly blue, and Harlow's cries. I try and squirm, kicking and struggling against the spell holding me back.

It's too late.

My mom lets go of me and Harlow falls to the ground as she takes a proud step back.

"Harlow?" I cry.

She's on her knees gasping. I barely catch the words as she chokes them out, "Kenadee, run."

"No, I—"

"*Run!*"

I take a shuddering breath, throwing a final look toward my mother, and race into the trees. I have to kill her, but… now she has Harlow. If she dies while controlling Harlow, what does that mean?

The camp is just in view. My heart stops as I see smoke billowing from its insides, orange flames licking at the walls. I'm too late.

Something grabs my feet from under me and tosses me into the air like a ragdoll. I slam into the ground, feeling all the air leave my chest as I stare at the starry canvas of sky above. Light footsteps approach, and Harlow kneels beside me. Only… it's not Harlow.

Her eyes are hard and empty, staring at me with unflinching raw hatred. Her signature crooked grin looks even more evil as it tugs up on her lips. "I'm not allowed to kill you, but I'm still allowed to have my fun." She hits me with a spell that feels like a knife to the gut. I scream, trying to crawl away. She only follows, prowling around me with that dark expression. "After everything that you've put me through, this is the least I can do to thank you."

"Harlow—" I sputter, hot liquid training down my nose and my ears. I wipe at it and find blood on my fingertips. "This isn't you. Fight back!"

She twists her hand and the blood pools faster. I taste it in my mouth, choke on it, as her hand cues a high-pitched scream. My head feels like it's about to burst. I press my hands against it, blinded with pain. I climb painfully to my knees and throw up all over the forest floor as the noise stops and Harlow's laughter replaces it.

"To be fair," says my mom's voice, light as she appears. "She warned you to run. Isn't this so fun, Kenadee? She's like a puppet held up on strings."

"Let her go," I choke. In the distance, screams fill the camp.

My mother taps her chin, as if considering. "No, I don't think I will."

"Then I'll make you!" I growl, leaping toward her. My mother gasps as water glistens in my hands. I turn it over, letting it grow and—

"Harlow!" my mother screams.

The blonde is on me in an instant, slamming my head back into a tree. My back scrapes against the hard bark, but I see my next move. I send my powers right into Harlow's bad leg. She cries out, leg buckling underneath her as I catch her momentarily off guard. Spinning around on my mother, I let the wave reform in my hands. It crashes in my palms, the tides tickling my skin. I throw it her way and she's swept underneath.

"Kenadee?" Harlow clutches a tree for support, looking around in horror. All signs of control are gone, her eyes are clear as she looks at me. "What…" she trails off, body doubling.

"No, Harlow!" I cry, "Don't let her in!"

"Get out of here." She chokes, flinching away as I reach out to help.

"I'm not leaving."

Troubled eyes flicker up, "I can't fight it. You have to go *now* before I—" She doesn't finish the sentence as, like a sigh of relief, she straightens up, body relaxing. The control sets back in, glazing over her pale blue eyes.

I begin to backtrack, feeling my heart trying to rip itself from my chest. "Harlow, stop. Don't let her do this to you—fight back!"

She laughs coolly.

I hear my mother in the distance and both of our heads turn, momentarily caught off-guard. My mother drags Jay beside her with a cruel smile. A huge bloody gash sits fresh above his eye. "Look who I found? He was looking for you, so I thought he could join in on the fun. Harlow, would you please do the honor?"

I charge forward, but my mother is the one to push me back. I watch, paralyzed in place, wanting to scream to Jay, to warn him. In an instant, Harlow's palms turn up to the sky. Jay gags, blood spewing from his lips. He chokes, wide-eyes set on Harlow, who stares expressionlessly back.

My throat is raw with the scream I can't let loose. Jay's eyes slide to mine as at last, he sags to the ground.

My mother's eyes are bright, "Who knew the things I could do with this girl? Now all I need is for you to have a death timer too. Imagine that power. Think of the possibility."

I can't respond, so I just stare back at her, hoping that she knows I'm glaring. She chuckles, throwing her hands in the air. "At this rate, there's no saving your friends. That poor little town. Your tiny home... you really thought it'd last?"

Paralyzed or not, I feel my powers hot, radiating through me. If I could just do something with them. Smoke billows in the distance, reaching my nostrils. Just out of the corner of my eye, I can see the dancing orange of the flames in the trees. Someone's setting fire to the town.

I can't move when I hear the shout, then suddenly, I'm falling to the ground. I gasp, testing that the spell is broken as I wiggle my fingers and Delia races to my side.

"Delia! Watch out!" Harlow's hand moves the trees, letting them wrap against Delia's body. She's swept away, gasping for air as the vines and the leaves crawl upward.

I strike again at Harlow's bad leg, this time whispering, *"confractus femoris."*

It snaps loudly like a twig being stepped on. I leap to my feet and free Delia as Harlow tries, and fails, to stand.

My mother appears in front of us. I reach for Delia's hand, trying to shove her behind me, but Emily Coria already has a hold on her mind. She smiles, not sweetly, at the healer. "We can't mend Harlow's injury over there, even with our elite power. Would you be so kind?"

"Yes," Delia replies robotically.

She's placing her hands on Harlow's leg as my mom wheels on me. "When are you going to give up? Hmm? Can't you see that you're outmatched?"

Delia finishes and without looking, my mother drops her to the ground. "Don't worry, she's alive for now."

I close my eyes, trying to find my power. It's weakened, taking longer now to build back up. My breath comes in pants as I spin on my heel and run smack dab into someone's chest.

"Benson!" I cry with relief, "You have to help!"

Something in his expression stops me. He watches me with calm dark eyes. He says softly, "I don't think that's going to happen."

Suddenly, I'm lifted into the air. I cry out as the branches of a tree wrap themselves around me, twisting around my arms and my ankles so that I can't move.

Benson stands over me, a sneer on his lips.

"It's been you all along!" I manage to hiss.

Benson raises a brow, "I've lived here for years and no one has suspected me. Then you came along and started spouting off about spies."

"How could you?" I growl, struggling against my binds. The smoke is thick on my lungs, making it hard to breathe. "I will kill you, Benson! I swear it, I will!"

He throws his head back and laughs. "You? You're *nothing*! Talk all you want, you won't win this."

It's the only challenge I need. I call all my remaining power forward, feeling it pooling in my palms. With one final burst, I let them explode.

41

EACH OF US FLY IN a separate direction. The tree releases its hold as I land neatly on my feet. Now I'm the one in control.

"Told you I would kill you," I sneer, stepping over Benson's crumpled form. He looks at me, but it's not the usual cockiness—it's fear, written into every line of his face.

His body tenses as my magic seizes control. I crush the air from his lungs, squeezing it slowly, painfully. To my right, my mother moves. She's waking up, and Harlow's already pushing herself into a sitting position.

I refocus my attention to Benson's pale face. The life is draining from him. I smile, feeling as wicked as Reed.

My mother sits up, eyes widening as she sees what's happening. "Don't you move!" I command.

She does as I ask, smiling sweetly. Her feet stay firmly planted, but her voice is loud, breaking the silence. "Harlow, be a dear and rip out your throat."

"No!" I shriek, watching in horror as the blonde's hands work like claws on her neck. Blood drips down her front as she wheezes.

My mother raises a hand, stopping her. Harlow's fingers freeze in mid-air, paralyzed in place.

"Let go of him," orders my mother. I do and she helps him to his feet. "I don't have to control your mind in order to get what I want. You try to run free, to disobey, but one tiny threat against your friend's lives and here you are. You're weak, protecting them over yourself."

"I'll do as you ask, just let her go. Please. Let Harlow go…" I beg, positioning my hands in a surrender position.

"Harlow's fate depends on your behavior."

I gulp back the fear. "Okay."

My mother presses the magic-proof cuffs against my wrists as Harlow waits on the side and Benson goes to fetch Delia. I'm shoved forward, headed back to town. I look at the place we once called home and let out a strangled sob. Bodies are everywhere. The buildings are nothing but a charred skeleton, mere bones of the home we all loved. A thin layer of smoke still curls from its remains, snaking through the air with a delicate, deadly grace.

All I can think of is my friends. Where did they go? Are they even alive?

Where is everyone? The town is empty. No signs of life.

I hear the dreadful cadence of his voice before I see him. Reed talks pleasantly, cheerful of his newest win. He beams brighter as my mother pushes me forward. "Ah, splendid, there she is, just in time! Now, you can see what you've done to your friends."

I fight the urge to spit at him. It's the least I can do chained up like an animal. The other part of me wants to kill him, to use the magic that he's so afraid of, use it for one final purpose, even if it kills me. He's the reason for so many cruel deaths, all for lies he uselessly started in the first place. Why does he hate us so badly?

We'll never live to know.

I look beyond him at the pitiful scene taking place. It makes my stomach reel. Military men, stand proudly as they clutch my friends.

"Eli?" I cry, "Bryce!"

Eli doesn't move, watching me quietly. Bryce, on the other hand, struggles against his binds, screams against the gag that muffles his voice.

"No!" I shriek as the guard puts a hand to his head. Bryce drops to his knees, blood dripping down his face.

The soldiers gripping me kick the back of my knees so I crumple too. When they grab my ponytail and yank my head back, I'm looking up at my mother. She chuckles quietly, "Next time, they'll kill him. Think carefully about your actions. They will affect Harlow's future, remember?"

"Ah, splendid! You managed to do it, Emily." Reed's watches Harlow proudly. "Look at you, Ms. Creston, finally playing nice after all these years."

He turns and begins to pace, slowly making his way down the line of new prisoners—a handful of them, my friends: Bryce, Emery, Kai, Kénzie. He stops at Eli, smirking.

"Tell me how it feels to be betrayed by your own team member? You were planning an attack on me, weren't you? Then she decided to intercept." All eyes follow Reed's accusatory finger, pointed straight at me.

"Now, I know what you're all thinking. I wouldn't lie! Kenadee is one of the biggest traitors of them all. She was about to leave you in your time of need. She took down the barrier for my nephew, Benson, and that is what gave us the advantage. She works for us, even if she doesn't always know it. She's more like her wonderful mother than she even knows."

"You were going to hurt them!" I shout back.

"Was I?" the president says pleasantly. "What do you think?" he turns around, and my mother steps forward.

"Eli," she says briefly, as if he's a stranger she's just encountered, "Glad to see you."

He glares at her with a mixture of fear and anger.

"Answer my question, please, Mrs. Coria. What do you think of your daughter? I think she's a great addition to our cause, don't you? You, her, and Ms. Creston here would make quite the magnificent group of witches."

"I was trying to save them!" I argue, but no one seems to hear me. Bryce looks to me hopelessly, for once looking small and fragile.

"I never meant for—" I continue, but the soldier behind me whispers and I find myself gagged and unable to speak.

Reed lets out a dramatic sigh, "The truth is out, whether you like it or not." Turning to his guards he says, "All this smoke in the air is taking its toll on an old man's lungs. Load them up. All the other prisoners we caught have been carted off. Take Kenadee and Eli to the White House. Everyone else can go to the internment camps, for all I care."

"Yes, sir!" I'm wrenched to my feet and shoves me forward. Dread washes over every part of me. If I don't side with Reed, what will happen to me? To my friends? To the people of the camp?

We will never survive this. Never.

"Alright, boys! Go!" the President grins maniacally as we're led towards the large military trucks. A long line of soldiers, who had been standing behind Reed, emerge, letting out angry roars as they sprint towards our beloved camp. Their powers unite like a grenade, sparkling, popping, sizzling through the air. The soldiers go running and our captors yank us closer to the trees for cover.

The camp explodes like a firework contrasting the baby blue sky. I can hear my screams, feel the tears rolling from my cheeks as I crumple. Everything's gone.

Reed claps his hands together slowly, enjoying the display of the cheering guards around us. I can barely make any of them out through the heavy smoke blanketing the air around us.

I don't struggle as my captor lifts me up, throwing me into the back of one of the many military vehicles at the edge of the highway. There's a bench on each side of the

THE TRAITOR'S CRUX

truck, stuffed now with our bodies, cramped together. Bryce's eyes meet mine, desperate, hopeless. Afraid.

A few guards cram their way in, standing alongside the tall walls as the door clamps shut behind us. The truck rattles to life and takes off down the rough road. They watch us nervously, guns clenched tight in their hands, as if waiting for one of us to make a move. They must fear us like everyone else—afraid we'll attack or harm them, believing the vile rumors the President has spread.

Next to me, Eli sways with the truck, eyes fixed on the floor.

Across from me, Bryce's foot taps against mine, like he wants to tell me something.

"Hey!" barks one of the guards.

Bryce shrugs innocently.

They must believe it, because they lean back, watching us with weary expressions. I meet Bryce's gaze, curious. He gives me a small smile.

Seeing him usually comforts me. Today, tears well in my eyes. I know his smile is a lie, no matter how much I want to believe his silent reassurance. He can't pretend that things are going to be okay. Reed got his way once and for all.

***

THE TRIP SEEMS TO LAST forever. I wish I could see outside. I want desperately to know what time it is, to breathe fresh air and see the sky. It reeks of sweat and smoke in the tightly-packed caravan, as bump after bump, my body grows sorer and restless. The stillness in the air is almost too much to bear, as we all avoid one another's gaze.

If only we could distract the soldiers that surround us with something... *anything*. If we could do that, maybe, just maybe, we could do a mind spell. If only I could tell the others...

My heart races. I can't do anything with these handcuffs on my wrists. They're the same magic-proof ones from before. I try to find Emery's gaze, but she won't look my way.

I sigh, plopping my head against the wall. I would do anything to discuss this with my friends again. If we could have a single second to come up with a plan, to distract them and take them down... that's all it would take. We could easily destroy them and get away, but not with them staring down every move we make. Gauging from their reactions, I actually think they're terrified of us. They know what we can do, and they're taking many precautions.

We were so sure of ourselves a few days ago. What changed blows my mind. Somehow, we need to do this. We can, I know it. We didn't come all this way to fail and lose at Reed's game. If we're going to play, I want to win.

With a rattling squeal from the brakes, the vehicle comes to a halt. All heads pop up in confusion. This wasn't a planned stop.

"Wait here with them," one of them barks. He has bright red hair that nearly matches Tess's.

THE TRAITOR'S CRUX

The others obey, looking around nervously as their fingers brush the triggers of their guns. Outside, it's silent. Still.

I share a look with Bryce, watching me with wild green eyes. This might just be our chance.

Another soldier decides to follow the red-head's lead. He opens the door, revealing the too-bright snow shining in the sun. I can hear his boots crackling against the crispy snow as he slams the door shut, leaving us in the dim.

It's quiet... eerily quiet.

Where's Reed? What happened? I hear nothing from them... maybe they're hiding, just like us.

A scream rings out, rattling my core. I sink lower in my seat, goosebumps now trailing my arms. The other soldiers throw each other scared glances, appearing to be at a loss of what to do next. They stand there stupidly, looking at each other with a lingering question in their eyes.

"Who was that?" one of them finally asks in a low voice. The others shrug.

"I guess we better... go... uh, check it out?" another says, his dark eyes betraying his fear.

"Why don't you go? We'll stay here and guard them." The first soldier shoves dark-eyes forward. He begrudgingly unlocks the door and pokes his head out. He gives an all clear sign behind him before sticking one foot out, then the other...

The door opens wide with his movement, and we all look longingly towards the open air, freedom, just beyond these binds. Suddenly, he's swept away into the air, flailing desperately as he goes higher and higher. The other guards scream, slamming the door shut and pressing their weight against it.

Eli elbows me, hazel eyes meeting mine. I can tell we're thinking the same thing.Magic. But who could be doing it? We're all handcuffed—there's no way it could be any of us.

"How'd you do it?" snarls one of the guards, gaining his composure as he waves his gun from face to face. "Huh? Fess up! We know it was one of you."

We only stare at him, bound and gagged, rendered completely useless.

Without another blink of an eye, the caravan explodes and we're swept away. Pieces of shrapnel rain down as my ears ring with that impossible high-pitched noise. There's a heat to the air as I gasp in pain and try and sit up, despite the binds holding my arms back. Fire now rages around us, encircling us completely as a few vehicles creak and moan. I see no bodies, nor the remains of the soldiers that surrounded us moments ago. They're gone, lost to the explosion.

Just as soon as it started, the fire around us begins to die, sinking lower and lower towards the group as the ash spits itself towards the bright blue sky. Only a second more and it's gone—just like a figment of my imagination.

Footsteps sound closer, as we huddle together, trying to understand what just happened. A few of us struggle to our feet, hands stuck behind our back. A girl appears, climbing gracefully through the rubble as she plants herself in front of us. Her hair is cut short, and she has cheerful eyes and a delicate upturned nose. She must be about my age, but looks incredibly young and fragile, despite the destruction I'm assuming she just caused.

"So, you wanna get out of here, or what?" She says with a raised brow, "Because I don't think you have much time."

42

DELIA'S THE FIRST TO ASK what we're all thinking, the gag falling around her neck. "Who are you?"

The girl sighs, snapping her fingers and producing a key, "Here let me get that." Her boots crunch loudly as she goes around to each person, using the same spell as Emery to rid us of the horrid cuffs. I rub my wrists, glad to have the weight off. I watch the girl move quickly and gracefully, looking more like one of those fairies I used to read about in books.

When she's done, the girl begins to walk away, glancing over her shoulder at us still frozen in place, "C'mon. We need to go. I'll explain as we go."

We do as she says, weary expressions across everyone's features. The girl doesn't seem to mind as she weaves in and out of the rubble, making a path without really watching where she's going. "I'm Anna," she says, not bothering to look at us, "I'm here to help save your sorry asses."

Bryce grabs my hand, squeezing it as I pipe up, "Where are you taking us? Where's the president?"

The girl doesn't respond, but stops dead in her tracks. We stop too, seeing exactly what she sees.

Reed stands, waiting for us with Benson, Harlow, and my mother at his side.

When he sees Anna, President Reed surprises us all by bursting into a fit of laughter. "Of course," he wheezes through his fits, "Why didn't I think of you? Dear, sweet Anna, how are you?"

"Just dandy, Reed. Thank you for asking! And you?" the girl's voice is calm. I exchange glances with my team, and we all get into position, prepared for the worst. They know each other... was this girl working for Reed? How does she know him?

"Oh, wonderful, except for seeing you. Anna, you always have a way of spoiling the fun."

What fun? What is he talking about?

"Oh well, I can't let you destroy the world now, can I?" the girl responds bitterly. I can sense the hatred from here.

Reed throws his head back and laughs. "Ah, but now it is your magic that is doing the destruction. Just like you swore you wouldn't. You always said that you weren't monsters, but I guess this proves that you're full of lies. A lot like your father."

Anna glares daggers at him, "I'm nothing like you."

He raises his hands in false surrender, obviously enjoying this.

I look to Anna, shocked. *She's* Reed's daughter? She gives him a forced smile, crossing her arms across her chest.

No one speaks, as the President's smile grows, "That hurts my feelings, sweet Anna. You know I don't consider myself a bad man. I consider myself a man that does what's necessary to save his country. Magic is a plague. It's been proven again and again."

"You're lying, Reed. What have we done but protect ourselves against you?" I growl, my voice low.

"Malen—"

"Was evil, yes. But we aren't—"

"Really?" he cocks his head, "Think of those innocent officers you almost killed. You couldn't control it, could you?"

"What's he talking about, Ken?" Eli asks, a crease between his brow.

Reed's horrid smile grows, "You even enjoyed it, didn't you?"

"Shut up!" I clench my fists.

Reed doesn't even flinch. "It didn't take much control from Benson on any of those attacks. The thing is, you're pulled to the darkness. No matter how hard you try, your powers destroy. They're evil. They'll take you over."

"Kenadee? Don't listen—" Bryce says, watching my balled fists. He's too late. My powers explode before I can even stop them, landing directly among the guards behind Reed. They scream in horror as their bodies thrash on the ground. Bones break and snap with sickening force as tears burn my eyes.

"I-I—" I feel myself taking a step back as Reed watches with a level expression. My friends stare at me, fear warping their features. The soldiers continue to wail in agony. It's too much, and I can't stop it.

"Kenadee!"

"No!" I struggle as Bryce grabs me by the shoulders. The soldiers' pleas fill my ears. It's too much...

His green eyes are steady, unafraid. "All you have to do is let go. Let go of the anger."

"I can't—" I choke. "I'm-I'm killing them. I can't stop."

The screaming fades as Bryce's eyes close and he lets out a soft sigh.

I killed them.

I rip myself from Bryce's grip, forcing myself to see the scene ahead. Their bodies are mangled and twisted, mouths open in soundless anguish. All the air escapes my lungs. They were so young, teenagers still, that believed everything the President said. They were kids, placed in a terrible situation.

Just like us.

"Don't touch me!" I shout as Bryce reaches for me. The others just stare, as if I'm someone unrecognizable.

Reed steps over his soldiers, then turns to my friends, a smug smile painted on his lips. "Now do you see what I'm saying? Believe what you may, Kenadee, but I swear to you on my grave this is the truth. You are dangerous, and someone needs to put a stop to your kind."

"So why don't you kill us?" snaps Kai, gesturing all around him, "Why put on this show? Hmm?"

"I didn't say that I couldn't still use you," Reed shrugs, closing the eyes of one of the mutilated corpses,

"I have an army for the magic, as you very well know. I usually only want those with certain powers, like Kenadee's, Eli's, Harlow's... Once they're trained and controlled, they can do quite miraculous things. Harlow's proven that to us today."

"You will all accept it when you realize how dangerous your existence is." Reed rises to his feet and watches us, "Malen was too powerful—I would've never been able to defeat him. It's all I ever wanted, and someone took care of him. The sooner magic is gone from the world, the sooner—"

"Oh please," snorts Anna, "Well all know what you really want, *daddy*. You want magic on your side so you can take over. You want to be just like Malen, but you can't with us here. You're threatened—"

His laugh is loud and cruel, his smile knowing. This has been his plan all along.

Suddenly, the laughter comes to an abrupt stop as blood begins spewing from his mouth. He coughs and gags, his mouth forming a surprised "O".

It's Anna that has him, lifting him slowly in the air as Reed chokes over his own blood, clutching his throat desperately. Dying.

Now it's Anna who laughs, breaking the silence with cruel giggles. "Well, dad, sorry to say this, but I'm not going to miss you."

She arches her arm back, then sends him crashing back hard against the cold metal of the trucks. Benson reaches for a transportation device.

"No!" I cry as my mother reaches for Harlow and Harlow obeys, "You promised you'd let her go!"

"Darling, when are you going to learn that you can't trust anyone?" my mother replies. And in an instant, they're gone.

Anna's voice yanks me back into reality. "Look, we need to go. Now! We can save her later!" she urges, turning towards us. My eyes turn towards Reed, now slumped against the truck.

Dead.

Anna shouts something that I can't understand, her eyes closing tightly. Before I can think, we're swept away, straight into the air—Reed far, far, behind us.

EPILOGUE
PRESIDENT REED

I CAN HEAR THE SOUNDS of the people through the White House walls like a steady roar. Undying, is their love for me. A hero, they think me to be. It's so simple—a few passionate words, a caring smile, and the Father of the nation has them eating from the palm of his hand.

"Are you ready for your return from death, Mr. President?"

Emily Coria stands behind me, a mixture of her two children. Her son's eyes, her daughter's worried mouth. She adjusts my tie with bird-like hands, glancing at me with moony eyes, just like all my admirers. I clear my throat, "Ready as I'll ever be."

"And how are you feeling?" she asks hesitantly.

"For rising from the dead, you mean? I'll be fine, Emily. You and Ms. Creston did a marvelous job. Where is she, by the way?"

"Right there," says Emily with a smile. Harlow Creston slinks into the room with the poise of a dancer and the deadliness of a wolf. Her stony blue eyes immediately fly to Emily for direction.

"Harlow, you look marvelous," Emily raves, pinching the girl's cheeks for color. I think to myself that if it were the old Harlow Creston, her fist would already be slamming into Emily's nose for even touching her. But this... this is the new Harlow. The improved one, a ghost of a girl who once was. I had my doubts when Emily showed me the spell. The girl put up a fight at first, but it wasn't enough. We catch her sometimes in glimpses—she tries to resist, but Emily is quick to beat her back into submission. All these years, all the time wasted trying to destroy her, and this is what's done her in. She's nothing but a puppet, a weapon.

A living, breathing, mindless weapon.

"Are you ready, Ms. Creston?" I hold out my arm for her to grab. She takes her place at my side, fingers curling around my inner elbow and replies with a robotic, "Yes, Mr. President."

Cameras flash and the crowd screams outside as the guards reach for the doors. "I look forward to our alliance, Ms. Creston."

She sets her pale eyes on my face, cruel and dark. "Me too, Mr. President."

And so, we step out on the balcony, and I rise from the ashes like a phoenix.

ACKNOWLEDGEMENTS

Where to even begin? This little dream of mine is only possible because of the amazing support system behind it.

First and foremost, a very large thank you to my family, for their endless love and support. To mom, for being my biggest cheerleader since day one. To dad, for teaching me the value of hard-work and a love of learning. To Jace, for all the bad jokes and brotherly love. To my grandparents: Lyle, my partner-in-crime and fellow trouble-maker. I'll never forget our adventures; Diane, who has inspired these stories since day one; and Mary-Ann, one of the strongest women I know. I can't name everyone (I wish I could), but I love you all so much. Your support means the world to me.

Mitch, Katlyn, Nicole, Mallory, Dawn, and everyone else that read the crappy first drafts of Traitor's without judgement: THANK YOU. Your feedback, advice, and encouragement made such a difference.

Riley: you're the truest of friends, the Tess to my Delia. Thank you for always being there.

To everyone at Oftomes Publishing, particularly: my editors, Jill and Xina, for the late nights and endless patience. For helping this novel grow. Chris and Claire, for formatting and designing this book. Tara Spruit, the amazing artist behind the cover. All the other authors, for the friendship, laughter, and insight you've provided. And Ben, for your boundless enthusiasm and dedication to this project. Words can't express how grateful I am for you.

CPSIA information can be obtained
at www.ICGtesting.com
Printed in the USA
FFOW03n1405261117
43697448-42545FF